THE ELEGANT LIE

Sam Eastland is the pen name of an Anglo-American writer, who is the grandson of a London police detective. He is the author of twenty books, including the Inspector Pekkala series, which he also writes under the Sam Eastland name.

The Elegant Lie

SAM EASTLAND

FABER & FABER

First published in the UK in 2019
by Faber & Faber Ltd
Bloomsbury House
74–77 Great Russell Street
London WC1B 3DA

First published in the USA in 2019

Typeset by Faber & Faber Ltd
Printed and bound by CPI Group (UK) Ltd, Croydon CR0 4YY

A CIP record for this book
is available from the British Library

ISBN 978–0–571–33569–5

FSC
www.fsc.org
MIX
Paper from
responsible sources
FSC® C020471

2 4 6 8 10 9 7 5 3 1

For P. Q.
My Captain and my friend.

Cologne, Germany
June 1949

When the guard came to his cell, Nathan Carter was already awake and sitting on the edge of his bunk. It was 5 a.m. He had not slept all night, afraid that this was only one of many dreams he'd had, in which the day of his release from Langsdorf military prison turned out to be nothing more than a figment of his imagination.

Carter was six foot tall with dark, short-cropped hair and brown eyes in which the irises could barely be distinguished from the pupils. His chin and cheeks were scruffed with a week's growth of beard and his normally slim build had been made considerably slimmer by the time he'd spent in prison. He had a habit of keeping his fingers tucked inside his palms, as if permanently conscious of their vulnerability. The expression on his face was thoughtful and closed, but otherwise unreadable. He looked like what he was – a man who kept his feelings to himself – but he also possessed the extraordinary ability of being able to walk into a crowded room and, with no outward sign of effort, emerge from that room with every other person having noticed he was there. Or he could step into that same space and leave again without anyone being able to recall with any certainty that they had spoken to him, or heard a single word he said, or even seen him there at all. To be remembered, or not remembered, was a skill he had turned to his advantage. It had also saved his life on more than one occasion.

The guard motioned for Carter to follow and, in the tomb-like silence of the prison before dawn, they made their way to the mess hall, which was empty at this hour except for the night duty staff, eating their breakfasts before they headed home.

Carter sat by himself at a table on the other side of the hall from the prison workers. A segmented metal tray was put in front of him, on which lay a splat of powdered eggs, half a slice of bread and a small, shrivelled apple. These were the same rations as the guards. It was the best meal he'd had in a long time. He ate everything quickly and without registering the taste of the food, gnawing the apple down to its core before eating the core as well. From a brown Bakelite cup, he drank a cup of water whose taste of dead leaves, the result of being passed through rusty pipes, was so familiar to him now that he had forgotten it could be any different.

After five minutes, the guard ordered him to his feet. What few words the guard pronounced were devoid of any feeling, as if he were speaking to some muted form of life which could not be expected to comprehend the complexities of human emotion.

Carter did not look at the guard, careful not to make eye contact or to move in anything other than a submissive, shoulder-hunched plod. To do anything else could be perceived, depending upon the mood of the guard, as a threatening gesture. The guards carried truncheons made from hard, black rubber and they always aimed for the face. One swipe across the cheek would shatter the delicate bone and either break the nose as well or else crack the skull's nearly paper-thin orbit around the eye socket. Both scenarios guaranteed an injury from which the victim would never fully recover.

With the guard following close on his heels, Carter passed through the first of several barred gates which separated prisoners from the outside world. Only now did he dare to believe that this might not be a dream, after all.

He was taken to a room that was crowded with racks of old trousers, shoes and coats. The place reeked heavily of mothballs. There, he stripped out of his denim prison overalls while the guard picked out a set of clothes, roughly eyeing him up for size, and threw them at his feet. As he dressed in the poorly fitting garments, he smelled the sweat of other men. The shoes he had been given, their leather cracked and heels worn down, were too small, but he was afraid to ask for a different pair, so he crammed his feet into them anyway and hobbled out of the room.

The guard opened a steel door and Carter stepped out into the hazy shadows of the morning, the clean air shocking his lungs. Still following the guard, he walked along a narrow path, bordered on each side by high fences topped with barbed wire. To his left stood the prison yard, where he had been allowed to wander for one hour each day. To his right was a wide strip of earth, ploughed once a week to keep the soil soft, so that it would reveal the footsteps of anyone who had managed to escape the twin layers of prison fence, as well as the attention of the guards, looking down from the watchtowers through the telescopic sights of their rifles.

At the end of the path, Carter arrived at a guardhouse, where he signed his name in a ledger, beside the signature he had made when he arrived nine months before. He received an envelope containing a bus ticket and a food voucher, and then he was escorted through a door to the street.

There was a moment when Carter imagined that the soldier might offer some words of consolation, or even an insult perhaps, anything to break the spell of sullen hatred that had been cast between prisoner and guard. But the man said nothing. He just shut the door to the guardhouse and was gone.

Having spent so long imagining his freedom, Carter's first thought on finding himself once more in the world was to knock on the door of the guardhouse and ask to be let back into prison. He worried that the months spent in Langsdorf had left him incapable of looking after himself, beyond the basic function of survival as a convict.

Before beginning his sentence, Carter had prepared himself, as much as he could, for the physical discomfort of prison, for the shockingly bad food and for the degradation of existing as a number. But what he had not prepared for and what, in retrospect, nobody could anticipate, was the effect of the monotony of prison life. The one thing he could not stand to contemplate – and thousands upon thousands of times he had batted it down into the darkness of his thoughts, only to see it rise again into the forefront of his mind, like an apple bobbing in a bucket of water – was the time he would never get back.

There was a saying at Langsdorf that a man only served two days in prison – the day he arrived and the day he left. Everything else, no matter how long the sentence, belonged in a separate world, in which the accounting of time was reckoned on a different set of clocks and calendars, which evaporated into nothingness the moment that door closed behind you.

And it was true. He could feel it – the terrible sameness of those days inside his cell, the brutality of wasted hours turning in upon itself, already half forgotten. But what the saying didn't clarify was that the place in your mind where those two days joined together, your first day and your last, could not be rendered with some tidy pencil line, like the one on which you signed your name inside the Langsdorf prison ledger. Instead, it was a ragged wound, Franken-stein-stitched like the chest of an autopsied corpse. And however you might succeed in wiping from your brain the months or years you spent inside, that scar would always be there to remind you.

The road that led away from Langsdorf was named the Selt-nerallee. It had once been bordered by rows of neat cottages, which provided housing for the prison staff. The prison itself had been built in the early 1900s to accommodate medium security convicts from the military district of Cologne. During the Second World War, the prison had been converted into an overflow for the barracks of the 153rd Infantry Regiment, which drew recruits from the surrounding area. At the time, there was no need for a military prison in Langsdorf, since anyone who might have served time there was either shot or transferred to penal regiments on the Eastern Front.

The Allied bombing raids that flattened most of Cologne had also severely damaged the Langsdorf complex. One wing of the horseshoe-shaped prison had to be reconstructed, but the damage to staff residences all along the Seltnerallee was so complete that they were never rebuilt. Once the rubble had been cleared away, only vacant lots remained, in which the ghostly outlines of where the cottages had stood could be seen amidst the blackened soil.

When the Allies overran Cologne in the spring of 1945, they immediately took over Langsdorf, restoring the compound to its original purpose in order to accommodate the growing number of criminals within their own ranks.

After the war, when Germany was partitioned into four zones, each one under the government of a different Allied power, the Occupational Government Prison System was formed to deal with military criminals from all the western countries. The Russians, who controlled most of eastern Germany, maintained a separate prison system for their own soldiers, but French, British and American soldiers were grouped together according to the severity of their crimes. Only the most serious offenders, those guilty of rape or murder, were returned to their own countries to face long periods of imprisonment.

Soldiers guilty of the least serious offences, such as going absent without leave, petty theft or drunkenness, were usually confined to barracks or held in regimental stockades.

Those whose crimes fell somewhere in the middle of these two extremes, who had engaged in violence causing grievous bodily harm, or large-scale theft or black-marketeering, served out their time at Langsdorf, which was located in the British zone of occupation. Their sentences ranged from one month to three years. No one stayed longer than that. At the end of their incarceration at Langsdorf, the majority of soldiers were dishonourably discharged, after being issued with civilian clothes left behind by German soldiers drafted into the 153rd Regiment during the war, who never returned to collect them.

Wearing the clothes of men whose bodies lay in shallow graves from eastern Poland to the gates of Stalingrad, the former convicts would travel to the nearest airfield or train station and begin the long journey home, after which time they would be abandoned and forgotten by the military.

Nathan Carter walked ten paces down the Seltnerallee before he caught sight of his face staring back at him from a puddle in the middle of the road. The sight of his sunken eyes and gaunt cheekbones stopped Carter in his tracks. The mirrors in the prison bathroom were all made of polished metal, which afforded a reflection so vague that most men learned to shave by memory instead of sight. This was the first time in almost a year that he had actually seen himself clearly and, at first, he was so shocked to see what had become of him that he could scarcely breathe.

Carter heard a creaking sound behind him and turned

to see one of the guards, who had opened the door to the guardhouse and was staring at him, his expression a mixture of impatience and hostility. Behind him, the first rays of sun glistened on dew that had coated the barbed wire coiled along the fences of the prison yard.

Hurriedly, Carter turned again and walked off down the street.

Since the Allies had ended their occupation of Germany in May 1949, only a few weeks before, the country had effectively been split in two. In the west, a new German government had established itself in the city of Bonn. In the east, another German government had been set up, although it was a government in name only, since every facet of its existence remained under Soviet control.

Marooned within the newly created West Germany, Langsdorf prison began the process of emptying its cells so that the premises could be returned as quickly as possible to their original owners. The prisoners closest to their release dates were the first to go, their sentences commuted.

By the time Carter's discharge papers came through, only about a third of the prison population remained.

Some days, the barren street that led away from Langsdorf would be crowded with poorly dressed men, but today that street was empty except for Nathan Carter, as he shuffled out uncertainly into a country that he knew wanted only to be rid of him.

In the distance, he could just make out the twin spires of Cologne Cathedral, still standing amidst the cadaver of a city that had been all but obliterated. Even though the war had been over for almost four years, the city had only just started to rebuild. In places, huge pyramids of brick, like the ruins of Mayan temples, were all that remained of taverns, hotels and department stores, which had once been the lifeblood of Cologne's economy. They stood as a reminder that certain things take on a kind of memory when they spend long enough in the company of flesh and bone. This city had once been like that, but the war had erased so much of its past that even the stones had forgotten. There was a smell to all this – a chalky, dry sweetness which caught in the throat and lingered there, and the smell of old fires long since extinguished, punctuated now and then by the reek of pickled cabbage and boiled meat from street food vendors, of carbolic soap from barrels where women washed clothes and hung them up to dry among the ruins, and the sharp, vinegary stench of poisoned rats rotting in the catacombs.

Carter began to walk towards the spires, slowly at first, in the shuffling gait of a prisoner. But then his pace quickened, and then, for the first time since his arrest, he began to run. Weighed down by his heavy clothes, he soon began to sweat, but it didn't slow him down. In the bright, early summer morning, Carter raced along the streets, past buildings that had somehow survived intact, and others that were patched together like poorly assembled dolls' houses. Men and women on their way to work and children heading off to school all stopped to watch him racing past.

Carter did not stop until he reached the cathedral square. Unused to the exertion, he bent double, gasping, with his hands upon the knees of his mildew-smelling trousers, and spat onto the ground.

When he finally got his breath back, he walked a little further down the street. Passing a grocery shop, he realised with a double take that the apples, plums and pears on display were actually made of wax. A little further on, in the window of a clothing store, a mannequin with plaster fingertips crumbled as if by leprosy modelled an evening gown, at the base of which was a small card that read 'not for sale'.

Far above, the contrails of high-flying planes cat-scratched the aquarium blue sky.

A few cars rumbled by, tyres popping on the cobblestones. One of them was a high-powered Tatra sedan, which he recognised immediately because it had three headlights set in a line across the front instead of the usual two, as well as an extraordinary fin sloping down from the rear of the roof, like the dorsal of a giant shark. The Tatra slowed as it passed him and then stopped. A well-dressed man climbed out from behind the wheel. He had a wide, smooth forehead, a square jaw and yellowish-brown eyes, which looked like chips of amber hammered into the sockets of his skull. He wore a pinstripe suit with wide lapels and shoes spit-shined as only a soldier would have done. His hair, cut short at the sides and left to grow long at the top, was combed back straight upon his head. 'Are you Carter?' he asked. 'Nathan Carter?' The man was German, but he spoke decent English.

Carter straightened up. 'I might be,' he replied, staring uncertainly at the stranger.

The man held out one hand towards the open door of his car. 'Please,' he said.

'What's this about?' asked Carter.

'My employer is anxious to meet you.'

'And who is that?'

'Someone who will get you a decent set of clothes and a proper meal, and after that . . .'

'I don't understand,' said Carter. 'Do I know him? Because I'm sure I don't know you.'

'My name,' he said, 'is Anton Ritter, and all you need to know about me and my employer is that we are your friends. From the look of you, if you will forgive me saying so, I am guessing you could use a few of those. Now, please' – he gestured towards the car again – 'I work for an impatient man.'

For a moment longer, Carter hesitated. Then he muttered, 'What the hell,' and climbed into the passenger seat.

A cigarette smouldered in the ashtray. It was American tobacco, not the perfumy, cigar-like stuff the Germans liked to smoke.

Carter was staring at the cigarette.

The man followed his gaze. 'Of course!' he exclaimed, the cigarette wagging between his lips. 'How rude of me.' Reaching into his chest pocket, he produced a silver cigarette case, which he opened, revealing a neat row of smokes, like the ivories of a piano keyboard.

Carter took one and the stranger lit it for him with a gold Dunhill lighter.

As the leathery smoke swirled around him, Carter retreated into silence.

Ritter left him in peace.

The car pulled out into the flow of traffic heading east along the Bischofsgarten road towards the Rhine. After only a few minutes, they arrived at the Bleihof club, a famous landmark in post-war Cologne. Only a stone's throw from where the river swirled past, grey and cold, the Bleihof was a tall, spindly and haunted-looking place, with red and white shuttered windows and a second storey which leaned out over the ground floor, making it seem as if the entire structure might, at any moment, stagger forward like a drunken man and pitch headlong into the river.

The hotel had once been the family home of a man who made his fortune selling bars of lead to barges moving up and down the river. The lead was used as ballast for empty ships and could be sold to other ships when the riverboats picked up their cargos downriver.

By the end of 1945, it had been transformed into the haunt of Allied soldiers, and the sad and beautiful women who kept them company in their long silk dresses and lips smeared red as arterial blood, laughing hollow-eyed at jokes they did not understand. Now that Germany had reclaimed its territory, the days of the Bleihof club were numbered. Each night, the drinking and the dancing took on a frenzied finality, as if the world itself were coming to an end.

Parked out in the street were British staff cars, as well as olive green US Army Packard sedans, Willys jeeps and Harley WLA motorcycles. Only a few of the vehicles were civilian and, unlike the military cars, these ones were all guarded by men like the stranger who had picked Carter up off the street, in their wide-lapel suits and shiny shoes with Mauser pistols tucked into the specially made leather-lined pockets in their trousers.

Ritter pulled up in front of the club and cut the engine. 'Come, Mr Carter!' he said. 'My employer must not be kept waiting.'

Carter emerged from the car, dazed and squinting in the brassy sunlight.

The doorman of the Bleihof, in a long blue coat which came down to his ankles, immediately sized up Carter's ill-fitting clothes, the hack-job prison haircut and the grey, half-starved complexion. Then he glanced at Ritter, as if to ask whether he really expected such a downtrodden wreck of a man to be allowed inside.

Ritter ignored this, if he even noticed it at all. The two men swept past the front entrance and made their way around to the back of the club to a small red door in between two curtained windows. From inside came the sound of a band playing 'When the Swallows Come Back to Capistrano'.

Ritter knocked on the door and then stepped back. He nodded and smiled at Carter. 'My employer knows how to throw a party. You wait and see!'

'Who's the party for?' asked Carter.

Ritter laughed. 'Why, Mr Carter! It's for you!'

The door opened and a man stuck his head out.

'Come on!' shouted Ritter. 'Let us in!'

The man swung the door wide.

Ritter put one arm on Carter's shoulder and guided him into the room.

The blare of the music struck Carter as if a ghost had shoved him in the chest. The darkened room was filled with smoke and voices. From the state some people were in, it looked as if the party had been going on all night.

Ritter steered him through the crowd, snatching up a champagne glass from a tray being carried past by a white-jacketed waiter. He drained the glass and handed it to the next man he came to.

Overwhelmed by the crush of bodies and the unfamiliar sound of women laughing, Carter stumbled along behind Ritter, who acted as a kind of battering ram through the maze of people in their way.

The low ceiling creaked and, in those moments when the music paused, he could hear different music playing upstairs, and the shuffling footsteps of people dancing in the room above.

At last, Ritter showed him into a second room, where a long table was crowded with plates of food. 'I'll wait for you outside,' he said to Carter.

At the far end of the room, lounging in a leather wing-backed chair, sat a tall man with thinning hair and a round, boyish face.

On one side of him sat a much younger woman with deep cloudy blue eyes, like those of a newborn baby, which Carter had often seen in Rhineland girls. Her hair was black and very shiny and pulled back in a ponytail, which showed more practicality than any attention to fashion, since most of the women wore their hair steam-curled into waves and held back from their faces with a mass of bobby pins. Neither was she wearing the same scanty, sequined clothing as the women in the outer room. Instead, she had on trousers and a navy blue turtleneck sweater, and her fingertips were stained with ink, as if she had just emerged from writing an exam.

'Mr Carter!' exclaimed the boy-faced man, leaping to his feet and vigorously shaking Carter's hand. 'It is an honour to meet you. My name is Hanno Dasch, and I am a great admirer of your country.'

'Including what they did to this city?' asked the girl with the ink-stained hands.

Dasch shot her a glance. 'That is in the past,' he snapped, 'and the fact is we should never have been enemies in the first place. As far as I'm concerned, everything you see outside we brought upon ourselves.'

'Why pick me to tell all this?' asked Carter. 'I'm not the only American in Cologne.'

'But none have resumes like yours,' said Dasch, 'or better prospects for the future.'

'From the look on your new friend's face,' said the girl, 'you might want to explain to him why a man in a second-hand suit who, I am guessing, cannot afford to shine his shoes, has suddenly found himself the guest of honour at a party thrown for him by someone he has never set eyes upon until today.'

'I do have a meal ticket,' said Carter.

The girl crumpled her lips in a vague, sarcastic smile.

'May I introduce my daughter, Teresa,' Dasch said with an exasperated sigh.

His daughter, thought Carter, as that piece of the puzzle fitted neatly into place.

'The reason I have thrown this party in your honour,' explained Dasch, resting his hand upon Carter's shoulder as if they had known each other for years, 'is that I am not only an admirer of your country, I am also a great admirer of your work, in particular.'

'My work?'

'Don't be modest! Explain to Teresa how you managed to complete one of the most successful robberies in the history of the US Army.'

Carter shifted uneasily. 'Well,' he began, 'I wouldn't call it that.'

'What he did,' said Dasch, picking up the story, 'was to send four trucks to the US Army's warehouse on the outskirts of Wiesbaden, in the American occupation zone, with bills of lading for more than three million American cigarettes which had just arrived there and which were due to be distributed to commissaries at every Allied base on the continent of Europe. The guards at the warehouse had been told to expect the trucks at a certain hour of the morning and they arrived exactly on time. The bills of lading were checked and the cigarettes were loaded on board. The whole thing took less than one hour. Then the trucks departed and, half an hour later, four different trucks arrived with identical bills of lading for the three million cigarettes. Of course, they were immediately arrested. By the time it was determined that these men were, in fact, carrying the legitimate bills of lading and that those in the first trucks were fakes, the cigarettes had disappeared, along with the men who had been impersonating American military personnel. The trucks were found about an hour away from the city, all neatly parked and with the keys still in the ignition, but the cigarettes and the men who stole them were never found. This was a success beyond the wildest dreams of anyone who's ever dared to contemplate such things.'

'Except for the fact that he ended up in prison,' muttered the girl.

'Ah!' Dasch raised one finger and sliced it back and forth through the air, as if he were extinguishing a match. 'But, Teresa, do you know why?'

'I imagine you are about to tell me,' she replied.

'He was betrayed,' said Dasch, and suddenly he was no longer smiling, 'by someone he thought he could trust. Is that not right, Mr Carter?'

'That's what the papers said.'

'So they did,' Dasch agreed, 'and there was something else they said, as well.'

'What's that?' asked Teresa.

'That Mr Carter never divulged his contacts, or the names of the people he had worked with. Even though he himself had been a victim of deceit, Mr Carter remained a man who could be trusted.'

'Bravo, Mr Carter,' said Teresa, without a trace of sincerity in her voice.

'Bravo, indeed,' said Dasch, turning to Carter and looking him straight in the eye. 'Such loyalty deserves to be rewarded.'

Teresa rose to her feet. 'Enjoy your party,' she said to Carter. 'I am going home.' Then she walked out of the room.

'Please forgive her,' said Dasch. 'She is singularly lacking in diplomacy.'

'At least she's honest about it,' said Carter.

'A little too much so, I'm afraid.'

Carter noticed that the music upstairs had stopped now, and the floor no longer creaked with dancing.

'The party is getting old,' said Dasch, apparently forgetting that Carter had only just arrived. 'Why don't we go out and get some air?'

As they left the little room with the wing-backed chairs, he saw that the band had finished for the night and were now packing away their instruments into battered, velvet-lined cases. The lights had been turned on and most of the guests had departed. A few sat unconscious on couches which, under the punishing glare of dusty light bulbs hanging from the ceiling, revealed stains of wine and the charred holes of cigarette burns.

Outside, almost all the cars had gone, leaving the street littered with cigarette butts, which the doorman was gathering one by one and stashing in the pocket of his long blue coat. It was a common habit for civilians to follow in the path of Allied soldiers, picking up the ends of cigarettes, which they would then take apart and reassemble into cigarettes of their own.

Ritter was standing by the door, hands folded across his chest and one leg tucked behind him so that the foot was resting flat against the wall.

Teresa had already vanished, and Carter wondered if he would ever see her again. It caught him by surprise that he would even wonder such a thing but, after the relentless sameness of prison life, almost everything he'd seen and every thought to cross his mind since he'd walked out of Langsdorf had been a cause for amazement.

'Walk with me, Mr Carter,' said Dasch. 'We have some business to discuss.'

With Ritter following behind, the two men strolled across the street.

Dasch led them down a pathway that had been cleared between two large grey piles of masonry, like heaps of dinosaur bones. Beyond the rubble lay the shell of a house. Pigeons swooped and fluttered out of holes punched through the slate roof tiles.

Dasch stepped into the hollowed remnants of the building.

Carter followed him in and then stopped and looked around. Above them, perched upon a fan of splintered floorboards, stood a bathtub that had somehow survived completely intact. A staircase led up to nothing. Shards of glass, powdered with soot, fanged the frames of broken windows.

'Breathe in, Mr Carter!' Dasch commanded, raising his hands like a preacher. 'Do you smell it?'

Carter vaguely caught the scent of fires that had been extinguished long ago. 'I'm not sure I know what you mean,' he said.

'In places like this,' explained Dasch, 'you can still smell the war. It is a very particular odour. Some people have told me that it comes from the ionisation of the air after an explosion. Others say it is the smell of bones that have been burned to dust. And some say it is purely my imagination, my own daughter included. I am often tempted to believe her, but when I walk among the ruins, I know for a fact it is real.'

Carter had thought he was joking, but now it seemed to him that maybe there was some kind of smell – different from the sweaty odours of the street that had flooded his senses when he first walked out of prison. This was sharp and piercing, like burned electrical wiring, like the reek of flint when it is struck against itself.

In that moment, Carter suddenly realised that he had made a terrible mistake following Dasch into the confines of this place. But there was no way out of it now. 'What are we doing here?' he asked.

'I just have one question for you,' said Dasch.

Carter sensed some nameless menace, hideous and lethal, lying just beneath the courteous formality of Dasch's words.

'I studied your technique,' continued Dasch. 'There is scarcely a detail of that robbery with which I am unfamiliar, and yet there is still one thing I do not understand.'

'What's that?' asked Carter. The moisture had gone from his throat and his lips felt like blades of dry grass rustling together as he spoke.

'What I don't understand is why.'

'Why what?'

'Why you did it. Why you would suddenly go from being a functioning, law-abiding member of society to carrying out such an audacious theft.'

Carter was silent.

'And I would like it very much,' said Dasch, 'if you could satisfy my curiosity on that small point.' And now he pinched the air between his thumb and index finger, as if to show what a tiny, insignificant matter it was.

'I did it,' said Carter, 'because I realised that I could.'

Dasch stared at him intently for a moment. Then his face split into a grin, revealing strong, white, perfect teeth. He tilted his head to one side and nodded.

It struck Carter as a strange movement, this tilting of the head, until he realised that Dasch had been nodding to Ritter, who stood directly behind him.

Carter felt dread sifting through his blood, like a slow silty explosion of black ink diffusing in water. Slowly, he turned around.

Ritter was only an arm's length away, a small automatic pistol aimed directly at Carter's face, but now he lowered the weapon and tucked it away beneath the folds of his coat.

Carter turned back to face Dasch. 'What the hell was that?' he demanded.

'That,' replied Dasch, 'was your job interview, which all depended on your answer to my question.'

'And how did you know what I would say?' asked Carter.

'I didn't,' admitted Dasch, 'but your answer was entirely to my satisfaction.'

'What if it hadn't been?' asked Carter.

Once more, Dasch's hand came to rest upon Carter's shoulder, like a bird that had been trained to settle there. 'There's no need to talk about that,' he whispered.

Carter and Dasch crossed the street to where the Tatra was parked, with Ritter drifting along behind them, like his master's second shadow.

The Bleihof club was closed now, its windows hidden behind shutters whose red paint still showed the dappled blistering of heat from the nearby buildings that had burned in the air raids years before.

'Climb in,' said Dasch.

'Where are we going?'

'Someplace where you can relax while you consider my offer.'

'And what is your offer?' asked Carter.

Dasch did not immediately reply to Carter's question. Instead he turned to Ritter and exclaimed, 'You see? This is what I like! This directness. This fearlessness.' He chopped the knife edge of one hand into the palm of the other. 'Cutting through the fog of ambiguity!' Only now did he respond to Carter. 'We may have our country back now, part of it anyway, but we have very little else. The lack of simple things we once took for granted, as you yourself did before you started living in a prison cell, has only increased our desire to possess them. The people who have these simple things – the cigarettes and chocolate and soap, which used to be such ordinary pleasures – are not the British or the French, and certainly not the Russians. They are the Americans, especially the soldiers over here. And I need somebody who can deal with them, preferably one of their own. But I can't just wander out onto the dance floor of the Bleihof club and hire the first American I see, even if he were amenable to my offer. I need a person with proven experience in the complicated business of separating these luxuries from those who have enough and delivering them to those who do not. That person is you, Mr Carter. I knew it from the moment I first read about your story in the paper. And since then I have been waiting for the day when you were free again, just as you yourself have waited for so long.'

After travelling along Aachenerstrasse, the car entered the Rudolfplatz and pulled up beside the Hotel Europa, which had been one of many grand hotels in Cologne before the war and was now, having somehow managed to escape annihilation during the war, the only grand hotel. 'Here we are,' said Dasch. 'Your home until tomorrow.'

'I can't afford to stay here,' Carter protested.

'Don't worry about that,' Dasch told him. 'Just tell them your name. Everything is taken care of. And here . . .' He rummaged in his pocket and pulled out a roll of money as thick as his fist. After peeling off a dozen bills, he handed them to Carter. 'This will get you some new clothes, and a visit to the barber, as well.'

'And what then?' asked Carter.

'I want you to make up your mind,' said Dasch. 'Either go home and try to make a life for yourself, ashamed of your past and hoping that no one learns about the things you've done. Or take that shame and turn it into something else. You can understand the actions which first drew you to my attention, and for which you have been punished, as evidence of the skills you have been granted in this life. I am offering you a chance to make use of those skills, among people who will respect you and welcome you, not turn their backs when they see you coming, or throw you once again into a concrete cell if given half the chance. I'll send Ritter by in the morning. If you're still here, you can begin your work immediately. If not,' he shrugged, 'then I will have misjudged your potential.'

Carter climbed out of the car and shut the door.

The Tatra sped away down the street, turned onto Hohenzollernring and was gone.

For a moment, Carter just stood there, staring up at the magnificent hotel with its revolving front door, lace curtains in the windows and flowers growing in window boxes on the balconies. But Carter did not enter the hotel right away. Instead, he waited until the car was out of sight, then he turned south and walked several blocks to the Zülpicher-platz, until he came to a little barber shop on the corner. A small, black and white enamel sign bolted above the door read 'Militärrasierstube', indicating that it was a place for soldiers to get their hair cut.

As Carter arrived, two British soldiers passed him on their way out of the shop. Buttoning their short, yellowy-brown wool overcoats, the men fitted their side caps carefully onto their freshly cropped heads and continued down the street. As they passed by Carter, the men barely seemed to notice he was there. To them, he was just another downtrodden survivor of a beaten army, struggling to forget the last five years of his life.

Carter smelled the aftershave that the barber had splashed on their necks. At the same time, he caught a breath of his own unwashed body, and the old sweat of a stranger steeped into the worn-out clothes that hung like scarecrow rags upon his undernourished frame.

Inside, a man in a white tunic was sweeping up the hair that had fallen around the barber's chair. Facing the chair was a large mirror, its backing flaked around the edges so that the reflection appeared as if seen through a pair of cataracted eyes. Along the counter were jars of different coloured liquids, red and blue, containing combs and scissors and a straight edge razor.

The man glanced up at Carter. He did not smile. 'The cost is three marks,' he said, 'and that is in advance.'

Carter pulled a twenty-mark note from his pocket. 'Do you have change for this?'

The barber's eyes widened at the sight of the large bill. Then he set his broom against the wall and spun the chair around for Carter to take a seat.

Carter removed his coat and hung it on a peg upon the wall, which was lightning-bolted with cracks, still unrepaired, from the seismic shock of a 10,000kg bomb known as a Grand Slam, which had been dropped by a Royal Air Force Lancaster on the night of 31st May 1942. The bomb had fallen six blocks away and where it landed, nothing remained in a two thousand foot radius but a crater, thirty foot deep in the middle, which had since filled with water, forming a pond in which old people, since there were only old people left in that part of town, sometimes went swimming. They floated peacefully, small islands of pale, sagging flesh, and stared down through the surprisingly clear water at the mosaic of broken stones, which were all that remained of the buildings they had once called home.

As Carter settled back into the chair, the barber folded down the collar of Carter's shirt and gently wrapped around his neck a thin strip of papery fabric. Then, with a movement like a magician wafting his cape, the barber covered Carter's upper body with a clean white cloth.

'How should it be?' he asked.

'Short on the sides,' said Carter, 'and leave it long on top.'

The barber fished out a pair of needle-nosed scissors and a comb and began to snip away at Carter's unkempt mass of hair.

At Langsdorf, prisoners received mandatory haircuts once every three months. The cuts were done by untrained soldiers using electric clippers and the hair was cut down to the scalp, frequently leaving gouges in the skin. It was possible to bribe the prison barbers with cigarettes or money, but all that got a person was a slower haircut; a little less painful, but just as ugly as everyone else's.

As Carter closed his eyes and listened to the metallic swish of the scissors, the muscles in his back relaxed for the first time in so long he had mistaken them for bone. Suddenly, and catching him completely by surprise, tears spilled out of his eyes and ran down his cheeks.

The barber stopped his cutting, produced a clean handkerchief and dabbed away the tears. He made no comment, nor did he pause in his work for more than a couple of seconds. In a moment, he was back to snipping away tiny strands of hair raised up along the black, medicinal-smelling tines of the comb.

For the remainder of the haircut, Carter puzzled over why the tears had come. It was something about the peculiar anonymous gentleness with which the barber performed his task, set against the dull, uncaring brutality that surrounded almost every memory he had of prison life.

When the haircut was finished, the barber held up a small mirror for Carter to see the back of his head.

For the first time in a long time, Carter recognised himself.

Then the barber produced a hot towel from a pot simmering on a heater in the corner. He squeezed out the water and then coiled the towel into a ring, laying it over Carter's face so that only his nose peeked out from the hole in the middle. Then Carter heard the dry shuffle of the straight edge razor blade against the leather strop. The warmth of the towel radiated across his face and down his neck.

A minute later, the barber removed the towel and painted Carter's face with soap, using a badger hair brush. Then he positioned the razor in his hand, tilted Carter's head very slightly to the side and slowly drew the blade down Carter's cheek, the straight edge rustling faintly as it cut through the bristles.

When the barber had finished his work, he closed the razor and wiped the white slick of shaving cream on a towel that hung across his sleeve. Then he used the clean side of the towel to clear away the last flecks of soap from beneath Carter's ears. Finally, he splashed rubbing alcohol onto his palms and, with practised movements, neither sensual nor complicated, he swiped his hands across Carter's face and neck. Carter gasped at the almost electric jolt of the alcohol upon his skin.

The cloth was removed, once more with a flourish, and Carter reached into his pocket for the money. 'There used to be another barber here,' he said, as he handed over the twenty-mark note. 'It was a while ago. I haven't been around much lately.'

'Do you recall his name?' asked the man, narrowing his eyes.

'Siegfried,' answered Carter.

The barber's face froze. His arm remained extended, fingers still clasping the money. 'Are you sure that was his name?' he asked.

'Positive,' said Carter.

The barber's face had turned very pale, like the belly of a fish floating upside down in a pond. 'I would be happy,' he began, his words sounding strangely rehearsed, 'to tell him we have spoken, and where he might find you, if you would care to let me know.'

'I'll be in the dining room of the Hotel Europa today at noon. Say that Carter wants to see him.'

The barber seemed to remember suddenly that he was still holding the twenty-mark note in his hand. He went over to a drawer in the counter, opened it and began rummaging about amongst a pile of coins and crumpled bills.

'Keep the change,' said Carter.

The barber turned and stared. 'What? All of it?'

'You earned it,' said Carter. Then he turned to leave.

'Mr Carter!' the barber called to him.

Carter stopped at the door but did not turn around. 'Yes?'

'Welcome back,' he said.

By the time Carter sat down at his table in the ornate dining room of the Europa, a large room located just off the main foyer of the hotel, he was wearing a new navy blue double-breasted suit, new shoes, new shirt, new tie. In fact, new everything. Every scrap of clothing he had been wearing when he walked into the little haberdashery on Bügeleisenstrasse had been rolled into a bundle by the quietly appalled sales clerk and tossed into the alleyway behind the shop, where it lay in a puddle for less than a minute before someone dashed out of a doorway to claim it.

Carter had chosen a small table in the corner, facing the entrance to the dining room and right next to the kitchen door, through which he might escape if necessary. He never sat anywhere except with his back to the wall and never more than three running paces from an exit. He had picked up a copy of the newspaper on his way in and glanced down at the headlines while he waited. The front page was taken up by an article about a woman whose body had been found washed up in bulrushes on the banks of the Rhine. As yet, she was still unidentified, but the police had ruled it as a suicide. It mentioned that, during the war, the suicide rate in Germany had been more than ten thousand people a year and, although the number had dropped considerably since the armistice of 1945, it was high enough to be a matter of national concern. Carter was not surprised to read this. As remarkable as the progress of rebuilding this country had been, it still had a long way to go. And it would be much longer still before the psychological damage of the war began to heal. If it ever healed. If it was ever meant to heal.

From what Carter had seen, not only would these mental scars remain, for as long as those who had lived through the war continued to draw breath, but the trauma itself would outlive them. It would be passed on from generation to generation, until it had altered the very substance of German identity. One thing was for certain – there could be no going back to the way things had been before, and yet that was exactly what Hitler had promised; a return to the greatness of some imagined moment in the past. By the time people realised that they had been tricked by one of the biggest con men in history, there was no choice except to link arms and march forward into a nightmare. The Germans even had a word for it: 'Ausharren'. It meant to proceed down a path that you knew was the wrong one to take, but to take it anyway because you had no other choice except to die. Carter wondered if the woman had thought about that as she slipped into the murky water of the Rhine.

Carter heard someone clearing their throat and looked up to see the waiter in his close-fitting tuxedo jacket. Before the war, this man had been a professor of physics at the university of Cologne, but considered himself lucky to have any job at all now, even as a waiter in a restaurant where he had previously been a regular customer. He was tall and thin, with a strangely blunted nose and the tops of his ears chipped away as if they had been carved from rotten stone

– all the result of frostbite, which he had received near the town of Tula Oblast while sleeping in the ruins of what had once been the house of Leo Tolstoy, in the winter of 1941. Beneath his collarbone, barely visible under the flimsy fabric of his shirt, was a large, X-shaped scar, where he had been stabbed with the cruciform blade of a Mosin-Nagant bayonet when a group of Siberians appeared out of a blizzard on the outskirts of Novgorod, and overran the snow-covered bunkers where the professor and his men had been waiting out the storm. There was also a mottled scar across his neck, like the drag of a long fingernail, where he had been grazed by a bullet from a Tokarev pistol, fired by a commissar in the seconds before he lost consciousness as the waiter choked him to death, waist deep in tar black water in the marshes of Pripet. Stories lost to all but him, and only half remembered now. 'Will you be having company, sir?' he asked.

'Yes,' replied Carter.

'Then would you like to wait before you order?'

'No,' said Carter. 'I believe I will get started right away.'

'Would you like to hear the special, sir?' asked the man.

'Whatever it is, I will have it.'

'Very good, sir,' replied the professor, bowing slightly and making a conscious attempt not to click his heels together, which had become a habit during the war.

In the stillness while Carter waited for the food, he found himself struggling to maintain an outward appearance of normality and calm while, inwardly, his heart felt clogged with a fluttering anxiety which, at first, he could not trace back to its source. As the minutes passed, the answer began to appear, dimly, like a man walking out of the fog, until finally it stood there in front of him and he recognised the demon that had dogged his path from the moment he set foot in prison.

During his time in Langsdorf, two things had obsessed Carter to the point where he could feel his sanity slipping away and madness scuttling towards him on its brittle, crabbing legs.

The first was that he had somehow been forgotten by the people who had sent him to prison, and that the days of his sentence, of which he kept obsessive track, were not even being counted by anyone other than himself. Carter had calibrated his sanity for the nine months he expected to serve, not one day longer. But what if they simply left him there to rot for the maximum three years, or even longer? Over time, it became a fixation. There was nothing he could do to pacify the voices in his head. All day, they gibbered at him from the rafters of his skull and, at night, they pursued him out onto the barren, moonlit tundra of his dreams. Now, even though he knew that he had not been forgotten after all, the fear of it still lingered in his mind.

His second obsession had been food.

He did not expect much from the prison kitchen, and he had never thought of himself as a picky eater, but the brain-coloured slurry that he scooped each day from a four-sectioned tray, perpetually greasy to the touch, was so mysterious in its composition and so consistent in its damp, sweaty smell – as well as the metallic tang it left in his mouth, like the taste of a penny resting on his tongue – that, most of the time, he did not actually know what he was eating. He was forced, in a short space of time, to recalibrate his whole idea of food. It was no longer about the enjoyment of the meal, neither was there any social aspect to the mealtimes since prisoners were not allowed to speak while they were eating. Instead the room was filled with the clatter of cutlery on trays, and men clearing their throats and the shuffle of boots on the linoleum floor.

To stop himself from going mad, Carter retreated far inside his head. There, in the treasure chamber of his memories, he relived the summers he had spent as a teenager working as a dish washer at a diner called Logan's in Dunellen, New Jersey. Like many such diners, the building had been constructed in the shape of a railroad car, with round-topped seats like giant mushrooms for people who sat at the counter and booths by the window which looked out onto the main street. It was right across from the police station where his father worked. For years, his father had been a regular at Logan's, with a seat reserved for him alone and apple pie served just the way he liked it, with a slice of cheddar cheese on the side. It was a personal favour to his father that Mr Logan gave Carter the job and his father had warned him what would happen if he did not live up to expectations.

'You shame me,' his father had told him, 'and I will wring your neck.' He always talked like that to his son, although he never laid a hand on him. But Carter had heard him speak to others using those same words, and had known that he meant what he said.

Carter worked from 6 a.m. until 5 p.m. and made fifty cents

an hour. He was also entitled to one meal per day, although he never got to choose what it would be. The meal would be whatever got sent back by some finicky customer whose order had not been taken down exactly right by the waitress. Or, if Carter was lucky, the chef would deliberately mess up an order – gravy instead of grated cheese, French fries instead of mashed potatoes – and Carter would eat that instead.

On Sunday afternoons, in the quiet time between lunch and dinner, the chefs from several local restaurants would gather in the kitchen of Logan's and take turns cooking for each other. Each week, a different chef would be in charge.

Carter would clean up after them, and the chefs would always make sure that there was a little left over for him. It always surprised Carter how ordinary these meals were – Shepherd's Pie, Meat Loaf, Tuna Casserole – but they were the best of their kind that Carter had ever tasted, and one day he asked the chef about it.

The chef, a moon-bellied man with small dark eyes and a double chin, which rested on a red and white checked scarf that he kept tied around his throat as if he meant to choke himself to death by wearing it at all, replied that the simplest things were always the hardest to cook. 'You want to know if a chef can really cook?' he said. 'Just get them to fry you an egg. You can eat eggs all your life and never know for sure how they can taste until a good chef cooks them up for you.'

For the most part, Carter had hated the job. Now and then, he would look up from the sink of dingy grey water and, through the open window that looked out on a vacant lot behind the restaurant, the fierce blue summer sky would flood into his eyes, and he would feel a terrible longing to just forget everything about these dreary days, to have them washed from his mind as if by some act of hypnosis.

Carter could never have imagined that, one day, he would return to those memories, selecting every moment that he could recall and holding it up to the light, turning it this way and that, like a man with a bucket full of diamonds. But each one of them brought him back to a time when food had taste and meaning and the fact that he had taken those things for granted made the resurrection of those thoughts even more precious to him in the boxed-in world of Langsdorf.

When the first course arrived – onions in beef broth and a piece of toasted bread with cheese on top floating in the middle – Carter felt a momentary twinge of guilt, knowing that even this small appetiser was more nourishment than some people out there in the streets of the city, the scavengers of coal, potato peels and the rags he had been wearing only a couple of hours ago, could expect in an entire day.

With the first sweet, salty mouthful, it was as if a part of him that had forgotten who he was during the months at Langsdorf prison suddenly remembered. The haircut and the new suit had not done that. All they had accomplished was to allow others to judge his appearance and to behave around him the way he had been used to being treated before he first put on the clothing of a convict. But that bowl of soup had brought him back to life.

As he ate, Carter kept his eye on the main door in the foyer, which he could see clearly from his table. It was a revolving door and the way the noonday light shone down into the street caused the whirling panes of glass to flicker blindingly as people came and went. Although this phenomenon obscured his view, he took comfort in the fact that anyone entering the hotel would need several seconds to accustom themselves to the darkness, time enough for him to disappear if necessary.

He had just finished the soup when Siegfried appeared through the whirling blades of the revolving door.

This man had never been a barber, nor was his name actually Siegfried. Carter had never met Siegfried. That was just an alias, agreed upon long ago, by which he could summon back to life the ghosts of his former existence.

In fact, the man's name was Daniel Eckberg. He was in his late twenties, with pale, slightly boiled-looking skin, small eyes and a dense crop of platinum blond hair. Aside from the CIA station chief attached to the US embassy in Bonn, Eckberg was one of only two people who knew the real reason why Carter had been sent to prison. The other was Carter's control officer, Marcus Wilby, whom Carter and Eckberg only ever referred to as 'our mutual friend'. At the time of their first encounter, Eckberg had only just arrived in Europe, having been recruited straight out of Yale. His task was to serve as the go-between in any dealings with Carter and Wilby – what was known as a 'cut-out'. That way, if Carter ever did something that caused his cover to be blown, it would be harder to trace his connections back to the CIA.

Back then, it had looked to Carter like the best chance of

getting his cover blown was by Eckberg himself, who possessed a nervous, naive energy which attracted unwanted attention. But Carter said nothing about it at the time, hoping that when they met again, Eckberg would have learned the kind of tradecraft that would allow him to blend in to his surroundings.

Looking at Eckberg now, it seemed to Carter that Eckberg had learned nothing at all.

Eckberg approached the tall, frostbitten waiter and spoke to him.

The waiter pointed at Carter and Eckberg made his way across the room. 'It's good to see you, Nathan,' he said, taking a seat at the table.

It irritated Carter that Eckberg called him by his first name, not because he should have used a different one but because it spoke of a familiarity between them that did not actually exist.

'I ordered whatever you're having,' Eckberg announced, unravelling his napkin with a flick of the wrist and tucking it into his collar.

Carter glanced around the room to see if anyone was watching. That gesture might have fitted in if they'd been sitting in a diner in New Jersey, but it didn't look right here. There was no doubt in Carter's mind that the other diners had noticed, but they were too tactful to show it. They remained hunched over their food, locked in quiet conversations, studiously oblivious.

Eckberg set his elbows on the white tablecloth and knitted his fingers together. 'So how's it feel to be a free man?'

'I think it's going to take a while before I know.'

'That looks like a new suit to me.'

'New everything,' replied Carter, 'except the man who's wearing it.'

The waiter arrived with the soup and put it down before Eckberg. As soon as the waiter had left, Eckberg pushed the bowl to one side. 'You almost gave the barber a heart attack. He wasn't expecting to hear from you for at least a couple of weeks, maybe even months. Frankly, neither were we.'

'If you're not going to have that,' said Carter.

'Be my guest.'

Carter reached across and pulled Eckberg's bowl over to his side.

'So why are we hearing from you now?' asked Eckberg. 'Did you already find who you were looking for?'

'I didn't have to,' said Carter. 'He came to find me. He sent a car with a chauffeur.'

The expression froze on Eckberg's face. It was a moment before he could speak. 'That is unexpected,' he said at last.

'Unexpected? That's the word you're going to use? How the hell did he even know that I was getting out today? How did he even know where I was?'

'I'll look into it,' said Eckberg.

'It's a little late for that. This guy is obviously better connected than you thought. You need to let me know where things stand.'

Eckberg scratched at his eyebrow. 'Listen, about that. About me letting you know. Our friend has decided to pull me from the operation. He sent me this time because I'm the one you were expecting to see and he didn't want to spook you. But I'm not the one you will be meeting from now on.'

'Why is he pulling you?' asked Carter.

Eckberg shrugged, but he looked more like a man in pain than one who was ambivalent. 'I don't know,' he said. 'I'm sure he has his reasons.'

Although Carter said nothing about it, he was relieved that Wilby had made the decision to remove Eckberg from field operations. It wasn't just Eckberg's mannerisms that made Carter nervous to be meeting him in such a confined space, when he knew others might be watching. It was also the way he looked, so obviously American in his low-heeled shoes, cuffed trousers and wide-brimmed fedora hat.

There was an art to blending in. You didn't have to look like you belonged. You just had to avoid standing out.

The most reliable way to achieve this was to find yourself a cafe in the neighbourhood where you would be working, sit at a table by the window and spend an hour watching people go by, particularly those who were about the same age as you, taking careful note of the way they dressed, the kind of things they carried and the way they wore their hair. After a while, you would get a sense of what passed for normal. Then you made your way to a second-hand clothing store or some kind of a charity shop where used clothing was sold. You picked out a set of clothes that came closest to the things you had seen – not what you liked or what you thought fitted best, but what people were actually wearing. You had to buy everything – socks, undershirts, belt, shoes –

and to make sure that all of it was used. New clothing would be noticed, no matter how local it was. And how did people carry their belongings in the street? Did they use briefcases, or canvas satchels or paper shopping bags? The final important detail was to get a haircut from a local barber, after making clear that you didn't really care what kind of cut you received. This would guarantee a disappointingly average hairstyle, which was exactly what you needed. There were many other tricks, adding layer upon layer of camouflage until a person could achieve a perfect anonymity.

Even if Eckberg had followed these strange rituals, which he clearly hadn't, something about his expression – an unmistakable and yet almost impossible to define sense of optimism which radiated out of his well-fed, rounded face – was markedly different from the ashen complexions of those Europeans of his age who had been poisoned by the bad food, smoke and horror of the war.

Ironically, it was this same lack of guile, which caused Eckberg to stand out so glaringly in these surroundings, that reassured Carter of his trustworthiness. But being trustworthy and being effective were two different things, and one did not outweigh the other, especially since Dasch had already proved himself to be more capable than anyone had expected. 'Who's going to replace you?' he asked.

'Nobody,' answered Eckberg. 'Our friend will come to the meetings himself.'

The news caught Carter by surprise. 'No cut-out?' he asked. 'I thought that was a basic protocol.'

'It was. I mean, it is,' he said, unable to conceal his frustration. 'It should be, anyway, if you ask me.'

'Then why isn't it?' Carter leaned forward across the table. 'What the hell is going on?'

'You'll have to ask our friend about that and, given what you've just told me, he's going to want to meet you right away.'

'I'm upstairs, room 201, but only until tomorrow morning, so tell him to hurry. I need some answers from you people or I'm getting the hell out of here.'

'Understood.' Eckberg rose from his chair and looked around. 'You know, this is the most expensive place in town. I can't afford to eat here. So how are you paying for it?'

'I'm not,' Carter told him. 'It's a gift from my new employer.'

Eckberg rapped his knuckles softly on the table. 'Good luck to you, Carter,' he said.

As Eckberg walked out of the room, people sitting at their tables raised their heads to watch him go, their eyes filled with a mixture of curiosity and the coldness reserved for all strangers.

That evening Carter was lying spread-eagled on his bed in room 201 of the Hotel Europa.

The mattress was so soft, and he was so unused to being comfortable when he lay down, that he wondered if he would end up sleeping on the floor that night.

He closed his eyes and listened to the rumble of cars out in the street, the soft clang of the elevator's bell as it moved from floor to floor and the clatter of the metal cage door as the elevator attendant opened it to let people in or out. And then there was the creaking of the carpeted floorboards as guests passed by his room.

Although he had no trouble identifying every sound, they seemed so distant in his memory that it was almost as if they had been borrowed from someone else's recollections. They had been overlaid by the sounds of the Langsdorf – the jangle of keys, the slamming of metal doors, the rustle of water in pipes. But more than anything else, it was the silence of the prison that had settled like a suffocating weight upon his chest, stifling the voices of the convicts, who never raised their voices without punishment. Out here in the world, the silence existed only in between the noises that made things normal. But in the jail, it was the silence that ruled over everything else, so that the noises became little more than punctuation in the terrible language of stillness.

Carter heard the floorboards creak outside his room. And then he heard them stop. He sat upright, no longer drowsy from the wandering of his thoughts.

There was a sharp knock on the door.

He waited, thinking maybe they would go away.

But the knocking came again.

'Who is it?' he asked.

'Room service!' was the muffled reply.

Carter slipped off the bed and went to the door. He opened it slightly, keeping the guard chain on and standing to one side, knowing that if someone tried to kick the door in, the chain would be of little help in stopping them. A man stood with a tray balanced on one hand. He was wearing a short, white jacket and a pillbox hat. The contents of the tray were covered with a silver metal dome, which also obscured his face.

'I didn't order any room service,' said Carter.

'Oh yes you damned well did,' said the man and, as he spoke, he shifted the tray so that Carter could see his face.

He was clean-shaven and sallow-looking, with thinning brown hair which was turning grey around the temples. Carter immediately recognised his control officer, Marcus Wilby.

'Hold on a second,' said Carter. He closed the door for a moment, undid the guard chain and then opened the door again, swinging it wide so that the man could pass through.

As soon as the door was shut again, Wilby thumped the tray down on a desk by the window, whipped off the pillbox cap and tossed it away into a corner of the room. 'Damn,' he muttered. 'I bet I get fleas from that thing!'

'Hello, Captain,' said Carter.

'It's Major now,' he replied, unbuttoning the white coat, 'and I heard Dasch offered you a job.'

'He did.'

Wilby paused. 'What kind of a job?'

'He wants me to use my contacts at the American military bases, so that he can start buying stolen goods from them directly. Except I don't have any contacts.'

'Don't worry about that,' said Wilby. 'We can take care of it. Just tell him you can get whatever he wants, then stall him for a couple of days. It might take me a while to set things up.'

'And if I need to reach you?'

'Use the standard protocols, the same as you'd have done with Eckberg.' Wilby flopped down into a wing-backed chair by the window, subsiding into the upholstery as if his bones were dissolving inside him.

'Why did you pull him?'

'Security concerns,' replied Wilby. 'Nothing you need to worry about.'

'Why don't you tell me what's going on and let me decide if I need to worry or not?'

Wilby paused. 'All right,' he said. 'A few days ago, we lost somebody who worked at the embassy in Bonn.'

'An agent?'

'Not exactly,' said Wilby, 'but I did have her working on some agency business, and I think that might have got her killed.'

'So who was she? What was she doing?'

'I got to know her when I was stationed in Berlin, right after the end of the war. All of us who worked for the CIA, or Strategic Services, as it was known back then, were quartered at what they called the Joe House on Promenadenstrasse. It was like a cross between a country club and a boarding school, and for all I know it may have been one of those things before we took it over. It was one of the only places in the city where you could get a decent meal and sleep in clean sheets. We were all lumped in there together, trying to figure out how to deal with the Russians, who were way ahead of us in almost every aspect of intelligence gathering. We knew that Soviet agents had penetrated British intelligence and that these agents had recruited people who were already working at MI5 and MI6. It became so bad that we hesitated to share information with the British, knowing it would be funnelled directly to the Russians. As a countermeasure to this happening in our own offices, we began placing agents in low-level but important positions at various stations around Europe. These agents had instructions to let slip comments which might make any potential recruiter for the Soviets believe that they had found a suitable candidate.'

'What kind of comments?' asked Carter.

'Just little things,' replied Wilby. 'A mention here or there expressing admiration for the Russians. Music. Writers. Food. Nothing too obvious.'

'But if you place an agent whose job is to catch Russian spies, how do you make sure that the spy isn't told about the operation?'

'Exactly,' answered Wilby. 'And the answer is, you don't tell them. You don't tell anyone at all. I put her in play at the Bonn station two months ago. I gave her a bottom-rung job as an archivist at the embassy. She wasn't even directly attached to the CIA branch.'

'And what happened?'

'Nothing, at first,' replied Wilby, 'but about two weeks ago, she informed me that she had been approached by someone she thought might be trying to recruit her.'

'And you knew this person?'

'No, and neither did she. It came in the form of a letter, which somebody left on her desk. It said it was from someone who shared her views and who wanted to meet to discuss them.'

'What did you do?'

'I told her to go to the meeting,' said Wilby. 'It was due to take place in the Poll district, just across the river from here. I was going to be there to make sure everything went smoothly. Then, at the last minute, her contact moved the time up. She left me a message but, by the time I received it, it was too late. When I got there, she had already been and gone.'

'Was she able to identify the person?' asked Carter.

'You don't understand,' said Wilby. 'She washed up in the reeds two days later.'

'I just read about that in the paper,' said Carter. 'They said it was a suicide.'

'I'll be damned if it was,' replied Wilby, 'although I can't prove it, of course.'

'So what you're telling me,' he said, 'is that Bonn station has been compromised?'

Wilby sat forward and touched his fingertips together. 'I don't know. Maybe. It might be nothing. Maybe she did kill herself.'

'You just said—'

'I said I don't know!' Wilby raised his voice.

'But you think Eckberg might be leaking information?'

'Not deliberately. Not him. But he's not ready for this. You could see that for yourself. The problem is, they're sending us people straight out of college who don't have any real world experience, let alone field craft. To them, the whole world is a Norman Rockwell painting. If there is someone working for the Russians at Bonn station, Eckberg is exactly the kind of person they'll go after. That's why I took him out of the loop – I stopped any problems before they could start.'

'Who else knows about me?' asked Carter.

'Aside from Eckberg, just the station chief, Colonel Babcock. And now that Eckberg is out of the picture, it's just Babcock and me. I'm keeping everything as tight as possible for now. The fewer links between you and me, the less chance there is of compromise. Surely you can see the sense in that.'

'It will do for a start,' replied Carter, 'and next maybe you can explain why Dasch had me standing in front of him within an hour of my getting out of Langsdorf.'

'I admit, there is plenty that we still need to learn about him.'

'Including un-learning some of what you thought you knew.'

'What do you mean?' asked Wilby.

'You told me he wasn't violent.'

'Dasch? He isn't, at least according to his profile.'

'Well, this morning, while he was giving me his version of a job interview, I had a gun stuck in my face by the gorilla that follows him around. He said his name was Ritter.'

'What did this man look like?'

'Medium height. Thinning hair. Wearing a suit. He had a military bearing. Looked like he could take a lot of punishment.'

'That's Ritter, all right. Anton Ritter. He spent a couple of years on the Russian front. Stay clear of him if you can, and from Dasch's daughter, as well.'

'Teresa?'

'So you've met.'

'What's wrong with her?'

'She's smarter than her father. Things that Dasch himself might put up with from you simply because you're an American are not going to fly with Teresa.'

'She made that perfectly clear,' said Carter, 'and Dasch himself was pretty clear that he would have ordered me killed if I had failed his little interview.'

'I'm sure he wouldn't have gone through with it,' said Wilby. 'You're still here, after all.'

'Listen to the words you are saying,' Carter murmured through clenched teeth. 'I didn't spend the last year of my life in prison for a crime that I not only did not commit, but that never even happened in the first place, just so I could get my brains blown out on the first day I get out of my cage, and all because you got your profile on him wrong.'

'There are always risks,' said Wilby. 'You knew that going into this.'

'But there are different kinds of risk,' said Carter. 'There are the risks you take, and then there are the risks I take. You and I both know those risks are not the same.'

'You have every right to be concerned,' Wilby tried to reassure him, 'but don't lose sight of how much is at stake here. If you succeed, we will have brought down one of the most profitable black market operations in this country.'

Dasch's success had been astonishing, especially since

he seemed to have begun with almost nothing, appearing out of nowhere just after the end of the war, driving a truck with which he began delivering goods around the city of Cologne. But not just any goods. From sources no one had ever been able to trace, Dasch had access to wine, champagne, cigars, canned fruits, vegetables and meat, as well as jams and chocolate. No one had seen anything like this in years. Even when such luxuries had been available, the prices were so astronomical that almost nobody could afford them, but Dasch had immediately grasped exactly what the market could bear. He began selling them off to restaurants, private clubs and a selection of diplomats, high-ranking officers and the wealthiest of them all – civilians who had secured contracts for the rebuilding of German railways, sewage plants, electrical power grids and telephone networks. The fact that almost all of his customers were either members of the Allied nations or those who catered to them meant that all attempts to investigate him somehow faltered when important documents were lost, or when Dasch would be tipped off about a raid. Added to this was the foregone conclusion that, in the years immediately after the war, when corruption in both civilian and military circles had reached epidemic proportions, any goods confiscated during one of these raids would wind up being consumed, and possible resold, by the same people who had ordered the investigation. The result of this was that no one seemed in a hurry to track down the source of Dasch's wealth, especially since, by keeping prices down, he was making them available to those who had never been able to buy them in the past, war or no war.

If Dasch had been dealing in guns or stolen works of art, all bets would have been off, but he kept his inventory limited to those things that might be overlooked from time to time, even by those for whom austerity had become like a second religion.

Roughly 60 per cent of Dasch's business was entirely above board: delivering construction supplies for the rebuilding of Cologne, transporting drinking water to areas of the city where plumbing had not yet been restored, even shuttling children to school. It was that remaining 40 per cent which fuelled Wilby's obsession with Dasch.

And Wilby was not just a man. He was a sign of changing times. As the time drew closer when the zones of occupation would be dissolved and Germany – the western part of it anyway – would be allowed once more to govern itself, the Allied governments began to crack down on the kinds of crimes that might previously have been ignored. The reason for this was that most of those crimes, specifically prostitution, gambling and the selling of black market goods, had served as pressure valves for occupation troops. With those days coming to an end, the French, British and Americans became concerned that the fledgling German government would not be able to cope with such levels of crime and might collapse as a result, even before it had been able to prove the worth of its existence.

Even more troubling to men like Wilby was the chance that Russia might find ways to exploit this marketplace of necessary evils in the western zones of occupation, as they had already done with medical supplies such as morphine and penicillin. Wilby knew how real a threat that was, because his own side had been doing it for years inside the Russian zone. For that reason, more than any other, war had been declared on Hanno Dasch.

'Do you know any more about him than you did before I went away?' asked Carter.

'Only that he's still in business, which is close to miraculous. Almost every other player has been rounded up, or fled the country or got themselves killed in some internal dispute. But Dasch is still out there, which tells me he's got contacts at very high levels. Customs. Law enforcement. Transport. Border police. Diplomats. He has to contend with all of these in order to maintain his supply chain, and yet we can't find anyone in any of those circles who knows how he operates, at least anyone who will talk. Usually, the way we break into these organisations is by chipping away around the edges. We get hold of one low-level contact and persuade him to give us what little he knows. Then we move on to the next one, moving up the chain until we can finally break into the inner circles where the real business is getting done. But none of that has worked. The only way we're going to make any progress with this guy is by going straight to the source. If you ask me, Dasch is the most accomplished criminal to appear since the end of the war, and there has been no shortage of contenders. If he was working for us, he'd probably be my boss right now.'

'So what exactly do you want from me?' asked Carter.

'Specifically, we have got to know how he is moving his black market products from one place to another, where he's storing them and who is supplying him. If you can get him to trust you, sooner or later you're going to start seeing some clues as to how he operates. There's no way he can keep that big a secret to himself. Judging from what he sells, he has contacts all over the continent – wine from France, chocolate from Belgium, cans of meat from Denmark, jars of fruit from Italy, Turkish cigarettes – and it's all best quality stuff. If you can just find us one piece of that puzzle, we can begin putting the whole picture together; but right now, in spite of all the times the British occupation police have raided his premises or searched his vehicles for contraband, we have come up with nothing at all. We're all relying on you,' said Wilby. 'Frankly, I don't think there is anyone else who could pull this off. For that, you have my utmost respect.'

'I don't need your respect,' said Carter. 'I just need you to keep me alive.'

'Then you can start by trusting me, because I'm one of the only people on this earth who knows you aren't actually a criminal. And I'm the only one who can give you back your life – which I will, just as I promised, as long as you hold up your end of the bargain.'

'It was never a bargain. It was blackmail.'

'Call it whatever you want.' As Wilby spoke, he lifted the metal dome of the food tray he had brought, revealing a half-eaten meal that he had picked up outside the room of another guest on his way up the back stairs. He pinched a piece of roast potato between his thumb and index finger and popped it in his mouth. 'Nice place you got here,' he said. 'You'd best enjoy it while you can.' Then he slipped out into the hall and closed the door quietly behind him.

Carter listened to the creak of Wilby's footsteps fading away down the carpeted hallway. Then he lay back down, exhausted but unable to sleep. After a few minutes, he climbed off the bed, stretched out on the floor and closed his eyes.

The final thought to pass through his head before unconsciousness washed over him was how he could not have predicted, never in a million years, that his life would have turned out like this.

*

It was Carter's own father, the chief of police in Dunellen, who recruited him straight out of college for a career in undercover work.

The year was 1937. With the Great Depression still in full swing, New Jersey was locked in a crime wave, much of it focused on the docklands of Newark and Elizabeth, just across the Hudson River from New York. The police were sorely in need of intelligence from inside and, after completing his basic training at the police academy, Carter was given the task of infiltrating the small, close-knit bands of thieves among the longshoremen.

He spent the next four years working as a stevedore along the docks, loading and unloading cargo from ships.

Despite his police training, most of what he learned about undercover work could not be taught, even if there had been someone to teach him. Since the crew rosters were constantly being reshuffled, Carter found it easy to move among the longshoremen without drawing attention to himself, constantly aware that even the slightest mistake could get him killed. To keep his cover intact, he rented out three apartments, none within a mile of each other and each one under a different name. He kept no bank account, always insisting that he be paid in cash. He made no friends, but made sure he was known to everyone. Since much of what he learned came from hanging out at the longshoremen's bars after work, he mastered the art of heavy drinking, or at least pretending to. Often, he would pick up half-empty glasses of beer when he had just ordered a fresh one, knowing that the owners of those half-empty glasses would gladly take his full glass without pointing out the mistake.

Carter became so adept at maintaining his forged identity that when, after a series of raids in which dozens of longshoremen were arrested, and rumours began to circulate that a police informant had penetrated the ranks of those who supplemented their income by stealing cargo off incoming ships, Carter was approached by his shift boss, a man named Alphonse Labrija. Labrija, whose work details were responsible for the majority of thefts at one of the largest docks in Elizabeth, entrusted Carter with the task of finding the undercover agent.

Now effectively in search of himself, Carter confronted

another member of Labrija's work detail, a twitchy, pinch-faced man named Harvey Kirsh, whom he knew had been stealing cargo in addition to that which had been sanctioned by Labrija. The punishment for these unauthorised thefts, devised by Labrija himself, was to have all five fingers of the man's right hand severed at the middle joint. It could be made to look like an industrial accident and that was how it would be reported, even by the man who had witnessed his own fingers being removed with a meat cleaver, because reporting the matter to the police would only have resulted in the loss of more critical body parts. Carter had no difficulty persuading Kirsh to disappear and, under the pretext of some imagined solidarity, even provided him with the bus fare out of town.

As soon as Kirsh was gone, Carter informed Labrija that Kirsh had been the informant all along. Since Kirsh had vanished without any other apparent reason, Labrija readily accepted Carter's story. Two months later, Labrija was arrested in a raid, along with most of his men, and was still blaming Kirsh for his misfortune when he began his ten-year sentence behind bars.

The River Gangs, as they were called, had initially made no distinction about what they stole. Often, they robbed crates without even knowing their contents. A profit could be turned from almost anything, and the River Gangs had many contacts in the areas around New York, New Jersey and Connecticut, where stolen items could be funnelled into the marketplace and sold, sometimes without any knowledge of the fact that they had been robbed, to the same shops where the goods would have been bought anyway.

But when war broke out in Europe in the autumn of 1939, the River Gangs turned increasingly to the theft of fuel. The reason for this was not only that the profit margin for selling fuel far outstripped the margins that could be earned from anything else coming off the ships in Elizabeth seaport, but also that most companies had switched from making products for the civilian marketplace to the production of wartime equipment, whether it was clothing, shoes or canned C-rations. Whereas there had always been a market for civilian goods, as well as a multitude of places where such items could be sold, military gear was issued as a matter of course, and only had to be paid for if it was lost.

But everybody needed fuel, and almost everybody wanted more than they were getting from the government. Attempts to colour fuel that had been designated for military use largely failed because military gasoline was sometimes issued legally to civilians when undyed fuel could not be found to meet the ration quotas.

The theft of gasoline and diesel became so pervasive that people who would never normally have considered buying stolen goods now did precisely that, since it had largely lost the stigma of criminality. People knew it was wrong, but it seemed like everybody was doing it, so it became easier to blame the government for over-zealous rationing restrictions than to admit that they were committing a crime.

Even before the attack on Pearl Harbor in December 1941 and the total mobilisation of the American war machine, the US military was losing twenty thousand gallons a day, 10 per cent of its total intake, to thefts ranging from a couple of gallons to entire tanker trucks which disappeared without trace.

From Carter's vantage point, the problem had grown far bigger than anything people in his line of work could handle.

Although he didn't know it at the time, the government had arrived at the same conclusion.

In October 1942, Carter received an order to appear at his precinct headquarters, an imposing stone structure called the Marquette Building, which took up half a block on Arcade Street in downtown Elizabeth. Although Carter had entered the building several times during his early days as a recruit, once he became an undercover detective he rarely went near the place. Even to be seen in the vicinity of the Marquette Building by a member of the River Gangs might be enough to blow his cover.

The order came with no explanation, only a date, a time and a room number. The only thing Carter could think of as to why he had been summoned in this way was that he had made some kind of mistake, for which he would now be facing an official reprimand and perhaps even suspension. In the days leading up to his appearance, Carter racked his brain for what he might have done wrong. His father, to whom he might have turned for information, had retired owing to ill health some years before and now rarely left his little clapboard house in Belmar, out on the Jersey shore. So there was no point in bothering him.

On the day he was due to appear, Carter called in sick and took a taxi to a place two blocks from the Marquette Building. From there, he walked to a vegetable market across the road from police headquarters. At the back of the market was a stairway that went down to a storeroom where vegetables were kept cool before being put on display. At the back of this storeroom was a door with a combination lock, which led to a narrow tunnel that ran under the street. The tunnel was lined with off-white tiles the colour of coffee-stained teeth and had no illumination, so Carter found his way by the greasy flame of a Zippo lighter. The tunnel ended at another door, which led up to the basement of the Marquette Building. This tunnel had been built for use by undercover police, and for smuggling informants in and out of the building.

In a room on the third floor he presented himself to a man he'd never met before and who did not identify himself. He did not wear a police uniform, but from his haircut – short but not a military crew cut – and from the clothes he wore – a starched, pointy-collared white shirt with a brown tie and suspenders – Carter guessed him to be a federal agent. He had learned to place people very quickly, based on nothing more than instinct and a glance. In Carter's line of work, the clothes a person wore told you almost everything you needed to know about them; not only where they came from but also where they imagined they were headed, in their careers and in society. Even the room told him something. It was bare, except for a desk and a filing cabinet with a clamshell for an ashtray on top. There was nothing to indicate that the man worked here. No pictures of his family. No diploma or citations on the wall. No cigarettes crumpled in the ashtray. Whoever this man was, he had come to deliver a message. That was all. Within the hour, all trace of him would have vanished.

All this made Carter very nervous.

'You are being transferred,' said the man, 'to the Office of Price Administration.'

'I've never heard of it,' said Carter.

'That's about to change,' said the man. 'We were created, by order of the President, to investigate the theft of military supplies. You will be responsible for the same areas you were working in before, but you'll be working for us from now on.' He reached down beside him and removed a manila envelope from a briefcase. He placed the envelope on the table and slid it across to Carter. 'This will tell you who you are reporting to. Your office is located in one of the disused warehouses on Cranston Street.'

Cranston Street was not really a street at all, but rather a wind-blown alleyway between two sets of warehouses where the sun only reached to the potholed concrete surface for about half an hour every day.

'Wait a minute,' said Carter. 'I think there has been a mistake.'

The man looked at him. 'How's that?' he asked.

'I work undercover,' explained Carter. 'That's all I've ever done, and the dockyards are the only place I've ever done it. I'm known there as a longshoreman. I push carts. I swing a billhook. Guys like me don't have offices. We don't have much of anything. My cover would be blown in a day. Do you understand me, sir? I can't do what you're asking of me.'

'I'm not really asking,' said the man, 'and I do understand what you're saying. But I'm telling you that things have changed. There's a war on. You no longer have the luxury of anonymity.'

'But wouldn't I be more useful to you if I stayed undercover?'

'The President doesn't think so,' said the man. 'It's his opinion that, with the Office of Price Administration, we are making a statement that the epidemic of thefts of government property across this country will no longer be tolerated. We are putting people on notice. Letting them know that they are being watched.'

'But we're already watching them!' shouted Carter, throwing up his hands. 'And I'm the one doing the watching!'

The man smiled a humourless smile. 'There's a difference,' he said, 'between going up against a local police force, which is what you were, and going up against a federal agency, which is who you are working for now. You used to put people away for, what, a year or two? And maybe you slapped them around a little bit along the way, just to remind them who's boss. But the people you work for now will throw a man into a concrete hole and leave him there for the rest of his life. It's a whole new game, Mr Carter. You know that now' – the man raised his arm and pointed towards the docklands – 'and they will too, soon enough.'

That same afternoon, Carter rode the Long Branch train down to Belmar and went to see his father. After retiring from the police, the old man had sold his house in Dunel-

60

len and moved permanently to their summer cottage by the shore. It was a three-room, single-storey house that stood amongst rows of identical cottages, most of which were empty since it was October and only a few papery leaves still clung to the sycamore trees that grew on strips of grass between the pavement and the road.

Carter visited his father most weekends, just to check in on him. There was a frailty to the old man now that seemed to have come upon him quite suddenly, catching both father and son by surprise. Through all the years of his growing up, Carter had thought of his father as being indestructible and had allowed himself to believe that things would always be this way. But the years seemed to have caught up with him at last, and it was almost as if he had become somehow opaque, fading from the world like a photograph left out in the sun.

Carter's father came to the door, moving slowly and using a rubber-tipped cane to walk. He wore a thick, waffle-grid undershirt and had not shaved in several days. His hair was thin and grey, but still cut short and a little spiky on top, the same way he had worn it in his days with the police. He had smoked heavily throughout his career, and his lungs had finally given out. Now he wheezed like a kettle coming to the boil. He spent most of his time in a chair whose leather cushions had moulded to the shape of his body.

It was cold in the house, and wind whistled in at the kitchen window.

They walked into what his parents had called the 'family' room, which had a couch and a couple of overstuffed chairs gathered in a semi-circle around a coffee table and facing a large radio cabinet, which stood against the wall. There were several copies of the local Asbury Park newspaper on the table, which did not look like they had been opened.

'You should get some insulation for this place,' said Carter, as they each took a seat in one of the overstuffed chairs.

'I have a stove,' said the old man, nodding to a potbellied clump of iron in the corner.

'Do you have any wood for it?'

'I can get wood when I need it.' The old man reached across to a little table beside the chair and fetched his cigarettes. With crack-nailed fingertips, he rummaged in a box for a match, which he lit by striking it against one of the brass button nails that ran down the length of his chair.

Carter's gaze followed the ribbon of smoke up to where a bloom of dirty yellow, the stain of a thousand other smokes, spread across the ceiling.

'This isn't your usual day for a visit,' said his father.

Carter told him about his transfer to the Office of Price Administration.

The old man sat very still as he listened, pausing now and then to draw from his cigarette.

By the time Carter had finished, his father had put away two more smokes and was scratching at his chin with soft raking movements of his fingertips, the way a barnacle sweeps its claw through the tide.

'I think they're trying to get me killed,' said Carter.

His father shrugged. 'The work we're in, it seems like they are always doing that. "Was", I should say.' With a gurgling cough, he cleared his throat. 'The work that I used to be in.'

Before Carter left, he strolled with his father down to the boardwalk. It took a long time, since his father often had to stop and catch his breath, hand resting on the dappled bark of the sycamore trees. On the boardwalk, they sat on a bench and looked out over the ocean. The beach, which in summer would be almost too crowded to see the sand, was almost empty now, except for a few people walking their dogs and some fishermen casting for striped bass.

For a while, they just sat there in silence.

It was his father who spoke first. 'You know why I picked you for undercover work?'

'You told me you thought I'd be good at it.'

'But do you know why I thought that?'

He had never asked his father, not because he wasn't curious but because it seemed like the kind of question his father wouldn't have wanted to answer.

'We're all part of one tribe or another,' said his father, 'and, for a lot of people, everything they think and say and do depends on fitting in with the tribe. They're terrified of getting out of line. Their whole sense of who they are depends on staying in the ranks. They'll do anything for that, suffer any indignity, betray their closest friends, whatever it takes to belong. But not everybody in the tribe is like that. Some of them know who they are without having to be told. People like that can survive on their own if they want to. And I always knew you could do that. It's why I knew you could handle undercover work, but I didn't think enough about the price you'd have to pay.'

It unnerved Carter to hear his father talking this way. He never spoke in these terms. Anything beneath the surface of emotions was taboo. 'What price is that?' he asked.

'By the time I was your age, I'd already been married for a while. We already had you, for Christ's sake! I had a normal life, as normal as it could have been until your mother died. I just don't know how you are ever going to have that.'

This, too, came as a shock. His father almost never spoke of her. She had died when Carter was six and these days he had trouble recalling what her voice sounded like, or the precise colour of her hair, or the smell of her; a mixture of coal tar soap, perfume and freshly folded laundry, which had lingered in the house for a while after she was gone. Sometimes, just before he fell asleep, she would appear suddenly in his thoughts. In those moments he would see her again as a whole person, but if he tried to focus on her, she would vanish and he would be left to assemble her from the jumble of remembered senses, like a bucket full of broken glass spilled out inside his brain.

His father looked across and smiled, then reached out an arm and gently patted his son on the back. 'I was thinking I owed you an apology, for getting you into this line of work.'

'Are you saying I should quit?' asked Carter.

The old man shook his head. 'You don't quit the job. The job quits you when you've got nothing left to give. I'm not talking about the years you spend punching the clock. I mean in here.' He tapped one finger against his temple. 'How deep it gets inside your head. And when you finally make peace with all the things you did and didn't do, what's left is only fit for sitting on a bench and staring out to sea. Unless.'

'Unless what?' asked Carter.

'Unless you find that precise moment in time when you can leave on your own terms, before you're broken, inside and outside.' His father stared at him hard, as if to show his words meant more than he was saying. 'And when that moment arrives, you cannot hesitate.'

'How would I recognise it?' asked Carter.

'When the time comes, you will know.'

'Have you ever seen it done?'

His father breathed out. 'No,' he answered, 'but I sure wish I could have given it a try.'

'I guess I'll keep a look out,' said Carter.

'Until then,' said the old man, 'just stick to the third rule.'

He did not need to explain what that meant. In that moment, the old man had switched from talking as father to son and was now speaking as one policeman to another. In addition to the duties of protection and service, there was a third, unspoken, unofficial rule: survival. This was not as straightforward as it seemed. To put oneself in harm's way was a part of the job, and anyone who did not have the instinctive ability to do that needed to find another line of work. The third rule meant knowing the difference between willingly going into harm's way and being put there by the ill-considered orders of someone who had not grasped the danger of the situation. There was sometimes a very fine line between those two things, but life itself could depend on knowing when that line was crossed.

The old man had turned his gaze towards some distant point on the horizon. Now he raised one arm and pointed out to sea. 'I heard that German submarines come up at night, not half a mile from shore, just so they can see the lights of the Ferris wheel in Asbury Park.'

'Why would they do that?' asked Carter.

'Maybe it helps them remember what their country used to look like before they got it in their heads to rule the world.'

Two days later, Carter showed up at his new office on Cranston Street. There, in the middle of a space that had once been the salesroom of a fish wholesaler, he found a man standing with his hands on his hips and a gun in a shoulder holster tucked under his left armpit.

'You must be Nathan Carter,' said the man. He was short and bald, with a head like a battering ram and a massive barrel chest. His name was Salvatore Palladino and he explained that, until the war had brought him back out of retirement, he had spent twenty-five years as a uniformed police officer.

'I didn't know they were sending me a partner,' said Carter.

'You used to work undercover, didn't you?'

'I did.'

'Well, you're in broad daylight now, son, and this is no place to find yourself alone.'

Once Carter had got over the surprise of working with a partner, he and Palladino quickly settled down to the business of tracking stolen shipments of fuel, as well as uncovering false-bottomed fuel tanks where hundreds of gallons could be secreted away.

At first, Carter had worried constantly that he would be spotted by one of the longshoremen with whom he had worked in his days as an undercover detective. He took the same precautions as he had done when he was working undercover, renting out three different rooms in town and never sleeping at the same one more than three nights in a row. Other times, he slept on a canvas cot in the office, a loaded pistol lying on the floor beside him. He took most of his meals at a little diner called Pavel's. It was wedged between a laundry and a cobbler's down on 12th Street, only a short walk from the docks. Pavel, an old Russian with watery blue eyes whose wrinkled forehead made him look as if he were always just about to sneeze, made pastrami and sauerkraut sandwiches, matzo ball soup and gravlax salmon marinated in lemon juice, pepper and dill, which he sliced paper-thin and served on pumpernickel bread.

As time passed, Carter slowly began to relax. His new work rarely brought him into direct contact with the long-shoremen. This, combined with the shifting nature of the crews, many of whom had been drafted or enlisted, and others who were constantly being shuttled around to different dock sites, allowed him to avoid being recognised.

They made very few actual arrests, since those whose task it had been to transport the stolen fuel usually bolted, leaving both trucks and fuel behind. It was Palladino who taught Carter not to bother chasing down the runners.

'Those guys are the smallest fish in the pond,' he told Carter. 'Even if you catch them, there's nothing they can tell you that's of any use because they simply don't have the information. And they're easily replaced. Better to let them go and have them explain to their bosses why they lost a whole shipment of gasoline, not to mention a five-ton truck. Believe me, by the time their bosses are done with them, they'll wish they'd surrendered to us.'

Even though Carter and Palladino recovered an average of five thousand gallons of stolen gasoline a week and prevented the theft of at least that much again, the problem continued to grow. Two years after Pearl Harbor, although the proportion of stolen fuel remained at 10 per cent, the overall consumption had skyrocketed after the Allied invasion of France and the amount of the loss stood at 2.5 million gallons per day, nationwide.

Against this tide of thieving, the question of whether these two men were doing enough good to justify their existences remained a mystery to them. They were never brought in for review, never received promotions or letters of commendation or of reprimand. Carter began to wonder if they might, somehow, have been forgotten. Until someone came along to tell them otherwise, however, they continued with the task they had been given. For a while, at least, it seemed as if their partnership might last until the Office of Price Administration vanished back into the bureaucratic haze from which it had emerged.

But that all changed one afternoon in the autumn of 1944.

They were down at the docks sitting in their V8 Packard cruiser, which was parked in an alleyway between two warehouses. A fuel barge had just arrived at Elizabeth port after a long journey up from Corpus Christi, Texas. According to the bills of lading filed with the port authority, the cargo was supposed to be transported to a refinery in Newark by three fuel trucks but, on the day of the transfer, four fuel trucks arrived.

It took several hours for the fuel to be unloaded, during which time Carter and Palladino sat in the car in the alleyway, hearing the wind moan through the broken windowpanes high up in the dust-smeared skylights of the corrugated iron sheds, their grey sides all tattooed with rust.

Finally, the trucks departed and, with Palladino driving, the two men slipped in behind the convoy, which was heading for the main road out of town.

Just before the trucks emerged from the tangle of roads that snaked across the docklands, one of them pulled out of the line and made its way towards an area of swamp known as the Meadowlands, where fields of tall bulrushes formed a shifting screen from everything but planes flying overhead.

The truck appeared to be heading towards a warehouse normally used for the storage of oxygen cylinders used in oxyacetylene welding, which required it to be set well apart from any other building due to the risk of explosion.

At a curve on the long, straight stretch of the potholed road, Palladino pulled in front of the truck and brought it to a stop. Then both men got out, carrying their guns.

The driver jumped down, wild-eyed and ready to bolt into the rustling thickets of bulrushes. But suddenly he stopped and stared at Carter. 'Nathan?' he said.

Carter felt his heart slam into his rib cage. He had almost

managed to persuade himself that this day would never come.

'It's me,' said the man. 'Johnny Shreve. We worked the South Pier together back in thirty-nine. I figured you must have been called up. Jesus!' said Shreve, his voice nearly falsetto with relief. 'I thought you were police.'

Before Carter could think of what to say, Palladino burst out laughing. 'I guess that spooked you!' he said.

Shreve laughed too. 'I'll say it did.'

Palladino holstered his gun. 'It's a misunderstanding is all. We just got our wires crossed. No harm done though, right?'

'Sure,' Shreve assured him. 'It's no problem. I guess I'll just be on my way, if that's all right with you.'

'Of course, and so will we.' Palladino turned to Carter. 'Why don't you go turn the car around?'

Carter wondered what Palladino was playing at, but he did as he was told and started walking for the car.

Shreve lifted one hand in farewell. 'So long, Nathan,' he said. 'I'll see you around.'

Carter waved goodbye and climbed into the Packard. The road was narrow at the curve and the way ahead was blocked by the fuel truck, so Carter had to reverse around the bend. Then he wrestled with the wheel, knocking the gears back and forth from forward to reverse, before he finally had the car facing back the way they'd come. He had just brought the car to a stop when Palladino came running around the curve. He opened the passenger side door and jumped in. 'Drive,' he said.

'What's going on?' asked Carter.

'Just drive!' Palladino commanded.

Carter slammed the Packard in gear and headed back towards the docks. Sunlight flickered off the windshield, as if someone were flashing a knife in front of his face. He waited for Palladino to explain what was happening, but the man said nothing at all.

They had been underway less than a minute when Carter saw a flash in the rear-view mirror and then he felt a tremor pass through him. He turned to see a ball of orange flame capped with thick black smoke rise, boiling, from the sea of rushes and unravel into the sky.

'Don't slow down,' said Palladino.

Carter glanced across at him. 'What have you done?' he asked.

'I stopped you from getting killed,' said Palladino. 'That's what. You just got made. Your cover was blown. I did the only thing that could be done. The third rule isn't just words. It's the thing that will keep you alive.'

'I never asked you for that.'

'No,' replied Palladino, 'but your father did.'

'What's my father got to do with it?' demanded Carter.

'Kid, do you know why I came out of retirement?'

'Because of the war, you told me.'

'I lied about that. It's because your father asked me to. I served alongside him for twenty years. You didn't know that, did you?'

'No,' admitted Carter. 'He didn't talk much about work, or anyone he worked with.'

'Well, knowing your father, that doesn't surprise me one bit. But he told me to look after you and that's what I've been doing all this time. How long do you think you would have lasted if the word had gotten out that you were working for the government?'

'What did you do to that guy?'

'What guy?' asked Palladino. 'There was no guy, and we were never here.'

The next morning, Carter was sitting on a round-topped stool at the counter at Pavel's, eating a bagel with butter and a slice of tomato, when the door opened and a tall man in the faded pea green trench coat of a US Army officer entered the diner. Aside from Pavel, who was sitting by the register reading the *New York Post*, Carter had been the only person there. It was raining and, judging by the amount of water that had sunk into the stranger's clothes, he had come quite a distance to get there.

The officer made no effort to remove his coat. Instead, he fixed his eyes on Carter. 'You're not an easy man to find,' he said.

Before Carter could reply, the expression on the officer's face suddenly changed. Slowly, he spread his hands out to the sides. 'Take it easy,' he said.

'I'm not pointing a gun at you,' said Carter.

'No,' replied the officer, 'but he is.' And then he nodded towards the cash register, where Pavel stood with a shotgun, its double barrels sawn off to the length of a man's forearm.

'Now how about you lower that old blunderbuss?' asked the officer. 'It looks like it could go off by itself.'

'It might,' said Pavel, 'and my fingers are shaky these days.' The gun stayed where it was, aimed at the officer's head.

'Who are you?' asked Carter.

'My name,' said the man, 'is Douglas Tate, and I am a captain in the Special Task Force division of the Military Police.'

Carter assumed that this must have something to do with what had happened out in the Meadowlands the day before. He had no idea what to do or what to say. Palladino's voice kept repeating in his head – *We were never here. We were never here.*

'And what do you want with my friend?' asked Pavel.

'To let him know that he has been relieved of his duties with the Office of Price Administration and that, effective immediately, he is being transferred to the US Army.'

'What about Palladino?' asked Carter.

'Who?'

'My partner.'

'I don't know anything about that,' said Tate. 'According to our records, you worked alone.' Slowly, Captain Tate reached towards his chest and paused. 'If I may?' he asked the pug-faced old Russian.

Pavel made a grumbling sound in his throat, which the officer took to mean he could proceed.

Tate slid his hand beneath the double-breasted fold of his trench coat and removed a manila envelope. He stepped over to Carter, moving with the careful stride of a man setting out upon a frozen pond with no idea whether the ice was thick enough.

Carter reached out and took hold of the envelope.

Tate raised his hands again and stepped back.

At this moment, Pavel sighed and set the gun down on the counter. 'I have decided, for the moment, not to kill you,' he said.

'For which I am eternally grateful,' said the captain, lowering his hands. He reached into his pocket and pulled out a packet of Lucky Strikes, its wartime wrapper olive green instead of peacetime white. Then he lit the cigarette with a black-painted Zippo lighter and, as the lid of the lighter flipped shut with the particular clunk-switch sound that only Zippos made, Carter noticed that the man's fingers were trembling.

'What does the army want with me?' asked Carter.

'Oh, it will be the same job, more or less.' Tate picked a fleck of tobacco off his tongue. 'We just need you to do it someplace else.'

'Some place like where?' he asked.

Tate pulled hard upon the cigarette until the end of it crackled and glowed. He spoke as he exhaled. 'How do you feel about Belgium?' he asked.

*

In his room at the Hotel Europa, Carter was woken by a heavy knocking on the door.

When he opened his eyes and glimpsed the stuccoed ceiling of his room, he could not, at first, recall where he was. For a few more seconds, his half-conscious mind attempted to refocus his eyes, sure that the wavy texture of the stucco must be some blurring of his sight and that he was, in fact, still in his cell at Langsdorf, where the ceiling was smooth and dreary, like a bone-white sky on a winter's day.

And then he remembered.

The pounding on the door continued.

'All right!' shouted Carter.

He put on a bathrobe and went to the door.

It was Ritter. He was wearing the same suit he'd had on the day before. 'Good morning, Mr Carter!' he said. 'Are you ready to begin?'

Fifteen minutes later, Carter was in the passenger seat of Ritter's car, heading towards the outskirts of the city on a long, straight road called Brühlerstrasse. Sunlight flickered through the abandoned buildings of the Raderthal district. On a morning like this, even the ruins looked pretty.

As the Tatra swerved along the potholed road, Carter felt a curious, familiar sharpening of his senses, like someone who had walked into a dark space and felt, without being able to see, the presence of another in the room. These same sensations came to him every time he went undercover, as a kind of mirage took the place of the person he actually was, coiling around him like a whirlwind of smoke, spinning closer and closer as it began to harden itself, like a shell, around his body, until at last the image of this new incarnation became, on the surface, indistinguishable from the man who hid beneath it.

As Carter had learned time and again in his years as a detective, his life would soon depend upon the flawlessness of this shell. Any cracks in the mask would quickly prove fatal under the scrutiny of those whose own lives depended upon trusting him.

For Carter, this transformation had become second nature. The only way he had survived this long was by learning to live behind masks, hiding who he really was in vaults so deep he sometimes forgot they were there. Everything else was illusion, the true art of which was to change as little as possible, leaving behind as much as he could of what was authentically him. Into this fabric of reality, Carter could then weave the threads of the lies, telling them with such conviction that as he spoke the words he actually believed what he was saying. He had taught himself not only to behave like the person whom others believed him to be, but also to react without thinking, so that half-truths merged with outright fabrications until one became indistinguishable from the other. Only then could those false parts of him, which had been stitched onto his soul like the borrowed flesh of Frankenstein's monster, take on the same life as those parts he knew to be real.

The most effective of Carter's traits, which he had imported from his real self into the chimeras by which some people came to know him, was a certain caustic bluntness with his superiors. This simultaneously irritated some of them and had the effect of reassuring them that he lacked the subtlety ever to be a threat. Dovetailed into this bluntness was a habit of asking questions, even at times when it might have been better to keep his mouth shut. Among the longshoremen, especially those who were engaged in the theft of cargo coming off the ships, the safest course was always to wait until you were told and to keep your curiosity to yourself. But there was a balance between being curious, which was natural, and making no attempt to satisfy that curiosity, which, ultimately, was far more suspicious. The man who never asked any questions was either too stupid to be relied upon or he already knew the answers, which made him dangerous. By asking the questions that any normal person would have asked in any given situation, Carter sometimes exasperated those for whom he worked. But his allegiance had never been questioned, while others with far less to hide than Carter had been singled out, not only for suspicion but for acts of disloyalty which existed only in the minds of those who swung the iron pipes that broke the bones of men who had stayed silent out of nothing more than ignorance and fear.

Carter's inquisitiveness became a kind of trademark of his personality, allowing him to gather information far more rapidly than he might otherwise have done and, at the same time, to ensure his survival among the people he was tasked with bringing down.

The hardest part was not the building of this parallel universe, but in finding his way back to the one he'd left behind, and in remembering who he'd been before he went away. Carter lived in quiet dread that one day he would become lost in this labyrinth of his own making. Even when he did find his way out, the journey did not come without a price. Like a piece of sea glass washed up on the beach and thrown back again and again into the waves, a little less of him returned each time he made it to shore.

Before Carter could even begin asking questions, Ritter had plenty of his own – some of which, at first, made very little sense.

Where did you come from? What did you do in the war? What was the name of your commanding officer? What was your serial number? What was your father's name? What was his job? How long have your parents been married? Do you have any brothers and sisters? Are you married? Are you right handed or left handed? What is your shoe size? What was the number of your cell at Langsdorf? Before the crime for which you went to prison, had you committed any other crimes? Do you have a police record?

Ritter fired these questions at Carter with such speed and relentlessness that Carter had almost no time to think about the answers. And he knew this was exactly the point. For almost every question, he was able to answer with the truth. Only when Ritter asked about the war did Carter shave away the facts and simply say that he had served in the Ardennes. Whoever Ritter was, he had experience in shaking people down to see if they were lying, and Carter knew that the answers mattered less than the way he answered them.

Finally, after Ritter had been pounding him with questions for more than fifteen minutes, Carter called out, 'Stop!'

To his surprise, Ritter did just that.

'Why are you doing this?' asked Carter.

'Mr Dasch considers himself an infallible judge of character,' replied Ritter, 'and maybe he is, but his methods leave much to be desired.'

'And are we done?' demanded Carter. 'Or do you need to ask what kind of toothpaste I use and which way I stir my coffee?'

'We are done for now,' said Ritter calmly.

'What are you?' asked Carter. 'A cop?'

'I am what you see,' replied Ritter. 'A driver for Mr Dasch, and nothing more.'

'But I doubt that's all you've ever been.'

Ritter glanced across at him. 'The war has forced us all to reinvent ourselves.'

'So how long have you worked for Dasch?'

'Since the time he almost ran me off the road.'

'And why did he do that? Was he trying to kill you or something?'

'Not at all. He wanted to purchase this car! I was driving it along the Oberländerufer in the southern part of Cologne, just along the west bank of the Rhine, when one of Dasch's yellow trucks flashed its lights and its driver began waving at me. At first I ignored him, but he kept at it for so long that eventually I pulled over to see what the hell he wanted. It was Dasch himself! He had spotted the Tatra and decided right then that he had to have it.'

'And did you sell it to him?'

'Of course!' Ritter turned to him and smiled. 'Mr Dasch can be very persuasive. You see, he not only bought the car. He bought me to go along with it.'

'You mean as his driver?'

'As a person who would do whatever he wanted me to do, no matter what he asked, without question or complaint. I have amassed some considerable experience in that department. But they were the kind of skills that I had imagined would be of no use from now on, especially for someone like me.'

'You mean you really would have shot me back there behind the Bleihof club?'

'Of course.' Ritter sounded almost offended. 'Mr Dasch admires you, which means we are friends now, you and I. But you should be aware, Mr Carter, that if the day ever comes when Mr Dasch says otherwise, I'll put you in the ground without a moment's hesitation.'

'Why would you commit a crime like that just to satisfy another man's curiosity?'

'Because he is not just another man,' answered Ritter. 'He is the one who saved me from myself.'

'And how did he do that?'

'By giving me a reason to live,' answered Ritter. 'When I was a child and it was time to go to bed, my mother would say, "Stay in your room. The night is full of monsters." When the war ended, I was forced to navigate my way through a world in which, from one day to the next, I changed from a hero – a knight of an empire that was to last a thousand years – into one of those monsters about which mothers warn their children. There was no longer a place for me in the world. For proof of that, all I had to do was look out of my window at the ruins of Cologne, a city that has stood since the time of the Romans. And just as the Romans belonged to the past, so did I. The only difference, it seemed to me, was that the Romans had the luxury of being dead. For years, I was torn between killing myself and killing everyone around me. On the day that I met Hanno Dasch, I had reluctantly arrived at the conclusion that killing everyone else was impractical.' He breathed in suddenly with a gasp of air, like a half-drowned man coming to life. 'I was on my way to the ruins of the Drachenfels castle, just a few miles down the road at Königswinter. I had chosen this spot because it stands upon a cliff looking out over the Rhine, from which I could be sure the fall would kill me. But Mr Dasch convinced me otherwise, and that is why I owe him everything.'

'And what about Dasch?' asked Carter. 'What did he do in the war?' The question seemed innocent enough, but in fact it was high on the list of Wilby's orders for Carter to discover exactly what Dasch had been up to before 1945. US intelligence had found nothing at all on him before that time. He seemed to have no record of service in the military, even though he was the right age to have been called up.

'Mr Dasch,' said Ritter, 'does not like to speak about his time in the war.'

'So you don't know what he did?'

'No.'

'And doesn't that bother you, not knowing?'

'I have learned to contain my curiosity,' said Ritter. 'You might do well, at least for now, to follow my example.'

At the outer edge of the Raderthal district they arrived at a large gated compound, surrounded by fences topped with thick coils of barbed wire. Inside the compound was a collection of German Army Hanomags, British Bedford lorries and American Dodge trucks, all with coatings of yellow paint and the words 'Dasch AG' stencilled in red upon the doors.

A guard opened the gate for them to pass. He wore a battered pinwheel cap and a hip-length, double-breasted wool coat with wooden toggle buttons, and he carried a hunting rifle slung over his shoulder.

The car pulled up in front of a large brick building, which had been divided into a mechanic shop on one side and an office area on the other. In the service bays of the mechanic shop, two trucks were being worked on by men whose upper bodies were plastered black with oil. The office building had a bench out front, flanked on each side by a terracotta pot in which geraniums were growing.

Dasch himself stood at the window of the office, hands in pockets, watching the car approach.

'As you see,' said Ritter, 'you are expected.'

At first glance, Carter could spot no place where it might be possible for quantities of black market goods to be hidden away, or any indication that the trucks in the lot could be loaded with contraband without being noticed, since everything was out in the open.

Far in the distance, across a tangled field of tall grass mixed with brambles, lay a railway siding in which goods wagons were being shunted back and forth by a small locomotive. The clank and rattle of the iron wheels sounded across the empty space, disjointed from the source of the noise, as if a ghostly crew of blacksmiths were hammering hot iron somewhere out there in the wasteland.

Entering the office, Carter caught the smell of coffee and cigarettes. The first person he saw was Teresa. She was sitting at a desk, tallying a stack of receipts which had been impaled upon a metal spike and whose many layers reminded Carter of the strips of meat he used to see on the kebab grill at a restaurant where he sometimes ate his lunch, down on the docks of Elizabeth. Teresa looked up at Carter, but did not smile. She seemed to be staring right through him and Carter wondered if this hostility was shared with everyone she met, or if it had been saved for him alone. 'I didn't think you would be so easily bought,' she said.

'I didn't think I was for sale,' replied Carter.

'Of course you were,' she told him. 'Everyone who walks through that door is for sale. The only difference between them is the price.'

'Nonsense!' boomed a voice.

Carter turned to see Dasch advancing upon him, his hand held out to shake. 'You must forgive my daughter. When the Nazis were here she hated them, and when the Allies drove the Nazis out, she hated them instead. It doesn't matter who's in charge. Teresa will hate them all equally. In this way, she is very democratic.'

Teresa sighed and went back to her work.

'Come,' said Dasch, and led him into a private room at the back of the office, which was furnished with objects of such lavish quality that they appeared absurdly out of place, hemmed in by clapboard walls and sheltered from the elements by a corrugated iron roof. There was a desk, veneered in ebony and inlaid with mother of pearl, showing scenes of pagodas and sampans poled along the inky blackness by men in conical hats. The curtains were red velvet, brocaded and tasselled and held in place with bell ropes made of silk. On one wall hung a picture of a woman with almost impossibly pale skin, who was sitting in a gilded chair wearing a ruffled white dress, with her chin resting in one delicate hand and staring out across the dusty compound towards the ruins of Cologne in the distance. Who she was, and in what stately home her portrait had once hung, Dasch showed no sign of caring. Neither did he appear to have any appreciation for his desk, which was cluttered with paperwork and old, half-empty cups of coffee, whose bases had left Olympic banners of overlapping rings upon the polished ebony.

The only thing that looked like it belonged there was a large map, which spanned from Ireland in the west to St Petersburg in the east and was still window-framed with creases from the folds of its original shape.

'Three years ago,' said Dasch, 'I had a map of Cologne on that wall. It seemed like the whole world to me and, in a way, that is exactly what it was. It was my dominion, so to speak. But now, as you see, I have a bigger map and, with your help, the name of Dasch will soon be known in towns I can't even pronounce. Have you travelled much in Europe, Mr Carter?'

'I've been around a bit,' he said.

*

It was late October 1944 when Nathan Carter, wearing a US Army uniform and with the provisional rank of lieutenant in the Military Police Special Task Force, climbed down the metal steps of a C-47 transport plane onto the matted grass of a runway near the city of Liège in eastern Belgium. At the edges of the airstrip he could see the wreckage of Luftwaffe fighter planes – ME 109s and FW 90s – which had been damaged on landing, bulldozed to the sides and abandoned when the Germans had retreated only a few months before. Outside of newsreels back home, this was the first sign Carter had seen of the enemy and, even though these machines had been left for junk, they still looked hostile in their black and green camouflage, rippled like the patterns on a mackerel's back.

There had been moments in that long journey, which had taken him through Gander airfield in northern Canada to Iceland, then to England and finally on to the Continent, when Carter had imagined he might visit some of the great cities – London, Paris, Brussels. But most of what he saw when he looked down was a shredded blanket of clouds, laid out over a pewter grey sea. And as for the great cities, he never even caught a glimpse of those.

According to the briefing Carter had received from Captain Tate on the drive to Fort Dix, his task was to investigate the theft of a US Army truck transporting more than two thousand gallons of gasoline. It had been stolen right off the streets of a village called Rocherath in the Ardennes Forest, not far from the Belgian–German border. The robbers had been civilians, all of them heavily armed. They had waited until the American driver had stepped out of the truck and gone across the road to a cafe to buy some lunch. As the thieves attempted to start the vehicle, the driver emerged from the cafe and drew a pistol from the holster at his belt. Before he could fire, he was shot dead by one of the robbers. At this point, the robbers panicked. They managed to get the truck started but one of the thieves, who was clinging to the back of the truck as it began moving, fell and hurt his leg. The other thieves either did not know what had happened or abandoned him to his fate. He was arrested by the local Belgian police and taken into custody. The gasoline had been dyed red to indicate that it was designated for military use only, which should have made it easy to trace. However, in spite of dozens of checks by military policemen at roadblocks set up all over eastern Belgium, none of the red-dyed fuel had been located. The truck had also vanished.

There had, Tate said, been countless instances of fuel going missing from US Army depots all over the world, but they were mostly small amounts, and rarely more than twenty or thirty gallons at a time. Some of this could be chalked up to poor record keeping, and some to the fact that the depots were constantly being moved around as the Allies advanced across the battlefield.

The assignment of special fuel-theft investigators had often been proposed, but no action had been taken until now, when the murder of a US Army soldier and the loss of so much fuel in a single robbery – not to mention the truck – had swept aside the bureaucratic dithering that had previously held up assignments.

Carter was under pressure to move quickly with his investigation, before such thefts emboldened other thieves and the situation got out of control.

Within minutes of leaving the plane, Carter had been bundled into a Willys jeep with MP, for Military Police, painted in large white letters on the hood, and began his journey east towards the Ardennes Forest.

The driver, who held the rank of sergeant, was a round-faced man with a Clark Gable moustache and eyes raccooned with fatigue. He wore a short canvas coat with a drab olive scarf thickly wound about his neck and a wool beanie cap pulled down over his ears. The clothing had a grimy sheen of dirt and engine grease and had moulded itself to his body, as if he had not taken it off in days or even weeks, which might well have been the truth. Even though he could not have been more than twenty-five years old, with the beanie pulled down over his ears he reminded Carter of one of the old men he used to see lined up outside a soup kitchen back in his hometown of Dunellen. The sergeant spoke so little and seemed so much a part of the machine he was driving that Carter sometimes felt as if he were being propelled across Belgium by some giant clockwork toy.

It was just as well the sergeant kept to himself, since Carter was exhausted by the trip. It was the longest journey he had ever taken and, throughout it, he had never been able to do more than doze in the freezing cargo hold of a plane over the north Atlantic or stretch out on a borrowed cot in a draughty Quonset hut, surrounded by a sea of mud next to the airfield in Keflavík, Iceland. He had struggled to keep up with the rising and setting of suns that made no sense to the workings of his mind. Eventually, his body just gave up and he lapsed into a kind of numbness, which surrounded him now in a fog, so that everything perceived by his senses seemed untrustworthy, half in and half out of a dream.

They travelled down roads lined with long ranks of beech trees, passing through slate-roofed villages with reeking mountains of manure heaped outside stone-walled barns and pastureland spreading out beyond into the rolling countryside. From men in wooden clogs and patched, faded corduroys, he caught the scent of unfamiliar cigarettes and, here and there, the iron railings of their gates had been curled back like the crooked fingers of old hags where bullets had cut through the metal. He saw houses where snipers had been routed, the windows shot away and the stonework chipped and dimpled by machine gun fire.

His thoughts kept drifting back to a short conversation he'd had with his father, just before his plane left Fort Dix on the first leg of his transatlantic journey. He had persuaded Tate to pull over at a gas station just outside the base, where a phone booth stood by itself at the edge of the road. He had to call three times before his father even answered the phone and, when he finally did pick up, the connection was so bad that Carter had been forced to shout down the line.

'You're going where?' his father had asked.

'Belgium!' Carter shouted, and he went on to explain what had happened, but his father didn't seem to grasp what he was being told.

'You've been drafted?' asked the old man.

'Not exactly, Pop,' said Carter, and he tried to explain it again.

'How long will you be gone?'

'I don't know,' replied Carter. 'A couple of months, maybe.'

There was no mention of Palladino. His father would probably have denied it, anyway.

'Pop,' asked Carter, 'are you going to be all right on your own?'

There was a pause on the line. Then finally his father spoke again. 'What are you talking about? I'll be fine. Why would you even have to ask?'

But that was only his pride talking. They both knew why he had to ask.

It had never been easy for Carter to say goodbye to his father, even on those short weekly visits when they sometimes just sat in the house and listened to the radio together. When the time came to leave, Carter would say, 'I ought to get going,' and his father would say, 'Yup.' There would be an awkward hug and then Carter would head out of the door, unable to escape the sensation that he had vanished from his father's thoughts before he even made it to the street.

With the telephone, it was even worse.

'Listen, Pop,' he said, 'I have to go.'

'Yup.' There was a pause. 'Well, you take care,' he said. And then the line went dead.

It had always troubled Carter that they lacked the words to go beyond the surface of things, and that everything beneath that veneer of emotions was simply understood – although even that they'd never talked about, so he never knew for sure. This time it troubled him especially. Carter had never been this far from home before, but he realised now, as he silently pronounced as best he could the names of the villages through which they passed – Aywaille, Stoumont, Trois-Ponts – that it was his father whom he thought of as home, more than the place itself had ever been.

Outside the town of St Christophe at a little crossroads called Baugnez, the driver pulled off the road onto the tall and winter-matted grass to consult his map.

Carter climbed out to stretch his legs. He studied the cryptic, hand-made signposts pointing to various military formations – CHAIN BAKER CP, D.A.O., DOMINO RC, QMSR – and one that just said 'COYOTE'. In the valley below, rising from the misty air, the rooftops of St Christophe and the crooked spire of its church showed signs of damage so recent that none of it had been repaired. 'That must once have been a pretty town,' said Carter, as much to himself as the driver.

The sergeant looked up from his well-thumbed map. 'Oh it was, sir,' he said, 'until our air corps bombed it by mistake. They were trying to hit some town across the border in Germany, but the navigator misread his map or something. People around here aren't exactly feeling warm and fuzzy towards us these days, and who can blame them?'

Carter pulled out a crumpled, almost empty pack of Chesterfields and offered one to the driver.

The sergeant's eyes lit up at the sight of American tobacco. 'Those are stateside smokes!' he exclaimed. 'Thank you, sir! Thank you very much!' With his black-nailed fingertips, he plucked one out.

Then the two of them sat smoking on the hood of the jeep, which was warm from the heat of the engine.

Carter was still unused to being called 'sir'. The concept of being an officer had not yet sunk in and he felt like a fraud in this uniform with a rank he had not earned. 'Did they tell you why I'm here?' he asked.

'I'm a sergeant, sir,' said the driver. 'They never tell me anything. But they didn't need to. After that fuel truck got stolen in Rocherath and the driver got shot, everybody knew they'd be sending someone from Special Tasks to find out what happened. And since my orders are to take you wherever you need to go until you're done with your work, I figured you must be the guy.'

'Then I guess I ought to know your name,' said Carter.

'It's Riveira, sir. Hector Riveira.'

Reflexively, Carter's arm shifted, ready to shake the man's hand. But then he stopped himself, embarrassed. 'This time last week,' he said, 'I wasn't even in the army.'

'No, sir,' said the sergeant. 'I figured that as well. You are what they call a "temporary gentleman", no offence intended.'

'I worked in New Jersey for the Office of Price Administration, chasing down people who stole government supplies which, these days, is mostly gasoline. I guess that's why they picked me for the job.'

'You could have told me you were a trash collector in Hoboken and I still would have been jealous,' said Riveira. 'Any stateside job sounds good to me right now.'

To find himself envied for his paranoid existence in the rust-cancered docklands of Elizabeth was something he had never thought possible. 'What do you know about where we are going?' asked Carter.

'You mean Rocherath?' Riveira nodded towards one of the roads that branched off from the junction and meandered into a dense pine forest on the horizon. 'It's way up on the German border. The 2nd Infantry Division and some of the 99th are bunkered down in the woods there, waiting out the winter. As soon as the snow melts, they'll move on into Germany and finish the job. The High Command keeps telling us there aren't enough German soldiers left to guard the border, and that the few they have left are ready to quit, but from everything I've seen of them so far, I kind of doubt it. Even though it's pretty quiet up there on the line, Rocherath is still no place you want to be, so the sooner you get your investigation squared away, the sooner you and I can get our asses safely back to Liège.'

One hour later, they arrived at a cluster of thick-walled stone structures with barns attached to the main houses, gathered around a church at the centre of the village. Pine smoke drifted from the chimneys and the smell of it, mixing with the by now familiar reek of manure, hung in the narrow streets. Unlike American farms, which usually stood by themselves, sometimes at great distances from their neighbours, the Belgian farmers seemed to concentrate in villages like these, with the land they worked spreading out in all directions. Most of the buildings appeared to have been taken over by the military and the streets had been churned into ankle-deep mud by the coming and going of army jeeps and trucks. Tucked in an alleyway between two buildings,

Carter spotted a Sherman tank, its barrel aimed across the open fields towards a line of woods in the distance.

Riveira dropped him off at the door to a large farmhouse. 'I'll be back tomorrow morning, sir. The major is expecting you.'

As the jeep rolled away down the muddy lane, Carter knocked upon the heavy wooden door of the farmhouse, which was answered almost immediately by a soldier wearing a tattered sheepskin vest. 'You must be the man from Special Tasks,' he said.

'That's right.'

The soldier stood aside to let him pass.

Carter had to duck as he stepped into the house. Inside, a narrow hallway branched off into small rooms with stone windowsills more than a foot thick.

In what had once been a dining area, a man stood staring at a map that he had laid out on a dining table so massive it must have been built inside the room.

'Major Wharton,' said the soldier, 'here's the guy.'

At the mention of his name, Major Wharton looked up from the map. He was a small, aggressive-looking man with high cheekbones and deep-set eyes, their colour hidden by a squint. He wore a double-breasted, hip-length coat made of faded pea green canvas with a shawl collar fashioned out of olive brown army-blanket wool. Strapped across his middle was a thick belt made of webbing, from which hung a brown leather holster and a pouch for extra magazines. His helmet lay upturned upon the table. Its surface, the colour of pine needles, was stippled with sand, which had been mixed into the paint to roughen up the texture. 'They said they were sending me a cop. A cop from New Jersey, they said.'

'That would be me,' replied Carter.

'Well, mister cop from New Jersey, welcome to the asshole of the world, where nobody cares about your fuel truck or the guys who stole it. We're just a couple of hundred men living like trolls out here on the border who are trying not to starve or freeze to death. As far as I'm concerned, you're just wasting your time. If whoever stole that fuel could have been caught, they would have been, and long ago, without your help.'

'So why weren't they?'

Wharton threw up his hands. 'Due to all the people here who hate our guts.'

'Why? Because that town got bombed?'

'That's part of it. But there's others who hated us long before we got here and others who didn't think about us one way or another until we arrived, and after what happened in St Christophe, some of them hate us even worse than they hated the Germans.'

'You mean collaborators?'

'No!' exclaimed Wharton. 'Anybody who seriously collaborated with the Germans during the occupation fled across the border when the German Army fell back into their own country.'

'Then who are we talking about?' demanded Carter.

'Just regular people,' said Wharton, 'who are looking to get back to living whatever they have left of their lives, and they can't do that while we're living in their houses, driving our tanks all over their fields and sometimes blowing them to pieces, even if it is by mistake. But don't take my word for it. You'll find out for yourself soon enough that people aren't going to like you snooping around here – and that goes for soldiers as well as civilians – any more than people back home in New Jersey like it when the police start knocking on their doors.'

'I'll keep that all in mind,' said Carter.

Wharton stared at him for a moment longer. Then he went back to looking at the map. 'Close the door on your way out,' he said.

*

Although many of the skills Carter picked up while working undercover with the police had prepared him well for working under Wilby, there were others he'd had to learn from scratch. The most important of these, Wilby stressed, was the necessity of following agency protocols as soon as he emerged from Langsdorf prison.

The first step on being released had been to make contact with the barber on Zülpicherplatz, who then relayed the message to Bonn station that Carter was now 'in play', as Wilby had termed it.

After their initial meeting at the hotel, all future contact was to be initiated with the use of a drop box. This was not actually a box, but a loose brick in a wall in an alley called the Höfergasse, right outside the Cologne central train station. The message was written on a piece of cigarette paper, which would be rolled up and stashed behind the brick. The message contained five numbers, the first being between one and six. Each of these corresponded to one of six pre-arranged meeting places scattered around the city. One was in Vorgebirgs Park in the Raderberg district, just south of the main city centre. Another, on the steps of St Heribert church, was in the Deutz district, on the other side of the river from Cologne. A third was in a meat market on Jennerstrasse in the Ehrenfeld district, in the far north-west corner of the city. For each meeting place, a safety sign had been arranged. A man holding up a sign emblazoned with the words 'Christ is Risen' was an indicator that the meeting place had been compromised. Curtains drawn in an apartment that overlooked the cold storage warehouse where the Jennerstrasse meetings took place were also a warning to stay away. The drop box was checked twice a day and the time of the meetings corresponded to the remaining numbers that were written in the message. If the numbers were underlined, the meeting time was p.m.

Although Carter had made use of pre-arranged meeting places when working undercover in New Jersey, these had never involved drop boxes or safety signs. The added security measures came as no surprise to him. He did not have to be told more than once that his life depended on their being used correctly.

Once the protocols had been established, Carter had to memorise them. No written record could be kept.

There was one final message he could send. It consisted of an X with one dot pencilled into each of the four open

V-shapes of the letter. This meant that his cover had been blown and that he was on the run. If this happened, he was to make his way to a safe house, located across the river at 106 Nassaustrasse in the Humboldt district. From there, if necessary, he would be smuggled out of the country.

For their first rendezvous using the numbered protocols, Carter chose the steps of St Heribert. Churches made good meeting places because they always had multiple exits and the layout of most provided excellent fields of view.

He chose eight o'clock in the morning, at the height of the rush hour. Joining a multitude of people passing over the Deutzer bridge, he turned right down a long set of stone steps, many of which still showed the marks of shrapnel damage from air raids which had pounded the district. He wandered through the narrow streets – Arminiusstrasse, Adolphstrasse, Mathildenstrasse – their names whispering themselves inside his skull, until he came to the church. It, too, had been badly damaged in the war, but enough of it still stood or else had been repaired that the structure had not been abandoned.

On his way he glanced in shop windows, studying the reflection of people passing in the street, in case he was being followed. Once or twice, he stopped and tied his shoes, glancing back to see if anyone came to a stop or suddenly changed direction, a sure sign that he had picked up a tail.

But there didn't seem to be anyone and, as he walked across the city, his nerves were not crackling like static, the way they sometimes did when something was wrong, even if he couldn't say exactly what it was.

Carter found Wilby sitting on the church steps reading a newspaper, a trilby pulled down over his eyes and a short-stemmed pipe jutting from between his clenched teeth. Before approaching his control officer, Carter looked for a person with a Christ is Risen placard, but there wasn't anyone around. As he approached the man, Wilby folded the newspaper, stood and walked away.

Carter followed him across the wide Siegburger road and into a narrow park that ran beside the river. They leaned against a railing that overlooked the Rhine. The rush hour had passed and only a few people were left from the throng of pedestrians travelling over the Deutzer bridge. A barge passed by, its engine chugging against the current. A Dutch flag whipped from a post above its wheelhouse.

'I found you a contact in the army,' said Wilby, 'someone who can get what Dasch is looking for. He's a quartermaster at the base in Oberursel. The base is closing down and he's responsible for shipping out about a hundred tons of supplies, either back to the States or else to bases that are remaining open. He can get you canned food, medical supplies, furniture. Whatever you want.'

'How do I get in touch with him?'

'He married a German woman whose family lives just north of here, near the old botanical garden. They visit once a month or so. His name is Tony Galton. He'll be at a bar called the Minerva at noon.' He handed Carter a piece of paper with an address in the Riehl district.

'How will I know him?'

'He's got a tattoo of a cloverleaf on his right hand. He'll

also be in uniform. I told him to wait for an hour, and if you haven't showed by then he'll know the meeting's off.'

'Does he know who I am?'

Wilby shook his head.

'Or who he will be working for?'

'As far as he's concerned, he's working for himself.'

'So he's really going to steal these things?'

'If Dasch is going to be convinced, he'll need to see some results.'

'Which means you're asking me to commit an actual crime, not like the imaginary stolen cigarettes that got me thrown in prison.'

'That's right,' said Wilby. 'This one's for real, which is why you really don't want to get caught. If you are arrested, it will be very difficult for us to disentangle you from the local police – that is if they don't shoot you on the spot. It would be a hassle finding somebody to take your place.'

'You expect me to take comfort in that?' asked Carter.

'What I expect,' replied Wilby, 'is for you to understand that you are a cog in a machine with many moving parts, and I can protect you, but only as long as you don't cause the machine to break down. I've been doing this job a long time now, and I have had to learn that sometimes you have to sacrifice a cog in order to keep the machine running. It's not an easy choice, but it is one you have to make.'

'Jesus, Wilby,' said Carter, 'how much blood do you have on your hands?'

'More than you know,' he replied, and as he spoke he removed his pipe, teeth clacking on the stem, and gestured with the stem across the fast-flowing, grey-green water towards the once densely populated streets of Rheingasse and Filzengraben, now mostly empty buildings with glassless windows like the eye sockets of skulls and heaps of stone still avalanched among those that had somehow remained intact. 'Back in the war,' he said, 'I flew thirty-five missions in a B-17 and we dropped bombs on this city more than once.

Carter said nothing. He kept his eyes fixed on the ruins, wondering about the people who had once lived there.

'I know what you think of me,' said Wilby, 'but don't kid yourself. We have more in common than you think.'

'I doubt that very much,' said Carter.

'Where do you think I go at the end of the day?' asked Wilby. 'Home to my wife and kids? To my neighbourhood bar, where I drink too much beer and talk sports? To confession every Saturday afternoon?'

'How should I know? I don't have any of those things.'

'And neither do I. That's my point. On the surface, we have to appear perfectly normal. And we're good at it. Nobody's stopping to stare at us as we walk by. We fit right in. At least, that's how it seems. But underneath, the whole thing is a scaffolding of lies. The only person who is ever going to understand your world is someone who has lived in it themselves. And as for finding anyone to share a life like that' – Wilby patted Carter on the back – 'well, all I can say is good luck.'

Wilby walked away, but Carter remained for a little while longer. He leaned against the railing and stared at the river swirling past. Much as Carter hated to admit it, Wilby had been telling the truth. He had known men, and women too, who had worked undercover and whose masks had come apart. More often than not, those people ended up dead, but Carter's masks had always held together, because he kept in mind the one thing he could never do, and that was fall in love.

There had been two women in his life, and neither one had stayed around for long.

The first had been a police dispatcher. Her name was Gwen. She had a round freckled face, green eyes almost the colour of jade and a soft, unflappable voice which had made her so perfect for her job. As part of his department's policy for undercover agents, Carter had been forced to ask his supervisor for permission to go out with her. The fact that she was also police made it easy for the supervisor to agree, but that turned out to be the only easy thing in Carter's relationship with Gwen.

There had been no secrets going in, and it was this which had convinced Carter that things had a chance of working. She knew he worked undercover, and that he could not talk about his work except in the vaguest of terms and usually not even then. She knew he could not say where he had been when he was gone all night or who he had spent time with. The moments when he might have spoken to her even about the littlest of things instead became filled with a silence that only became deeper and more pressurised as time went by.

She started to mistrust the silence, even though she knew the cause of it. Her imagination, which might have tolerated such a crippled shared existence if he had spun for her a skein of believable lies, instead began to prey upon itself.

In the end, it was not lies that broke up what they had, as they break up the lives of many others. Instead, it was simply the absence of truth.

The second woman was named Penny, and he lied to her all the time. His supervisor had summoned Carter in one day and ordered him to begin a relationship. When Carter asked why, the supervisor told him that men who kept to themselves all the time always fell under suspicion, and even more from women than from men. Not having a girlfriend was putting Carter at risk, the supervisor said, and he was given one week to set that straight.

It took him only one day to settle on Penny. Penny acted as a landlord for one of the three buildings where Carter had rented an apartment. Penny didn't actually own the building, but she collected the rent and oversaw the cleaning crews and all of the repairs. She was a nervous, energetic woman, brash and flirty and pushy, and she made no secret of her affection. Penny had been flirting with Carter ever since he rented the apartment, always asking him why he only stayed there one or two nights a week, and where he was from and what he did for a living and what kind of movies he liked. And to every one of these questions he told her the stories, some of them true, that belonged to the mask he was wearing.

They went out to dinner and ate the food his alter ego would have liked. They saw the movies both of them would have enjoyed if one of them hadn't been lying. She talked a lot, fast and nervously and with a twang in her voice – clipping off the ends of some words and rounding out others as if she had forgotten how they ended – that belonged, unmistakably, to the ironbound section of Newark.

One night, as they were walking out of a showing of *Drums Along the Mohawk*, she stopped on the pavement and turned to look at him. There was a softness in her gaze, which said more than all the rapid-fire chatter with which she had concealed any vulnerability until now.

The next day he broke it off, moved out of the apartment and never went back, not even to that part of town.

When his supervisor called him in to ask what had happened, Carter reached across the desk, took hold of the man by the collar of his shirt, and through clenched teeth and with a lowered voice cursed him with every barbed, daggered word that he could find inside his head, as angry at himself for following the order as he was at the man who had given it.

From then on, Carter stayed on his own, as wary of loving as he was of being loved, because he knew that no camouflaging of his soul, no matter how elaborate and deep, could stand for long against the weight of true affection lived out in the framework of a lie.

*

In the cold, grey dawn, Lieutenant Carter woke from his first night in the Ardennes in the attic of the farmhouse that Major Wharton had chosen as his command post. He lay on the floor, wrapped up in an army blanket which he had scavenged from a room downstairs. Its previous occupants, to judge from the mess they had left behind, had been steadily making their way through every piece of furniture in the house, smashing chairs, tables and entire chests of drawers and burning them all to stay warm. Now the fireplace was heaped with ash and the stubs of iron nails and brass hinges, folded in upon themselves by the heat until they resembled the petals of flowers. Scattered in the corners of the room were little foil envelopes that had once contained powdered lemonade and Nescafé from American C-ration packs. Where these men had gone, Carter had no idea. He already had the sense that people and vehicles were constantly in motion around him, and that no one seemed to know or care where anyone else was headed as long as they could fend for themselves. No wonder, he thought, that someone could disappear with an entire truckload of fuel. It was probably parked in some village square not far from here and no one was paying attention, because it wasn't their business to look after it. The exasperation that Major Wharton had vented at Carter upon his arrival was starting to feel entirely reasonable, and he hadn't even started work yet.

For a while, Carter just lay there, staring up at the thick plaster of mud and straw that made up the underside of the attic roof. Outside, he could hear vehicles moving around in the muddy lanes between the houses. Already he was learning to tell the difference between the Willys jeeps and the deep, throatier engines of the Dodge trucks. Now and then he heard the clattering roar of a tank, but that was always in the distance.

Making his way downstairs, he found Riveira cooking rations on a stove in the kitchen. The sergeant had emptied out a can of spaghetti into the shallow pan of a mess kit, on top of which he crumbled a handful of bone-coloured army biscuits.

'Is that breakfast?' asked Carter, nodding towards the plopping slurry in the mess kit.

'I'm afraid so, sir. You're on the front line now. There's nothing but C-rations out here, and that means either pork and beans, spam or spaghetti, all of which taste pretty much the same after a while.' He gestured at a pile of cardboard ration boxes on the counter. 'Help yourself,' he said.

Carter scrounged a mess kit for himself and fried up some slices of spam.

'Where's Major Wharton?' he asked.

'Inspecting the front lines,' said Riveira. 'He does that every day.'

'How far is it to Germany from here?'

'You could walk there in under an hour, but I wouldn't recommend it.'

'Do you ever see them – the Germans, I mean – out there in the woods?'

'No,' replied Riveira, 'but that doesn't mean they aren't there.'

There was no table in the kitchen, so Carter sat on the floor with his back to the wall while he ate the greasy strips of spam, washing them down with a canteen cup of powdered coffee.

When he had finished, he washed out the mess kit in a

cattle trough behind the house and climbed into the jeep, where Riveira was already waiting.

'Where to, sir?' asked the sergeant.

'I need to talk to the man they arrested for stealing that fuel truck.'

'Well, they've got him at the police station over in Büt-genbach. It's not too far away. I got to warn you, though. I've heard he is out of his mind.' Riveira knocked the jeep in gear and pulled out of the alley. Soon they were driving along narrow lanes, with earth and hedges built up so high on either side that only at the crossroads could they see across the landscape.

They passed lines of soldiers shuffling along the road. The men were red-eyed with fatigue from sleeping in foxholes in the woods. Many had blankets wrapped around their shoulders, which made them look, at a distance, like a procession of stooped old women.

Bütgenbach was a slightly larger town than the one where Carter had spent the night. A group of women in stained and tired-looking dresses, all of them clattering along in wooden-soled shoes, gave the jeep the same look of weary impatience as it passed.

Riveira pulled up in front of the police station beside a monument to the dead of the Great War. A Belgian soldier cast in bronze looked out over the square, his eyes sea green with corrosion. The clouds had gathered, seeming almost balanced on the rooftops of the sleepy little town, and the first Morse code flicks of rain darkened the grey slate tiles.

Inside the police station, Carter was led to the one prison cell in the building by a guard who wore a dark blue tunic with silver buttons, polished like gunmetal at the elbows from where he had leaned on his desk, chin resting in his hands, and slept away the quiet afternoons. He also wore a pillbox hat that was slightly crushed, as if he had sat on it by mistake. What the guard lacked in bearing, he made up for with a magnificent moustache and a reassuring air of dignity.

The cell was barely wide enough for a man to stretch his arms. An opening near the ceiling looked out through a dirty pane of glass towards the eggshell sky. The prisoner sat on a bed, which was attached to the wall by hinges and two chains, allowing it to be folded up flat. He was a heavyset man with shaggy hair and a grey wool vest, beneath which he wore a brown collarless shirt. One trouser leg had been rolled up, revealing a bandage wrapped around his ankle. The man looked blearily at Carter and muttered something that caused the guard to raise his head slowly until he was staring at the man down the length of his formidable nose. The prisoner immediately fell silent.

'Do you speak English?' Carter asked the man.

'Enough,' replied the prisoner.

'What is your name?' asked Carter.

'François Grandhenri.'

Carter turned to the guard. 'Do you have an interrogation room?' he asked.

The man did not answer, but turned and walked back to the foyer of the building, returning a moment later with a small stool, which he placed in the corridor opposite the cell. Then, squinting with one eye, he gave Carter a look, as if daring him to ask for something more.

Carter sat down and the guard left them in peace.

The first thing Carter did was to offer Grandhenri a cigarette. He did not do this out of compassion, but rather as a sign; a laying out of rules – which any prisoner would understand, whether tied up in a chair in a warehouse in the docklands of New Jersey or stuck in an airless concrete hole somewhere in eastern Belgium – that Carter needed something from him, and that his first attempt to get it would be with gestures of civility. Whatever happened after that was up to the prisoner.

Grandhenri reached through the bars and plucked the cigarette from between Carter's outstretched fingers.

Then Carter removed a lighter, spun the little striker wheel until the wick caught fire, and held it to the bars.

Grandhenri leaned forward until the tip of the cigarette just touched the shuddering flame. Then he sat back, drawing in the smoke.

'How did they catch you?' asked Carter.

The man exhaled two grey jets of smoke through his nose. 'I was climbing into the back of the truck. The driver did not wait. He started moving. I lost my grip and fell. When I hit the ground, I twisted my ankle so badly that I could not run away. My friends did not come back for me.' He shrugged and smoked again. 'There is nothing more to tell.'

'They don't sound like very good friends,' said Carter.

Grandhenri paused. 'There are different kinds of friend.'

'Where are they now?'

Grandhenri leaned towards the bars. 'Listen,' he said quietly. 'You should not be worrying about my friends, or your precious truck or even the man who was killed.'

Carter narrowed his eyes. 'What are you talking about?' he asked.

'Death is coming,' said Grandhenri. 'That is all you need to know.'

'Who paid you to steal the truck?' asked Carter.

Suddenly Grandhenri leapt up from his bunk and threw himself at the bars.

Startled, Carter rocked back, cracking his head against the wall so hard that flecks of light appeared to dance around the prisoner's face.

'You are not listening!' Grandhenri's voice rose to a crackling hiss.

The guard reappeared, striding down the corridor. He unlocked the steel door, not even glancing at Carter, who had no choice except to stand aside.

Grandhenri just stood there, trembling. 'I'm telling you the truth!' he said.

As the guard stepped forward into the cell, a short black object suddenly appeared in his hand, which had slid down through his sleeve. It was a ball of lead about the size of a man's thumb, fitted with a metal spring that formed a handle, with the whole thing wrapped in horsehide. With a movement so slight it appeared almost gentle, the guard knocked Grandhenri in the temple with the leather-padded ball of lead. The tap from this weapon was so perfectly placed that the man just dropped to his knees and then fell forward onto his face. The guard emerged from the cell, locked the door again and turned to Carter. 'The interview is over,' he said. Then he walked back down the hallway.

By the time Carter had returned to Rocherath, Major Wharton was back from his inspection of the lines. He was sitting in the dining room, still wearing his gloves and a heavy woollen scarf around his neck. 'Well?' he asked Carter, setting the heels of his muddy boots upon the dining table.

'I went to see the prisoner.'

'Did he tell you anything?'

'He said that death was coming.'

Wharton laughed. 'You see? You were wasting your time.'

'It sounded like he meant it.'

'Of course he did!' said Wharton. 'For the past four years, that man has been living under German occupation and if he had tried the same stunt when they were around, he would have been shot days ago. But he didn't think twice about stealing from us, even though we came to liberate his sorry ass. We're all thieves here, Lieutenant. It is what time and circumstance have made us. Even you.'

'I haven't stolen anything.'

'Of course you did!' laughed Wharton. 'You stole that blanket you slept in last night, and chances are it's already been stolen from you. The rations you ate this morning were stolen from a depot back in Stavelot.'

'Who stole them?' asked Carter.

'Nobody!' exclaimed Wharton. 'And that's the beauty of it. Rations were simply requested for men who are no longer with us. Some of them have been dead for months.

But we're still picking up their rations so that we can get enough to eat. Is it a crime? Of course it is! Does everybody know what's going on? Of course they do! Does anybody really care?' Now Wharton stood, set his fists upon the table and leaned forward until he was towering over Carter. 'Not when they're sleeping in bunkers in the woods. Not when they haven't been on leave in more than half a year. Not when they know that, for every soldier stuck here at the front, there are twenty back in France, or England or even in America, who have no idea what it's like to get shot at by sixteen-year-old German kids who've never been taught how to play football or baseball, or how to dance with their girlfriends or to do anything you and I would think was normal for a teenage boy. All they know how to do is kill you. And they know how to die. And after you've been fighting them, all day every day, for so long you can't remember what it's like to do anything else, trust me son, you don't lose too much sleep over a truckload of fuel, or a case of goddamned pork and beans.'

Carter sat there for a while in silence. 'All right, Major Wharton,' he said at last, 'assuming that's all true, what would you do now if you were me?'

The question seemed to catch Wharton by surprise. 'Do you really want to know?' he asked.

Carter held open his hands in a gesture of surrender. 'I'll take whatever you've got.'

'All right,' said Wharton. 'I guess I'd answer the question by saying that, from time to time, everybody gets handed jobs which seem like a good idea to whoever thought them up but which, when you actually put them into practice, have no hope at all of success. The problem is, the people who usually come up with the ideas aren't interested in how you get it done. All they think about are the results, which leaves the poor bastard who's been given the job, people like you and me, with no choice but to struggle with a task he knows will fail. So what you have to do is make it seem like you're getting things done. You file a lot of paperwork. You disappear into dusty little corners where no one will come looking for you. You don't ever tell them that it can't be done. They'll figure that out for themselves. Between that time and this, the best you can do is not get anyone killed, including yourself.'

*

The Minerva bar, where Carter was due to meet the quartermaster sergeant, was tucked away down a narrow street called Pliniusstrasse. Tall, steep-roofed buildings with scallop-fringed slates cast heavy shadows on all but a sliver of road. Several of the shopfronts were closed with metal shutters, even though it was the middle of the day.

But the Minerva was open. Dance music blared into the street. Inside, a heavily made-up woman, stripped to the waist and wearing a white silk skirt which came down almost to the floor, was performing what looked like some kind of flamenco dance. Several men sat around at tables that had green and white checked tablecloths, leering at the woman's breasts.

A US Army soldier was leaning up against the bar, his back to the woman, tilting a glass of honey-coloured liquid back and forth. He wore a short jacket patched with his sergeant's chevrons, a wound stripe at the bottom of his sleeve and three gold bars below them, to indicate a year and a half's continuous overseas service. His hair was grey and his cheeks looked dry and pink. When Carter walked over to the sergeant, squinting as his eyes adjusted to the dark, the man slid the drink away, allowing him to see the cloverleaf tattooed on the top of his right hand. Then Carter knew for certain it was Galton.

'Let's get out of here,' said the sergeant.

A moment later, Carter was back on the street and the nerve-jangling music was already fading from his ears.

'What did you think of the dancing girl?' asked Galton.

'I didn't really have time to pay attention,' replied Carter.

'That's a pity,' said Galton. 'She's got talent.'

'If you say so.'

'Oh, I know so. She's my wife.'

Carter glanced at him. 'Jesus,' he said.

Galton laughed. 'One thing you have to learn about this place, and by that I mean this whole godforsaken country, is that you're either buying or you're selling, and that absolutely everything is for sale. That's why you came to see me, after all. It's the only way people can survive. Anyone who thinks otherwise is either starving or already dead. Nobody wants it that way, and maybe it will change some day, but right now that's the way it is.'

The two men walked along the road that ran beside the

city's botanical garden. Galton strode quickly, facing straight ahead, but his pale blue eyes shifting nervously as he noted everything in his path. At the entrance, Galton turned into the gardens and only then did his pace slacken. There were high brick walls around the gardens and Carter was surprised to see that, far from being filled with exotic plants and trees, the whole place had been converted into a giant vegetable patch. A man wearing a rubber apron and the long-brimmed, field-grey wool cap of a former Third Reich soldier was using a fire hose to water a small field that had been planted with lettuce.

At a bench on the far side of the lettuce field, Galton sat down and stretched his arms, suddenly relaxed. For now, Carter stayed on his feet.

The location for their meeting had been well chosen. No one could get near them without being noticed, and their voices would be drowned out to all but each other by the swish and patter of water raining down as the old soldier played the hose back and forth across the lettuce patch.

'They didn't tell me anything about you,' said Galton, 'except that we spoke the same language.'

'That ought to be enough,' replied Carter.

'I figured I'd be meeting with the buyer, but you don't look like some big spender to me. My guess is you are working for a German, and this guy is smart enough to know I wouldn't work with him if he came to me on his own. That's why he sent you as a middleman. Am I right?'

Carter said nothing.

'All right.' Galton turned away and spat towards the

miniature forest of lettuces. 'Then at least guarantee me that your buyer is legit.'

'What do you mean?'

'I mean can he pay? I don't want to show up to a meeting and have you, or somebody else, whining in my face about how they're running short on cash or trying to renegotiate the deal.'

'He is not that kind of guy,' said Carter, finally taking a seat beside Galton.

'So you can vouch for him?'

'I wouldn't be here otherwise.'

'Well, good' – Galton aimed a finger at Carter – 'because if there are any problems, you're the one I'm going to hold responsible.'

Their conversation paused as a woman passed by, pushing a pram whose wheels creaked with rust, and followed by two wide-eyed little boys in clunky boots which were too big for them. Seeing his uniform, the boys stopped and stared at the sergeant. The mother walked on a few paces, then turned and hissed at them. The boys snapped out of their trance, and ran to catch up with her.

The men went back to their discussion.

'So what are you looking for, anyway?' asked Galton.

'The usual stuff,' replied Carter. 'Food. Candy. Medicine. Cigarettes. Soap.'

'I got plenty of that, at least for now, but you need to understand that I don't know how long I can keep the gravy train running. American bases are closing all over the zone we used to occupy, and this has given me an opportunity, but it's not one that I'm going to be able to hold on to forever.'

'How does it work?' asked Carter.

'The warehouses for the few bases that are remaining open are already filled to capacity. This means that literally hundreds of pallets of material are being shipped to storage areas which are being rented out wherever we can find them.'

'Why not ship them back stateside?' asked Carter.

The sergeant laughed. 'They don't want them! Some of the stuff only just got here. By the time it goes all the way back to America, it will either have expired or else whatever it is will have been replaced by newer equipment. In the last year alone, changes in the regulation of tunic patterns meant I had to destroy over a thousand perfectly good uniforms.'

'Destroy them?'

'Burned them! Those were my orders. So what I'm trying to tell you is that tonnes of material is basically getting blown to the winds while we get ourselves untangled from this country. It's going to stay locked up in warehouses until people either forget about it altogether or else decide that they don't want it anymore.'

A sudden, momentary spray of water from the hose rained down on them. They looked back at the old soldier, who smirked at them to show he had done it on purpose.

Galton swiped his hands across his sleeves to wipe away the droplets. He smiled back at the gardener, but his eyes stayed cold and hostile. 'If this had been five years ago,' he muttered through clenched teeth, 'that would have been a flame thrower in his hands, and I bet he would have had the same shit grin on his face as he does now.'

Carter returned to business. 'Tell me what you can deliver, and I'll get the message across.'

'All right.' Galton sat forward and rubbed his face with his big, pink hands. 'Let's say two hundred packets of American cigarettes – Camels, Chesterfields, Lucky Strikes – whatever I can get my hands on. And five cases of canned fruit – it'll probably be peaches and pears – and I can also get you twenty pounds of coffee. The real stuff. That comes in one-pound cans.'

'And the cost?' asked Carter

'The price is eight thousand marks. That'll get you everything I mentioned and maybe a little bit more.'

'It'll need to happen soon.'

'Let's say the day after tomorrow at noon, on the corner of Bachemerstrasse and Stelzmannstrasse. That's close to the Lindenburg hospital. There'll be a blue delivery van with yellow writing on it. I'll be sitting in the passenger seat. You're going to get into the driver's seat, hand me the money, and then I'm going to get out and walk away. You're going to drive the van to wherever you need to go to unload it. Then you're going to drive it back to the Lindenburg hospital and leave it in the parking lot reserved for delivery vehicles. You got all that?'

'I'll tell him what you said.'

'I'll wait for half an hour,' said Galton. 'If you don't show, don't come back to me later with a mouthful of excuses, because it won't make any difference. It'll be the last you'll ever see of me.'

They walked out of the garden.

The old soldier had finished watering the lettuce patch. Now he was coiling up the hose, looping it over his shoulder so that he looked like a man being crushed by a python.

They were on the street now, about to go their separate ways. 'I have to know,' said Galton. 'What are you doing here? In Germany, I mean. You aren't a soldier. I can see that. But I'm guessing you might have been one, so why didn't you go home?'

'I have nothing to go home to,' Carter told him.

For a moment, Galton's expression changed and he looked lost, as if he suddenly couldn't recall how he came to be here, standing in this place. 'You and me both,' he said.

After his meeting with Galton, Carter travelled out to Dasch's compound in the Raderthal district. He took a bus as far as Höningerplatz, the end of the line, by which time it was just him and the driver. As he stepped out onto the cobbled square, Carter couldn't even tell what Höningerplatz used to look like. Now it was nothing more than a large circle of smashed bricks and masonry, amongst which several enterprising people had constructed little shops selling brooms and buckets and shaving brushes. One stall was run by a man with no legs. He sat on the pavement at a table whose legs had also been removed, with his wares laid out in front of him – razor blades, combs and nail clippers.

From there, Carter walked south along a path called the Leichweg, with the wide expanse of a cemetery spreading off to his right; stone angels, some of them fingerless, others handless and others with their arms gone altogether, looked down from shrapnel-pocked pedestals upon the tilted gravestones.

Dasch's compound stood at the intersection of Leichweg and Militärstrasse, a wide road that ran in an arc around the southern edge of the city. Carter arrived just as Dasch and Ritter were piling into the Tatra. Teresa stood off to one side, arms folded, studying Carter as he wiped the sweat from his face after the walk from Höningerplatz.

'Come!' shouted Dasch, beckoning to Carter. 'We're taking a little trip.'

'Are you certain it's a good idea,' asked Teresa, 'bringing him along?'

'It's a brilliant idea!' Dasch told his daughter. 'I know, because it's mine. Now get in, Mr Carter' – he gestured at the cramped back seat of the car – 'or we will be late for our appointment.'

With Ritter at the wheel, Dasch up in front and Carter wedged into the back, the Tatra skimmed along the main road that ran down the western bank of the Rhine, passing from the devastated suburbs of Cologne into the hilly countryside to the south. Ritter and Dasch were puffing away at cigars, filing the car with so much smoke that Carter finally wound down his window, sending a cloud of grey billowing out onto the road.

Carter told them about his meeting with Galton.

'Perfect!' boomed Dasch. 'I will have the money ready.'

'How do you know this man?' asked Ritter. 'Have you ever worked with him before? Is he known to the authorities?' He seemed to be winding up for another barrage of questions.

Carter wasn't sure that he could answer them this time, at least not to Ritter's satisfaction, and he felt his throat tighten with fear.

This time it was Dasch who saved him. 'What does it matter,' he demanded, brandishing his cigar in Ritter's face, 'as long as he gets the job done? It's my money, after all. Why must you always be so suspicious of everyone and everything? You're worse than Teresa sometimes!'

Just outside Bonn, Ritter cut in from the highway, circling around the city towards the town of Bad Godesberg. At a village called Ippendorf, which was nothing more than a tiny cluster of houses clinging to a shred of pastureland, Ritter turned off the main road and they began to climb into a thickly wooded area which, according to the road signs, was called the Kottenforst.

The tarmac surface of the road quickly gave way to dirt, which gave way to mud, and eventually the car was just slipping along through potholes. They passed a sign with a skull and crossbones painted on it, as well as the word 'Tollwut' – rabies.

Dasch turned and grinned at Carter. 'That keeps away the spectators,' he said.

Carter looked out at the forest. The branches of large trees growing on either side of the narrow road met in a tangled archway above their heads, cutting out most of the light.

He glimpsed a clearing up ahead and, a moment later, the car emerged into a large, open area, about three times as wide as a football field and maybe six times as long. Here, the trees had been cut back and the ground made level. Off to one side, about a third of the way down, he could just make out the arching metal roof of a large, camouflaged building with two huge sliding metal doors at the front, both of which were closed.

Ritter pulled over at the edge of the clearing, a short distance from the building.

The passengers climbed out.

'What is this place?' asked Carter.

'It used to be the private airstrip of Franz Wendel, a military governor in southern Poland during the war, who had a holiday home around here. It was his idea to put up rabies warning signs.'

'And now?'

Dasch held his arm out towards the building that was set back among the trees. 'It is the haven of my pride and joy,' he said.

As they entered through a side door, what Carter saw so stunned him that for a moment he found it impossible to breathe. A C-54 cargo plane, complete with what appeared to be Canadian markings on the sides and on the wings, filled up the giant hangar. Dozens of wooden boxes, each one the size of a milk crate, were being loaded into the plane's storage bay by men who barely glanced at the newcomers as they went about their task.

Dasch slapped Carter on the back, as if to dislodge something that had got caught in his throat. 'You seem a little pale!' he laughed.

'Where the hell did you get this?' asked Carter.

'That is an interesting story,' said Dasch. Putting his hands in his pockets, he strolled around the aircraft, pausing now and then to examine the splintery wooden crates that were being loaded aboard.

Carter followed behind, forcing his mind through the cloud of confusion that had enveloped him since he walked into the hangar, and to concentrate on every detail he could see. *Wilby will want to know everything,* thought Carter, *if he doesn't drop dead from a heart attack when I tell him what Dasch has got his hands on.*

'In the spring of 1945,' explained Dasch, 'a Royal Canadian Air Force transport plane loaded with medical supplies set off from Kilmarnock airfield in Scotland, bound for an airfield just outside Oslo, Norway. Crossing the North Sea, it encountered an ice storm, which ran it off course. It overshot its destination and crossed into Sweden, where it made an emergency landing at Bulltofta airbase. By then, Bulltofta had become a parking lot of Allied as well as German planes, some of which had landed there in emergencies and others which had flown there deliberately to escape the war. Regardless of which country they belonged to, all of the planes were impounded and their crews sent to live in separate military barracks until the war was over. When the war did end, three months later, the aircrews were all sent home and most of the planes were destroyed. Due to a misunderstanding between the Canadians and the Swedish about its condition, this C-54 was initially slated for scrap. By the time the mistake had been cleared up, paperwork showed that the plane had already been junked. In fact, when the plane took off for the Arctic city of Kiruna, where it was to be stripped of usable parts and its aluminium frame recycled in a furnace, it travelled south instead, across the Baltic, landing on a frozen lake in northern Germany. The pilots were two deserters from the German air force, who had managed to avoid forced repatriation by the Swedes to an area now under Russian control. Once the plane had landed, its wings and engines were dismantled and the aircraft was put into hiding until a suitable buyer could be found. And that buyer turned out to be me. I had heard about this plane, but at first I didn't believe the story. It took me two years to track down the men who had stolen it. They were working in a cement factory in Poland. They had all but given up hope that their great adventure would ever pay off, and you should have seen their faces when I offered not only to buy the plane but also to hire them as its pilots.'

'And what are you going to do with it?' asked Carter.

'Tonight, we will be making our first delivery by air. I told you I would need that bigger map up on my wall!'

Just then, they were startled by a crash.

One of the loaders had been handing a crate through the side door of the plane. The man who stood in the doorway had taken the crate from him, but lost his grip and dropped it. The crate had fallen several feet to the concrete floor of the hangar and its glass contents had shattered.

'Damn you!' roared Dasch.

The man who had dropped the crate stared in terror at Dasch, his hands still clasping the air where the crate had been only a second before. 'I'm sorry,' he stammered. 'It was an accident.'

Dasch walked towards him and then suddenly stopped.

Carter wondered for a moment if he was going to pull a gun.

But Dasch just stood there, rooted to the spot. 'An accident may be the reason,' he said, his voice low and threatening, 'but it is not an excuse.'

'There is always some loss,' said Ritter, trying to calm his master. 'Every businessman knows that. Garlinsky will understand.'

Dasch turned and stared at him. 'You may be right about the loss,' he said, 'but as for Garlinsky understanding, I wouldn't be so sure about that.'

By now, a puddle of liquid had formed around the crate, one corner of which had splintered with the impact of its fall. Carter could smell alcohol.

The man who caused the accident had clambered down from the plane and now picked up the crate. Broken glass shifted inside. More liquid poured out over his legs. 'I don't think they're all broken,' he said. 'Mr Dasch, what would you like me to do?'

'Put it aside,' ordered Dasch, 'and see if you can finish your job without ruining anything else.'

Waddling under the weight of his burden, the man carried the crate over to a corner of the hangar, set it down and returned to his work, head bowed and silent as he walked by.

Dasch walked over to the puddle, dipped a finger into the

liquid and touched it to his lips. 'Scottish whisky,' he said. 'Apparently, the Russians acquired a taste for this stuff when it was brought to them as gifts by British sailors delivering supplies to the Arctic port of Archangel, on what they called the Murmansk Run.'

'This plane is flying to Russia?' Carter asked in amazement.

'Not quite that far, my friend, but close enough that you might hear their balalaika music.'

A man jumped down from the cargo door, a clipboard hugged against his chest. He was one of the pilots and wore an olive green gabardine flight suit, the cuffs tucked into a pair of black sheepskin-lined flight boots. 'We have a small problem, Mr Dasch,' he said.

'What problem?' asked Dasch.

'As you know, sir,' explained the pilot, 'since there appears to be no provision for refuelling once we land, we are carrying our own gasoline for the return journey. This has taken up a significant portion of our cargo space but, more importantly, it has also limited the weight of cargo we can carry. According to my calculations' – he held out the clipboard – 'if we try to load every case on board, we will be dangerously over our weight limit for the kind of flying we are going to have to do. If we unloaded some of the crates—'

'No! You'll already be one short!' Dasch pointed to the corner of the hangar, where the crumpled box was still leaking whisky. 'You could unload some of the fuel.'

For a moment, the pilot's face froze. 'Then we would not

have enough to make it home.'

'Surely there must be some place where you can refuel,' said Dasch.

The pilot thought for a moment. 'There is a small commercial airstrip not far off our route. Planes come and go from there all the time. The man in charge is an old friend of ours. He can sell us fuel and make sure our plane is not recorded on the manifests. But it might mean a delay in our return.'

'How much of a delay?'

'A day. Perhaps two.'

'I think I can spare you that long,' said Dasch.

It took another hour to load the plane and for the pilots to conduct their pre-flight check. By then the sun had gone down, and the deep and sleepy green of the pines all around them vanished into coal-black silhouettes.

When the great doors of the hangar were finally rolled back, the stars were already out, balancing like Christmas ornaments upon the jagged treetops.

Dasch walked outside, followed by Ritter and Carter. It was cold, and a light wind rustled through the tops of the pines, filling the air with a hiss like running water, as if the moonlit runway were, in fact, the ruffled surface of a lake.

The engines of the plane fired up, exploding from the cavern of the hangar. The wedge-shaped chocks beneath the wheels were pulled away and, by the glow of a light in the cockpit, Carter could see the pilot and co-pilot, their heads cocooned in flying helmets, eyes fixed upon the instrument panel in front of them.

The cockpit light was extinguished and then the plane

began to move, the great buzz saws of its propellers flattening the grass as it manoeuvred out of the hangar.

'I meant to bring champagne!' Dasch shouted over the bone-rattling thunder of the engines. He took Carter gently by the arm. 'See if you can find an unbroken bottle in that crate. We ought to celebrate with something, after all.'

Carter made his way back into the hangar. The main lights had been switched off, and only a few bare bulbs along the walls lit the huge space. The men who made up the ground crew had already set off on their bicycles down the road that led out of the forest, clattering on metal rims for lack of rubber tyres.

Carter knelt down in front of the box. The lid had been nailed shut, but the drop had jarred it partly open and it required only a little effort to remove the wooden slats covering the whisky bottles, which had been packed in straw. Three of the nine bottles on the top had shattered, and Carter had to be careful as he moved aside the jagged shards of broken glass. The smell of the whisky drilled into his senses with a sharp mustiness that reminded him of new leather. He noticed that one of the slats had split in such a way as to reveal a hollow centre. *No wonder it snapped,* thought Carter, *if they're going to use such cheap materials.* He prised it back carefully to avoid getting splinters in his wrist as he lifted out one of the unbroken bottles. The fragile slat snapped again where it had been nailed to the body of the case, coming away so suddenly that Carter almost lost his balance as he crouched there in the dimly lit corner of the hangar. As he regained his balance, something fell to the floor just by his feet. Glancing down, he realised it was a bundle of money. At first he thought it had tumbled from his pocket but, as he picked it up, ready to stash it back into his coat, he realised that the money wasn't his. It was too crisp. Too new. In fact, it wasn't even German currency. Peeling away one of the notes from the bundle, he found himself squinting at a Russian twenty-five-rouble note, its bluish-green tint underlaid by corn-pollen yellow, showing the face of Lenin on one side, and the hammer and sickle crest of the Soviet Union cupped between two sheaves of wheat, as if by hands at prayer. Fanning his thumb through the stack, he saw that they were all twenty-five-rouble notes. He picked up the broken piece of wood and shook it, and another slab of money slid out into his hand. Studying the wood, he could see that the slat had been cut in half, hollowed out and glued back together before being sanded so that the seams were almost invisible.

Carter looked around him in case someone else might have seen. But there was no one else in the hangar, and the attention of Dasch and Ritter was taken up by the plane, which had come to a stop at the beginning of the runway. Off to one side, Carter could see the tiny orange sun of Dasch's cigar.

Carter's pulse was thumping in his neck as he pocketed the bills. He rose to his feet and was halfway out of the hangar before he remembered the whisky. He spun around and ran back to grab a bottle, arriving at Dasch's side just as the C-54's wheels left the ground. For a moment, it looked as if the plane wasn't going to clear the trees, but then it wobbled into the sky and, keeping close to the ground, soon vanished beyond the saw-toothed horizon where the runway dissolved into the blackness of the forest.

Dasch turned to Carter, his teeth starkly white in the darkness as he smiled. 'You almost missed it,' he said.

Carter handed over the bottle.

The cork was soon removed and the whisky passed around.

'I wonder how much the Russians pay for this,' Dasch said. 'I ought to start making it myself.' He took a drink, growling at the fire in his belly, then pressed the bottle against Carter's chest.

Carter took it from him and knocked back a mouthful, but his mind was racing so fast that he barely tasted the alcohol. Smuggling whisky he could understand, but why hide Russian money in the crates? Dasch obviously had no idea about the roubles, so why keep it secret from him? Why hide one crime inside another? It made no sense to him at all.

When the droning of the plane's engines had faded at last into the night, Ritter and Carter slid the hangar doors shut and returned to the car, where Dasch was already waiting.

For a while, as the car slipped along the muddy track, nobody spoke. Only when they turned again onto the main road back to Cologne, mud from the wheels spattering against the cowlings, did somebody finally talk.

'Well, Mr Carter,' said Dasch, 'what do you think of my new toy?'

'You were right about needing a bigger map,' replied Carter.

'My thoughts exactly,' replied Dasch, and he lit up another cigar.

Back at the compound, Teresa was there to meet them. She did not ask where they had gone or what they had seen.

Dasch stepped inside his office to collect a briefcase full of paperwork. Ritter followed him in, leaving Carter alone with Teresa.

Teresa fidgeted awkwardly, stuffing her hands in her pockets and tapping a foot in the dirt as she kept time to some rhythm that was pounding in her head. Suddenly she turned to him and pointed out into the dark, down the long, twisting dirt road that led back towards the city. 'Leave,' she murmured to him. 'Go, before it is too late.'

'I've been meaning to ask you,' said Carter. 'Is it personal, or do you treat everyone like this?'

She stepped closer to him.

Even in the dark, Carter could see the anger on her face.

'All my life,' she said, 'I have watched people gather around my father, like hyenas around a lion when it has made a kill. They wait for the scraps he leaves behind and my father mistakes this for friendship, when the truth is that those hyenas would vanish in an instant if the food ever ran out. So the answer is no, Mr Carter. It is not personal. But I know your kind, and that is usually enough.'

'You're forgetting something,' said Carter.

'And what is that?' she asked.

'I didn't come to him. He came to me.'

At that moment, Ritter and Dasch emerged from the office.

'Climb in, Mr Carter,' ordered Dasch.

'Where are we going?' he asked.

'To your new luxury accommodation! And by luxury, I mean it has a roof that does not leak.'

'To have any roof at all,' said Ritter, 'is luxury enough in this town.'

As they drove along the moonlit roads, streetlamps, neglected since the war, cast hurdles of shadow across their path.

Carter thought about Teresa's warning to get out while there was time. It seemed to him now like less of a threat, and more of a warning by which he might still save himself. He wished he could have told Teresa it was already too late, not only for him but for her as well.

Carter's luxury accommodation turned out to be a one-room attic apartment on Bertricherstrasse, overlooking Vorgebirgs Park. It was located above an electrical appliance repair shop which did not even seem to have a name although, judging from the number of vacuum cleaners, lamps and toasters in the front window, all of them tagged with the names of their owners and ready to be collected, the shopkeeper and his customers were already well acquainted.

'And here is your luxury transport,' said Ritter, pointing to a rusted bicycle with a sagging leather seat which was leaning up against the wall of the building.

As soon as they had gone, Carter made his way up to the apartment, which was reached by climbing a narrow staircase attached to the side of the building. It had two windows: one at the front, which looked out over the street, and one at the back, which had a view of a brick wall and an alleyway below. Under any normal circumstances, it was too small to be comfortable, but the prison cell in which he had spent the best part of the previous year had altered his sense of surroundings. Open spaces made him nervous now and Carter had begun to doubt if that was ever going to change. Besides, it had a roof and, more importantly, it didn't have bars on the windows.

*

When Carter walked out of the farmhouse and into the mud-plastered streets of Rocherath, Riveira was already waiting with the jeep. It was the morning of his second day. The sky had cleared and it was cold. Fangs of ice hung down from leaf-clogged gutters.

'Where to, Lieutenant?' asked Riveira.

'I thought I'd take another crack at that civilian they've got locked up in Bütgenbach.'

'So he's not out of his mind, after all?'

'He probably is,' answered Carter, 'but right now he's the only lead I've got.'

'Before we go,' said Riveira, 'I learned something last night which I think you ought to know about.'

Carter settled into the stiff-backed seat of the jeep, waiting to hear what Riveira had to tell him.

'I was over at the field kitchen,' continued Riveira, 'talking with some of the guys who've been rotating in and out of the forest for the past bunch of weeks. They all take three-day shifts living in foxholes and bunkers before they get to come back into Rocherath for hot food and a bath. This place may not look like much to us, but it's practically a resort to those soldiers.'

'What did they tell you?' asked Carter.

'Well, it didn't take long for word to spread that someone from Special Tasks was here in town, looking into the theft of that truck, and when they figured out that I was the one driving you around, they said it was about time somebody investigated why that fuel got hauled across the border.'

Carter sat forward. 'Son of a bitch,' he muttered. 'It went across the border?'

'They said that truck drove right through town and out along the road which goes direct to Germany.'

'Nobody said anything about this to me when they were giving me the job.'

'Maybe they didn't know.'

'But didn't anyone try to stop the truck?'

'I guess they didn't.'

'Why the hell not?'

'You'd have to ask them that yourself, Lieutenant.'

'Where are these guys?' asked Carter. 'The ones you talked to last night.'

'They were rotating back into the woods. They should be on their way right now.'

'Get me to them,' said Carter. 'Please. And quickly.'

'What about the prisoner you wanted to see?'

'He's not going anywhere for now,' replied Carter, 'and he won't be any less crazy tomorrow than he was yesterday.'

As Riveira and Carter drove out of Rocherath and under the dense canopy of pines that seemed to stretch on endlessly towards the east, Carter spotted no trace of any of the Americans who were bunkered down in the woods. Instead, he saw only the ranks of trees, which seemed to rush dizzyingly into the half-light. It was only as his eyes became accustomed to the perpetual twilight of the forest that Carter began to make out shelters the soldiers had made – low-lying bunkers fashioned out of logs and roofed with pine boughs. Now and then he glimpsed a soldier, the olive green of their combat jackets and the darker brown of their wool trousers blending so perfectly with their surroundings that they looked to him less like men than like trees which had been conjured into life.

'There they are,' said Riveira, pointing to a squad of six soldiers walking along the side of the road, equipped with an assortment of Garand rifles, Thompson submachine guns and a Browning automatic rifle. 'Those are the guys I talked to last night.'

'Pull over,' said Carter.

Riveira braked hard and the jeep swerved onto the muddy shoulder of the road.

Carter had, by now, grown used to Riveira's jerky handling of the vehicle, as well as the potential at every corner that he would be pitched out into the road. He gripped the side of the fold-down windshield until the jeep had come to a stop. Then he climbed out. As he walked towards the soldiers, he could see them glancing at the white letters MP on the hood of the jeep.

The men shambled to a halt. They had no discernable

signs of rank, so Carter just spoke to the soldier who was first in line. 'I'm looking into a report that a US Army truck passed through here, headed for the border.'

'That was a while back,' said the man.

'But it happened?' asked Carter.

'Hell, yes,' said the man. 'It almost ran me over.'

'Why didn't anybody stop it?' asked Carter.

The man sighed. 'We have orders to stop, search and turn back any traffic that comes along this road, whether it's motorised, on foot or being pulled by a horse. But until that truck came along, nobody had been crazy enough to do it. By the time we realised what was happening, the truck was already gone.'

'Did you see who was driving it?'

'No. Sun was reflecting off the windshield.'

'And did you have any idea what it contained?'

'It was sitting low on its shocks. I saw that after it had passed. But the canopy was battened down and I didn't get a look inside it.'

'You didn't wonder what it might have been hauling?'

'Of course I did,' said the soldier.'

'What did you think?'

The man looked at him suspiciously, as if afraid that he was being tricked into saying something that would recoil upon his head. 'I know what I heard afterwards,' he said. 'That it was stolen gasoline.'

'Did you report it?'

He nodded. 'To my platoon commander, and he took it directly to the major.'

'That's Major Wharton?'

'Right.'

'And that truck never came back?'

'Not this way it didn't, but these woods are full of trails. It could have come around some other way. I never said it went all the way to Wahlerscheid.'

'What's at Wahlerscheid?' asked Carter. 'Is that across the border?'

'It *is* the border,' said the man. 'It's a little customs house stuck out in the middle of nowhere.'

'And do you hold it?'

The soldier shook his head. 'That place is no man's land. We send patrols out there and so do they. Most of the time, we just avoid each other. But you go a mile or two down that road and you'll see them sure enough. These woods are crawling with Krauts.'

'I thought there weren't supposed to be any.'

One of the other men in line breathed out sharply through his nose. 'Where'd you hear that?' he asked. 'Back in Paris?'

At that moment they heard a clattering roar, far away among the trees.

The men in the line flinched.

For a while, nobody spoke as the sound rose and fell and then died away, swept up in a wind which came hissing through the tops of the trees.

'What the hell was that?' asked Carter.

The man smiled faintly. 'That depends on who you talk to. If you're listening to the same generals who are saying there's no German army at the other end of this forest, then that noise is from some kind of giant record player, broadcasting the sound of a German tank engine.'

'That didn't sound like any damned record to me,' said Carter.

'I would be inclined to agree with you, sir,' said the soldier, 'if given the opportunity to do so.'

After the soldiers had gone, Carter climbed back into the jeep. 'Did you hear all that?' he asked Riveira.

'Yes, sir, unless you'd prefer that I hadn't, in which case I have no idea what you were talking about.'

'Major Wharton didn't say anything to me about a truck heading into these woods.'

'I can't say I blame him, sir, seeing as this whole mess could come down upon his head if those rumours turn out to be true.'

*

'He has *what*?' Wilby was sitting in a meat locker on the frozen carcass of a pig. More frozen pigs hung all around him, split in two and gaffed upon iron hooks whose metal was tinselled with frost.

The night before, Carter had left a message at the dead drop behind the train station. Choosing from the pre-arranged locations, he had selected the butcher shop on Jennerstrasse, whose owner was paid a regular wage to look the other way whenever strangers appeared out of nowhere in his freezer.

Outside the butcher shop, the cobblestoned street glistened red with blood and the piercing metallic reek of beef and pig carcasses hung over the place like a fog. The meat markets of Jennerstrasse catered to the wholesale trade. It was a crowded, chaotic place, echoing with the guttural sounds of men and women speaking Rhineland dialect, and punctuated with the soft thuds of cleavers hacking through bone. All this, and the fact that it was still early in the morning, the busiest time at the market, made the butcher shop an ideal place to meet.

They had made their way to the meat locker at the back of the shop and there, his breath condensing in that upside down forest of gore, Carter began to tell Wilby about the aeroplane he had seen the day before.

He had only been speaking for a few seconds before Wilby interrupted. 'What kind of plane?' he demanded.

'A Canadian C-54,' said Carter, and he went on to explain how it had been stolen from the Bulltofta airfield in Sweden.

'Please don't tell me Dasch has started flying contraband around the country.'

'Actually,' said Carter, 'he's flying it out of the country.'

Wilby put his face in his hands. 'Oh my God,' he muttered.

'Last night it took off with a cargo of whisky. I'm not sure exactly where it was going, but Dasch told me the buyers are Russian.'

Wilby rose to his feet and began to pace about between the carcasses, which twisted on their iron hooks as if some life was still left in them. 'Where the hell did he get his hands on all that whisky?'

'It wasn't his,' explained Carter. 'He's transporting it for a man named Garlinsky.'

'And who's he?'

'I don't know. He wasn't there. I can tell you that Dasch seems very anxious not to get on the wrong side of him.'

'What did I tell you about Dasch?' Wilby threw up his hands. 'The man's a genius. Hell, I'd apply for a job with his company if all this was even half legal.'

'You know,' Carter said uneasily, 'I'm not sure this guy is everything you say he is.'

'What do you mean?'

'He has a lot of big ideas, for sure, but I'm not seeing signs of any huge operation. He has a few people working for him. His daughter does the books and this man Ritter keeps him safe. But I've heard no mention of any diplomats or law enforcement under Dasch's control and, apart from what they loaded on the plane, which wasn't even his, I haven't seen a single piece of contraband since I set foot on his compound.'

'That doesn't mean it isn't there. It has to be. Just look at what he has accomplished. How many black marketeers can you point to who have their own damned air force?'

'It's just one plane,' said Carter.

'You're missing the point, son. He has an *aeroplane*!' He slumped back down on his dead pig bench. 'As much as I want to see this guy rot in a prison cell for the rest of his life, I can't deny I am impressed. But this is also troubling, Carter, deeply troubling. I don't mind telling you that. So far, it's just contraband he has been moving, but what if he turns his hand to something else? Something that could cause us even more problems?'

'I'm afraid he already has,' said Carter, 'although he doesn't even know it.' As Carter spoke, he removed from his pocket the money he had retrieved from the crate.

Slowly, as if convinced his eyes were playing tricks on him, Wilby reached out and took the stack of roubles from Carter's hand. The blood drained out of his face. He seemed completely overwhelmed.

'Are you going to be all right?' asked Carter. It worried him to see Wilby so rattled by this news.

But the question snapped him out of it. 'Of course I am!' he said. 'What are you talking about?' He shook the wad of bills at Carter. 'And what do you mean Dasch doesn't know about this?'

'I only found it because one of the whisky crates broke,' said Carter. 'Garlinsky didn't tell Dasch about the money.'

'Are you certain?'

'Positive. When the crate broke, all he cared about was the whisky. What I don't understand,' said Carter, 'is why Garlinsky would take the risk of hiding all that cash in something that was already illegal.'

'That's easy,' said Wilby. 'It's because whisky is the kind of thing Dasch would be expecting. Since he deals in black market goods, it makes perfect sense that someone might approach him for help in transporting stolen or illegal merchandise out of the country. How else would they convince him to get involved? Whoever Garlinsky is, and whoever he's working for, they're obviously in a hurry to get that money to its destination, or else they'd never take such a risk.' Wilby peeled one bill from the stack, held it up to his ear and crumpled it between his fingers. Then he scratched at it and studied the rim of his fingernail.

'You think it might be fake?' asked Carter.

'I have no idea,' replied Wilby, 'but we're going to some-one who does.'

'Now?'

'Immediately! This kind of thing can't wait. This is big, Carter. This is really big. It's one thing to be moving food around. A man can get rich doing that. But money! And Russian money! This is exactly what I was afraid might happen.'

'But if it's counterfeit—' Carter began.

Wilby didn't let him finish. 'That's what we're going to find out.' Once more, he climbed to his feet. 'Come on!' he said. 'Get up!'

Wilby's confusion was gone, replaced by a nervous, almost frantic energy that worried Carter even more.

'Wait two minutes,' ordered Wilby, 'then follow me out. Make sure you keep twenty paces back.' And then he was gone.

For a few seconds after Wilby had departed, Carter stood alone in the meat locker. He felt like one of those bell-helmeted deep-sea divers plodding around with lead-weighted shoes on the ocean floor, depending on a single hose connecting him to his air supply up on the surface. The only thing that stood between Carter, the agent with an invented criminal past, and Carter the actual ex-convict, now working for one of the biggest black marketeers in the country, was a man who had just appeared to be on the verge of losing control.

Carter stepped out of the freezer and the warm, early

summer air wrapped itself around him like damp towels. He emerged from the butcher shop just as Wilby was turning the corner from Jennerstrasse onto the main road, leaving a trail of bloody footprints for Carter to follow.

Wilby's path meandered over into the Nippes district; a warren of little streets and alleyways in which, if he had not kept his eyes on Wilby, Carter would soon have become lost.

Carter tried to memorise the names of the streets – Cranach, Steinberger, Wilhelm – but he soon gave up since Wilby was not moving in a direct line, as if he feared that he was being followed by somebody other than Carter.

They arrived, eventually, at a small antique bookshop on Erzbergerplatz. It was wedged between two closed storefronts, their windows whitewashed blind and doorways clogged with dead leaves and scraps of old newspaper. Above the dusty window of the bookshop, painted in dull red letters outlined in gold, was a single word – Thesinger. Behind the window, placed on fragile-looking stands, were even more fragile-looking volumes whose gilded Sütterlin script was indecipherable to Carter. Between the cloth-wrapped bindings, their once-bright colours rubbed away to the white canvas threads beneath, their crumbled pages looked ready to disintegrate even at the slightest touch. Carter found himself marvelling at the fact that something so delicate could have survived the storm of war when everything else around here, even the mighty cathedral that might once have protected these books, looked as if it had been picked up by a giant and shaken apart before being dropped to the ground in a heap.

Ahead of them, just entering the shop, was a thin man with a tattered-looking suitcase and a brown trench coat which sagged so far off his shoulders that he had been forced to roll up the sleeves.

As Carter and Wilby walked into Thesinger's bookshop, a little bell tied to the doorframe jangled to announce their arrival. They passed by the man with the suitcase, who was now sitting in a tired but comfortable-looking chair in front of a little round table, on which rested an ashtray crammed with the charred twigs of burned-out matches. Two other men, almost as gaunt and dishevelled as their companion, sat around the table, lounging in mismatched furniture. The tattered man was in the process of rolling himself a cigarette with a shred of newspaper. Open on his knee was a battered little tin, from which the man plucked shreds of tobacco mixed with what appeared to be strands of dried corn silk.

The others at the table watched him patiently, their eyes softened with pity. Their friend had obviously fallen on hard times, and Carter wondered if that suitcase contained books he had come to sell to Thesinger, or whether it was everything he owned.

Wilby was talking to a short, heavyset man with thin, curly white hair resting on his head like a cloud. He wore a wool cardigan with leather patches running from the cuff all the way to the elbow and a pipe stem sticking from one of the pockets.

'This is Mr Thesinger,' said Wilby. He made no attempt to introduce Carter and the man with the white hair didn't ask about his name.

'I hear you have brought me a treasure,' said Thesinger.

'It might be,' replied Carter, 'and it might not.'

'We shall see.' Thesinger motioned for them to follow him into a back room, where books were stacked waist deep in every corner. In the centre of this crowded space stood a drafting table. Bolted to one end was a long-stemmed lamp which stooped over the table like a heron. On the table itself lay a large magnifying glass, of the kind Carter's father had used for tying fishing flies.

Wilby removed one of the Russian notes from his pocket and laid it on the table. 'What do you think of that?' he asked.

Other than a slight narrowing of his eyes, Thesinger betrayed no emotion. He turned on the lamp. Then he fished a pair of glasses from one pocket of his cardigan and put them on. He manoeuvred the magnifying glass until the bill seemed to rise up into the air, a jumbled mass of colour and words. For a long time, Thesinger hunched over the table staring at the bill, his breath blooming and fading and blooming again on the lens.

The two spectators remained almost motionless, as if afraid to break the spell under which the old man appeared to have fallen.

At last Thesinger straightened his back, removed his glasses and, with a gesture of fatigue, pinched his thumb and index finger into the corners of his eyes. 'It's counterfeit,' he whispered.

Wilby and Carter breathed out simultaneously.

'But it is a very good one,' added Thesinger. 'In fact, it is the best I've ever seen, and Soviet currency is notoriously difficult to fake.'

'Why is that?' asked Carter.

'In the engraving of the plates from which the currency is printed,' explained Thesinger, 'they use a laborious process called "micro-intaglio". The creation of the platens – the copper plates on which the design of the note is engraved – can take months and is extremely time-consuming. In micro-intaglio, ridges are made in the plate which are then filled with ink and pressed into the paper, rather than just resting upon the surface. The resulting grooves in the note are too slight to be detected by the human hand, but they give an overall appearance that is genuinely three-dimensional, even if the person looking at the bill can't quite understand what gives it the look of authenticity. Some people mistake it for metallic compounds in the inks that give it a particular lustre, but in fact it is caused by the interplay of light upon the minutely recessed grooves in which the inks themselves are embedded. Another trick they use is borrowed from the makers of Persian carpets.'

'Carpets?' asked Wilby.

'The Persians would always work a deliberate flaw into their design, in the belief that only God could achieve perfection. In a similar way, the plate engravers for Russian bank notes work in very slight faults: a minuscule break in a single line amongst hundreds of other lines which are cross-hatched together for the purpose of shading a number or a person's face – a technique engravers call "guilloche". A counterfeiter mistakes these details for printing errors and corrects them but, in doing so, creates an actual flaw in the design. The composition of the Russian paper is also highly unusual. They use rayon fibre mixed in with the cotton, which means that if you crumple one of the bills' – he picked up the twenty-five-rouble note and, holding it by his ear, folded it into his fist – 'it has a characteristically softer sound than if you crumple an American dollar or a British pound.'

'I wonder why they bother with all that,' remarked Wilby, 'seeing how little it can buy. The moneychangers in the west won't even take it in exchange!'

'Have you ever thought,' asked Thesinger, 'that this might be the way the Russians want it? By keeping the value of their currency so low, they discourage all those capitalists, whom they despise, from meddling in their economy. And as for the complexity of their printing methods, it is an acknowledgement of how much damage could be done if they lost control of their monetary system – a lesson the British very nearly learned the hard way during the war, when the Germans came up with a plan to flood Britain with counterfeit five-pound notes. If the plan had worked, it would have caused total chaos.'

'Why didn't it work?' asked Carter. 'Were the fakes not good enough?'

'On the contrary,' said Thesinger, 'they were nearly perfect. When German agents travelled to Switzerland with some of the counterfeit money, they approached a bank in Zurich with concerns that the money might be fake.'

'I don't understand,' said Wilby. 'They went to the bank with fake money and told them it was fake?'

'Not exactly,' said Thesinger. 'What they did was actually very clever. They wanted the money to be examined by experts, to see if it would pass the test of authenticity, but the only way they could do that was to approach the bank as if they had their doubts.'

'And what happened?' asked Carter.

'After examining the currency themselves, the Swiss bank then forwarded it to representatives of the Bank of England, who assured them that it was authentic. This was how the Germans knew that it had passed the ultimate test – to be approved by the very people whose job it was to safeguard the British monetary system.'

'Then why didn't they go ahead with it?' asked Wilby.

'In the end,' replied Thesinger, 'they were unable to distribute the money in a way that would have allowed the fake currency to mingle effectively with the real currency. The only plan they had was to throw it out of aeroplanes and let it rain down over the English countryside, in the hope that people would immediately gather it up and start spending it. The trouble with that plan was that the fraud would have become known immediately, and it relied on the dishonesty of anyone trying to spend it. Whatever damage it might have done would have been extremely short-lived. The only way it could have worked was to let the money trickle in slowly. The art of the counterfeiter is not simply in persuading someone to exchange something that is real for something that is not. It is, in fact, in making them believe in a lie, and the more elegantly that lie is told, the more likely it is that those who are being lied to, even when they realise it is a lie, will cling to it regardless, because they have invested themselves in the idea that it is the truth. It is not just their wealth that is at stake. It took the average British worker almost a month to earn five pounds. Trust in the authenticity of that money also represents their peace of mind. The only thing that prevents even real money from being just a pretty scrap of paper is an agreement between you and your government that this paper' – he waved the rouble note in the air – 'is worth what they say it is. And once the counterfeit bills have found their way unnoticed into the arteries of commerce, even the innocent become complicit in the deception. When the fraud is eventually revealed and, more importantly, accepted as a fraud, the result is that nobody knows anymore what or whom to trust. The Russians have virtually perfected the art of misinformation in their dealings with other countries. It can be very effective in undermining the governments of their adversaries, but they use the same tactics just as vigorously on their own people, which leaves them open to the same vulnerabilities they exploit in others.'

'So is that why somebody is smuggling counterfeit Russian currency back into Russia?' asked Carter.

'Maybe,' answered Thesinger, 'or it might be much simpler than that. Perhaps these counterfeiters simply want to buy something and don't have the money to pay for it.'

'Have you ever heard of a man named Garlinsky?' asked Wilby.

At that moment, the little chime attached to the front door tinkled softly.

'It seems I have a customer,' said Thesinger.

'But the name?' Wilby persisted. 'Do you know it?'

'Unlike my door,' replied Thesinger, 'it does not ring a bell. Excuse me, gentlemen.'

Wilby reached into his pocket, pulled out a roll of American bills and handed it to Thesinger. 'That's the real stuff, by the way,' he said.

'If it wasn't,' answered the old man, folding the money away in his hand, 'I would have been sure to let you know.'

Leaving the shop, Carter noticed that the three men were gone. The sound they had heard was them departing and not the arrival of a customer, after all. Out in the street it was raining and Carter felt sorry for the ragged man, scurrying along before his suitcase disintegrated in the downpour. But, these days, there were so many like that ragged man, wandering like tramps from town to town in search of food and shelter, that you could not feel sorry for them all and not go crazy in the process.

With the collars of their jackets held against their throats, Carter and Wilby walked south along the wide boulevard of Neusserstrasse, heading for the central station where Wilby would catch the train back to Bonn.

'Who is Thesinger,' asked Carter, 'and how does he know what he knows?'

'At the end of the war,' replied Wilby, 'he turned up in a refugee centre somewhere in Austria. Before that, he had been in a concentration camp. In the debriefing given to all refugees, he said he had been employed before the war as a technician at the Reichsbank. His specialty was what's called "rotogravure", which means engraving the copper plates used for printing currency. His story checked out and he was released from the refugee centre. He may be a book dealer now, but that old man used to work at the heart of the German banking system. The reason he knows what to look for in a counterfeit note is that he used to be in charge of making the real stuff.'

'But why go to him?' asked Carter. 'Surely you have people in your organisation who could have told you what you needed to know.'

'I told you I had concerns,' replied Wilby.

'But you answer to people at Bonn station, just like I answer to you. If this is as big as you say it is, surely you can't keep it hidden from everybody.'

Wilby had been striding along, but suddenly he skidded to a halt. Beads of water dripped from the brim of his hat. 'I can keep it hidden,' he said, 'and that's exactly what I'm going to do.' He took hold of Carter's arm and led him under the red and white awning of a bakery to get out of the downpour. The two men faced each other, rain thrashing down so hard around them that they almost had to shout to hear each other. Except for a tramcar sliding past, sparks trailing from where its overhead connector touched the wires, the streets were empty. The windows of the bakery were fogged with condensation. Dimly they could make out the shapes of people moving around inside.

'Up to now,' said Wilby, 'even if Russian intelligence had known about your assignment with Dasch, it wouldn't have been a major concern for them. They're much more interested in stealing military secrets, or finding out which ones of theirs we've got our hands on. The currency you found has changed all that, since it poses a more serious threat than a whole battery of missiles. Your life, and Dasch's too, won't be worth much if they find out. That's why we went to Thesinger. He's one of my contacts, not one of the agency's. I kept him off the books in case something like this ever happened.'

'So what do I do now?' asked Carter.

'Stay close to Dasch,' said Wilby. 'The sooner you can get him to confide in you, the quicker you can find out what the hell is going on.'

Carter knew that learning secrets, on its own, was not enough. Every criminal organisation he had ever infiltrated required the perfection of three different lies. The first lie was to merge seamlessly into his surroundings. It was possible to be unknown, at least in the beginning, and yet still not be taken for a stranger. The art was to look and sound and move like he belonged. This lie formed the surface of his shape-shifting world. Beneath this lay the second lie – the earning of trust, which demanded only the relentless following of orders; or at least the appearance of it, since a man did not need to be liked in order to be trusted. The third lie was to become a friend, and this was the most difficult of all because it could not be cobbled into existence, like the armour of outward appearance, or engineered, as trust could be. It could only be given away. Once this had been achieved, the fate of his opponents was sealed.

*

When Major Wharton stepped in out of the rattling hail that had begun to fall on Rocherath, hissing and bouncing and stinging the knuckles of the men who darted through the muddy streets, he found Lieutenant Carter sitting in the front room of the house. 'Something I can help you with, Lieutenant?' asked Wharton, irritated to find this cop from New Jersey making himself comfortable in his chair.

'Why didn't you tell me that the stolen fuel truck was spotted heading down the road to Wahlerscheid?'

Wharton removed his helmet and placed it on the table. He smoothed the hair back on his head. Then he removed his leather gloves and tossed them into the bucket of the upturned helmet. 'Who told you that?'

'Is it true or not?'

'I don't know,' snapped Wharton. 'Trucks come through here all the time.'

'But they don't all vanish into the forest in the direction of the German border.' Carter stood suddenly, his chair skidding back across the floor. 'You didn't think that it might be relevant?' he asked, struggling to contain his anger.

'Look,' said Wharton, 'there are three divisions strung out along this section of the Ardennes: the 1st, the 2nd and the 99th, as well as a tank destroyer battalion and support personnel from all over the damned place. One thing you learn pretty quickly out here is that anything short of a total logistical nightmare is the absolute best you can hope for. If I tried to chase down where that truck came from and where it was headed, it would have taken me a week of phone calls. Make the calls yourself. Be my guest. Just try it and you'll see.'

'Why didn't you at least tell me about it?'

'Because I didn't want to have the conversation we are having right now. And I knew that we would, if I told you.'

At that moment, their conversation was interrupted by the sound of a woman screaming just outside the house.

'What the hell . . .' muttered Wharton.

Both men walked out into the hailstorm to see what was causing the commotion.

Four soldiers stood in the street. One of them was German. He was young – sixteen or seventeen at the most. He looked exhausted, his eyelids rimmed with reddened flesh. He wore a dirty grey-green tunic made of poor-quality wool, worn through at the elbows and cuffs. On the left side of his collar was a plain black rectangle of wool and on the right, two crooked lightning bolts. Stitched to his left sleeve at the level of his bicep was a small spread-winged eagle in greyish-silver thread on a black background. His baggy wool trousers were tucked into canvas gaiters and his ankle boots were slick with grease. He wore no belt or cap and the forelock of his dirty blond hair hung down over one eye. He was bleeding out of one of his ears and more blood had splashed from his nose, which had just been broken with a rifle butt whose imprint was still clear on his cheek. The boy seemed terrified and, looking at the soldiers who surrounded him, Carter thought he had good reason to be frightened.

In front of them, a woman was picking herself up from the ground, her dress plastered with half-frozen mud. Seeing Wharton, she pointed at one of the American infantrymen and began to shout, gasping and crying as she made her accusation.

Carter had no idea if the woman was speaking French or German. It sounded like a mixture of the two.

'How did she end up on the ground?' demanded Wharton.

'I put her there,' said the soldier who was out in front, with no trace of regret in his voice.

'And why did you do that?' asked Wharton.

'Because she spat on me.'

The woman continued to rant at the Americans, clawing at the air with her fingers, teeth bared as she cursed.

'I can't understand you!' said Wharton. Then he turned to the soldiers. 'Can anybody tell me what she is saying?'

It was the German who answered. 'She is asking for the soldiers not to kill me, because that's what she thinks they will do.'

'You're SS,' said the soldier. 'Why the hell wouldn't we?'

'Shut up,' barked Wharton. Then he turned to the boy. 'Where did you come from?' he asked.

The boy pointed back towards the forest.

'We found him walking down the middle of the road,' said one of the soldiers.

'Was he armed?' asked Wharton.

'No, sir,' replied the soldier. 'Looked like he was trying to surrender. He had his hands up and everything.'

'Is that right?' Wharton asked the boy. 'Were you giving yourself up?'

'I came to warn you,' said the boy.

*

The sun had not yet risen above the fractured rooftops of Cologne when Carter left his apartment, treading carefully on the rotted wooden staircase that brought him down to ground level. His meeting with Sergeant Galton was scheduled for noon and he needed to make an early start.

Carter headed to a cafe across the street, hoping to find some breakfast. It was a tiny place with only three tables and, after a moment of squinting around for a menu, he arrived at the conclusion that the only things they served were coffee and sausages cooked in wrappings of dough. A woman sat behind the zinc-topped counter, wearing a grey dress with a navy blue apron which matched the colours of the restaurant decor. She had a wide, smooth forehead, shallow-set eyes and thin, unsmiling lips. Even though the cafe had only just opened, she appeared already to have lapsed into the trance-like state Carter remembered from the long summer afternoons of washing dishes at the diner, when he would stare in quiet desperation at the hands on the wall clock as if to nudge time forward by force of will alone.

He ordered a sausage roll and a mug of hot brown liquid, which he realised from its smell was not real coffee at all, but what they called 'Ersatzkaffee', made from ground acorns and chicory root. He sipped at it as he made his way over to a table. The drink left a papery, liquorice taste in his mouth. It didn't taste so bad, but it didn't taste like coffee, either.

Sitting at a table near the back, Carter swept away some crumbs left by a previous customer and was turning the plate around, examining the sausage roll and wondering whether he should eat it with his hands or with a knife and fork, when a man walked in and ordered a cup of coffee at the counter.

Carter glanced at the customer and the breath caught in his throat when he realised it was Eckberg, his old contact from Bonn station.

Eckberg did not look his way and Carter assumed his presence here must simply be a coincidence.

Eckberg still had the unmistakable look of a foreigner. There was no sign that he had made any attempt at all to blend in with his surroundings. *With any luck,* thought Carter, *he'll leave without ever realising I was here. And even if he does recognise me, I hope he has been well enough trained not to show it.* He kept his head lowered, listening to the clink of crockery as the woman behind the counter fetched a cup, then the rattle of coins on the metal countertop and the almost musical clunk of the cash register opening. He waited for the creak of the door as Eckberg departed, but it never came. Instead, he heard the soft tread of Eckberg's rubber-soled shoes as the man approached his table.

'Mind if I sit down?' he said.

Carter looked up. 'Do I know you?' he asked, with a meaningful glance.

'Relax,' said Eckberg as he took a seat across the table. 'The waitress is a friend of ours.'

Carter glanced over to the counter, but the woman had disappeared.

'How did you find me?' asked Carter.

'Dasch has properties all over the city and I figured he'd have put you up in one of them. This is the third place I went to. I got lucky when I spotted you crossing the street to this place. I thought I'd be out there all day.'

'I didn't think I would be seeing you around,' said Carter.

'Neither did I,' said Eckberg, 'but things have changed.'

Carter felt his stomach muscles clench. 'Is it our friend?' he asked. 'Is he OK?'

Eckberg nodded. 'It's him. And no he's not.' He sipped at the coffee and winced. 'Jesus,' he muttered. Then he set the cup down and pushed it to the side.

'What's going on?' asked Carter. *Wilby must be dead*, he thought. *There's no way he would have sanctioned this meeting.*

'We're not exactly sure.'

'Who's "we"?'

'The station.'

'Does that include the chief?'

'Of course,' said Eckberg. 'He's the one who sent me.'

'Does our friend even know you are here?'

'No,' replied Eckberg, 'and it needs to stay that way. What I have to tell you is strictly off the record. Do you understand?'

'I understand what you are saying, but that doesn't mean I agree.'

157

Eckberg smiled and sat forward. 'I'm not asking for your permission. I'm telling you how it has to be. It's that important. Otherwise, I'd never have come here and you know it.'

Carter remained silent, wondering how bad this was going to get.

'People are concerned that our friend is becoming unstable,' said Eckberg.

'What do you mean by that?'

'Have you noticed a change in his behaviour lately?'

'I don't know him well enough to answer that,' Carter said evasively.

'For example, he might have spoken to you about a colleague of ours who died recently.'

'Maybe.' He thought of the woman who had washed up on the river bank.

'Well, he took it very hard,' said Eckberg. 'He had his eye on her. There's no point in denying that. But he's coming up with a bunch of crazy ideas about what happened. Things which, believe me, just aren't true. He told me all about it. It's not just that he's got a whole conspiracy worked out in his head. To be suspicious is a perfectly healthy attribute in our line of work, but if you're not careful it can take over your mind. And when you start inventing things to back up your suspicions, that's when you've gone down the rabbit hole.'

'You mean she wasn't working for him?'

'As a secretary, yes! But all that other stuff?' Eckberg shook his head. 'That's in his mind.'

'If that's true, then why the hell don't you pull him out? Or me, for that matter?'

'It may come to that, in time,' said Eckberg, 'but the station chief will only take action if he feels that your specific operation has been compromised. From now on, though, he has authorised you to communicate with me about the details.'

'How am I supposed to do that?'

Eckberg reached into his shirt pocket, pulled out a pack of Camel cigarettes and slid it across to Carter. 'Unroll the cigarette in the top right-hand corner of the pack and you'll find a telephone number where I can be reached.'

Carter tucked the cigarettes into his pocket. 'I might not see eye to eye with him on everything – on most things, actually – but I still don't like going behind his back.'

'And you think I like being put in this position?' asked Eckberg. 'This isn't what I signed up for, any more than you did. But this problem isn't going to go away by itself. Pretty soon, if we don't get this situation under control, people are going to start getting hurt. When that happens, you'll either be part of the solution or part of the problem. You need to choose, right now, which side you want to be on when the crap hits the fan. What happens next is up to you.'

Carter suddenly felt as if he needed to get out of this place. The air had become thick and unbreathable. His heart seemed to be stumbling in his chest. 'I have some place to be,' he said. It was all he could do not to bolt into the street and keep on running until his legs gave out from under him.

'You go on, then.'

As Carter walked out of the cafe, the first rays of sunlight pooled like molten copper in the puddles left from last night's rain. His mind was spinning. Even if it was true that Wilby seemed to be losing control, that didn't make him wrong. The idea of turning on his own control officer was something Carter had never considered. Even now, in spite of all he had heard, and what he'd seen for himself, he could not bring himself to do it. But Carter knew that this might have to change and, if it ever did, to hesitate would be the end of him.

Carter crossed the street and, glancing back towards the cafe, he glimpsed a movement behind the glass.

Eckberg was gone. He must have slipped out the back.

The waitress had reappeared and was eating the remains of Carter's meal. She stared at him with a mixture of shame and defiance, cheeks bulging with food and pastry crumbs falling from her lips.

*

'You came to warn us?' asked Major Wharton, glaring down at the German soldier.

The young man sat at the table in the command post, perched on the edge of a dining chair, his hands pressed together and clamped between his knees. His shoulders were hunched and he breathed in short, whistling breaths through his broken nose.

Carter was sitting against the windowsill, arms folded, watching.

The boy kept glancing at him and then looking away again.

Carter left his perch by the window and set a pack of cigarettes down on the table in front of the boy. Then he took out his lighter and set it on top of the pack.

The boy looked at the cigarettes and then at Carter, but he made no move to help himself.

'Go ahead,' said Carter.

The boy reached out and took a cigarette. After fumbling with the lighter for a moment, he managed to get it to spark. Then he lit the smoke, inhaled and settled back into the chair.

'Warn us about what?' demanded Wharton.

'There is going to be an attack,' said the boy.

'When?'

'I do not know exactly,' he replied. 'Soon. Maybe very soon. Everything has been prepared.'

'What kind of attack?'

'A big one.'

While the boy and Wharton spoke, Carter studied them both.

Wharton's hands were constantly in motion, now clasped into a double fist and resting against his mouth, now resting on the table.

The boy was clearly in a lot of pain, since Wharton had not offered him any medical attention. From time to time his eyes glazed over and he blinked rapidly, as if to return them to focus.

'Big?' asked Wharton. 'You mean like a platoon? A company. A battalion?'

'Divisions,' said the boy.

Wharton exhaled sharply. 'What divisions?'

'The 1st SS. The 12th SS. A division of *Volksgrenadier*. *Fallschirmjäger*. Those are the ones I know about. There may be more.'

'And you're sure about all this?'

'Why else would I be here?' replied the boy.

'All right,' Wharton said quietly, his tone almost gentle. 'I think you've told me everything I need to hear.' He twisted in his chair and called out to the two soldiers whom he had ordered to remain in the hallway.

The soldiers appeared, peering around the room as if they had forgotten that such luxury as tables and chairs still existed in the world.

'Get him out of here,' said Wharton.

'You think I am lying,' asked the boy.

'Young man,' said Wharton, 'I know you are. The 12th SS was destroyed in Normandy. I'm one of the guys who destroyed them! And the 1st SS is reported to be somewhere out in Russia right now. The only thing you may be right about is the *Volksgrenadier* – a bunch of wheezy old men and teenagers like yourself, freezing their asses off in the woods outside of Wahlerscheid.'

The boy looked as if he had not understood everything that Wharton had been saying. But some of it had clearly sunk in. 'No,' he protested. 'No, that is wrong.' He pointed to the lightning bolts on his collar. 'I am SS.' Then he reached a hand inside his shirt and pulled out his dog tag; a grey zinc disc perforated down the middle. He held it out. 'I am from the 25th Panzergrenadier Regiment of the 12th SS Panzer Division *Hitlerjugend*.'

Wharton turned to one of the soldiers. 'You don't usually find them so eager to confess a thing like that.'

Now Carter spoke. 'Did you see a truck?' he asked the boy.

'What kind of truck?'

'An American one. It might have come past you the other day, up by Wahlerscheid.'

'No,' replied the boy.

Wharton clapped his dirty hands together. 'There you go,' he said.

'But I heard about it,' added the boy.

'You lying sack of shit,' said Wharton. 'Now I know you're just playing with us.'

'What did you hear?' asked Carter.

The boy shook his head slightly. 'Only that there was a truck, that it was driven by Belgians who had stolen it.'

'Anything else?'

'That's enough!' snapped Wharton. 'Just get him out of my sight.'

One of the soldiers slapped the cigarette out of the boy's mouth. It spun away across the room, trailing smoke and sparks. Then he took hold of the boy's arm, hoisted him to his feet and led him out of the room.

Carter waited until he and Wharton were alone again. 'What are you going to do?' he asked.

'Do?' Wharton got up from his chair, walked over to where the cigarette butt still smouldered on the floor, and ground it out with the toe of his boot. 'What is there to do? I'll send him over to divisional headquarters in St Christophe and, if he ever makes it, they can ask him all over again.'

'If he makes it?' asked Carter. 'You mean they're going to kill him?'

'You don't understand,' said Wharton. 'You didn't fight those little bastards back in Normandy. I can tell you one thing for sure. If you'd walked into their camp, there is no way you'd get out of there alive, no matter what news you were bringing. So is he going to make it back to headquarters? I don't know. And I don't particularly care, especially since I didn't believe a single word that came out of his mouth.'

'Why not?'

Wharton banged his fist against the wall, sending a crack zigzagging across the plastered surface. 'Because his whole division got destroyed in France! Somebody over there on the other side of the border' – he waved his hand vaguely in the direction of the woods – 'thought it might be a good idea to scare us with some story of a big attack. Get us all running around like chickens with our heads torn off. It's just like those damned recordings we keep hearing.'

'What about the truck?' asked Carter. 'Why would he lie about that?'

Wharton shrugged. 'So maybe a load of gasoline got across the border. Maybe it happened. So what? You think that will win them the war?'

Carter walked out into the street to get some air. It was dark now and the night was cold and clear. He passed by the church, whose doors were open. Inside he saw the flicker of candles. Outside the house that had been converted into a field kitchen he spotted Riveira, lounging in his jeep with his heels up on the dashboard, reading a magazine with a flashlight.

'Hey, Lieutenant!' he said. 'Looks like it's going to be a cold night.'

'They've all been cold,' said Carter.

'I saw them drive that German kid away.'

'Which way were they going?' asked Carter.

'Back towards St Christophe.'

'At least they were headed in the right direction.'

Riveira understood the meaning of his words. 'I wouldn't go too hard on them, Lieutenant. Out here, the rules are different.'

'The rules are the same,' Carter told him. 'It's just how they're followed that's different.'

*

After the meeting with Eckberg, Carter climbed onto his rickety bicycle and pedalled through the backstreets of the Sülz district – Kyllburger, Blankenheimer, Leichtenstern – until he came to the Lindenburg hospital. The pavements were crowded with people on their way to work. When Carter reached the corner that Galton had chosen for the meeting, he paused and looked around. There were still a few hours before the rendezvous, but he wanted to make sure he was familiar with the place.

Above him, in what had once been a large and solidly built stone building, an old lady sat on a balcony behind an ornate iron railing, knitting. Behind her, the building seemed to be nothing more than a gaping hole, the interior having collapsed in upon itself. Carter could not understand how she had got there or where she lived among the bare-brick walls and glassless window frames.

Below her on the street corner a young man played a small accordion. On his left sleeve he wore an armband painted with three black dots to indicate that he was blind, although the fact was plain enough to see already, since his empty eye sockets were only partly hidden behind a pair of dark round glasses.

Carter wondered what had stolen his sight: a grenade blast in a bunker, or a rush of fire in the burning cockpit of a plane, or some terrible hand-to-hand fight. There were so many of these wounded, half-assembled men gimping and shuffling and feeling their way with the tap of flimsy canes that Carter almost felt ashamed to stand there in one piece.

A horse and cart trundled past, its iron-rimmed wheels clattering upon the cobblestones. The back of the cart was filled with children on their way to school, each carrying a small satchel and watched over by a stern-looking woman in a headscarf who sat on the buckboard with the driver, only facing backwards so she could keep an eye on her students.

Painted in white letters on an iron girder, which was all that remained of a shop, were the words, 'We want action. Words are not enough.' Across from that, a theatre had opened showing *The Best Years of Our Lives*, with Fredric March and Myrna Loy. Although the movie was already a couple of years out of date, it was still the only business open on that street.

Carter lingered there, studying the doorways and the alleys and the rubble-filled dead ends where he might be cornered if he ever had to run. Satisfied at last, he pedalled along the military ring road on the southern edge of town, wooden brake pads smoking as he raced between the luminous green of neatly tended sports fields and the jagged shapes of empty, bombed-out buildings until he arrived at last at the gates of Dasch's compound.

Dasch and Ritter were waiting. Dasch was tallying receipts and Ritter lounged in a chair, reading an old copy of the US Army magazine *Stars and Stripes*.

'Do you have the money ready?' asked Carter. 'The meeting is in an hour and I have to get back across the city on that bicycle.'

Dasch lifted a grey canvas satchel onto his desk. 'All here,' he said, patting the lumpy contents of the bag.

Carter stepped forward to take it.

But Dasch's hand remained upon the satchel. 'I was thinking,' he said.

Carter stopped in his tracks. 'Thinking what?'

'I just wondered if it might make sense for you to have an escort. This is an awful lot of money, after all.'

'Are you worried about him stealing it or about me stealing it?' asked Carter.

'I am worried about it getting stolen,' replied Dasch. 'It won't make much difference who has taken the money if it's gone. For this reason, Ritter has persuaded me that I should allow him to accompany you.'

'And he's going to drive me there in the Tatra?'

'Of course.' Ritter tossed aside the magazine. 'Why wouldn't I?'

'It'll stand out too much,' Carter told him.

Ritter glanced across at Dasch. 'But that's the car I drive!' he protested.

'Carter is right,' said Dasch. 'You can take the Wanderer instead.'

The Wanderer was a small, lopsided sedan whose rear springs had almost given way, so that the back of the chassis appeared to be resting on the wheels. Carter had seen the old car parked behind the garage, a silhouette of oil gradually seeping out from beneath its leaking engine. He hadn't even thought it was still running.

'You can't be serious!' Ritter growled indignantly. 'It's humiliating even to get behind the wheel of that thing.'

'You can swallow your pride for a few hours,' said Dasch. He removed his hand from the bag and Carter picked it off the desk, surprised at its weight.

Ritter soon appeared from behind the garage, hunched inside the Wanderer and revving the engine savagely since it seemed on the verge of cutting out. Clouds of bluish smoke belched out of the rusty tailpipe. 'Hurry up and climb in!' he shouted at Carter. 'Otherwise we won't get there at all.'

Soon they were rattling along towards the meeting point. The passenger-side window was missing and wind shrilled past the poorly fitting piece of plywood that had been put there in its place.

For a while, each man kept to himself. Then suddenly

Ritter began asking questions, in the same relentless fashion he had used when they first met.

How do you know this man? Where did you first meet him? Is he known to be a criminal? Did you approach him or was it the other way around? Are there others like him or is he the only one you can deal with for black market goods? Does he know where you live? Does he know you were in prison? Does he know why? Do you trust him? Does he trust you?

Once more Carter endured the barrage, the answers, true or false, forming in his mind before Ritter had even finished his questions. Finally, though, he threw up his hands and said, 'Enough!'

'That isn't for you to decide.'

'In case you had forgotten,' said Carter, 'you and I are driving to this rendezvous with a bag of Dasch's money and we're coming home with a truckload of contraband. So whether you trust me or not, we're headed in the same direction, whatever that turns out to be.'

'There is some truth to that,' admitted Ritter.

'I asked you once before if you were a cop,' said Carter. 'You dodged the question then. Are you going to dodge it now as well?'

Ritter considered this for a moment. 'I suppose it wouldn't hurt to tell you, just to pass the time. I was an interrogator during the war. I operated mostly on the Eastern Front, questioning high-ranking enemy officers.'

'You speak Russian?'

'I do,' he replied. 'My father was a businessman who

often travelled to the Soviet Union. He sold parts for steam turbines that were used at hydroelectric plants. He was convinced that the future of Germany lay not in our alliances with the west, but to the east, in Russia and beyond. Because of that, he insisted that I learned Russian. He refused to believe that our two countries would end up in a war and when the Molotov–Ribbentrop Pact was signed in August 1939, guaranteeing peace between Russia and Germany for the next ten years, he felt sure that his instincts had been correct. And then, when Germany disregarded the pact and invaded Russia in 1941, it broke my father's heart. And for myself, instead of using my language skills to sell steam turbines the way my father had imagined, I ended up firing questions at Soviet commissars, majors, colonels and even a general or two.'

'Only officers?'

Ritter shrugged. 'They were the only ones who knew anything of value. In the opinion of the German High Command, the average Russian soldier could barely sign his own name, let alone tell you where his division was about to be deployed. It wasn't true, but the High Command were very fixed in their ideas about what the Russians could and couldn't do. That was what cost us the war, something they might have been able to avoid if they had only listened to me.'

'What do you mean?' asked Carter.

'In June 1943,' explained Ritter, 'a Russian transport plane strayed over our lines during a snowstorm and crash landed. There were ten people on board, of whom three survived. They were all officers attached to the headquarters of General Zhukov's 14th Army and I was given the task of interrogating them. I took my time. No violence. The trouble with pain is that it will make a person say anything, no matter how far-fetched, just to stop the process, even if only for a while, and that is of no use at all. The shock of finding out that one is not going to be tortured is often more effective than any infliction of pain. So they began to talk, although not about anything they thought I could use, such as Russian troop movements or rates of desertion or the failure of tank engines or anything like that.'

'Then what did you learn?' asked Carter.

'What those men told me was something I already knew, which was that Germany was planning an attack. They threw it in my face, to show how much they knew about us and how little we would learn about them. And I allowed them to believe they had succeeded. I showed surprise. Even astonishment. And this made them even more boastful, adding details about the attack designed to humiliate our delusions of conquest. Unknown to them, however, what they had actually given up was far more valuable than anything they could have told me about their own army. You see, this was not just any attack we had been planning. This was to be the greatest assault of armour in the history of mankind, punching a hole through the centre of the Russian forces, not far from the city of Kursk. If it succeeded, it would snap the entire Red Army in two, draining them of their resources in a way from which even they would be unable to recover. It would finish the war in the east, allowing us to concentrate our forces on the impending invasion of the Anglo-Americans in the west. In short, it would have decided the war in our favour. I informed the High Command of my findings and advised that the attack should be called off, but they told me it was too late. Hitler had already made up his mind. He believed that, even if the Russians did know what we had planned, they would be unable to stop us. He also believed that secrecy had been maintained, so it was, in fact, impossible that these Russian officers would have known. They told me I was being duped, and that the Soviet officers were saying anything that came into their heads, just to lead me away from acquiring any real information.'

'Was there no one who believed you?' asked Carter.

Ritter laughed in a single, humourless bark. 'There were plenty,' he replied, 'but none who were prepared to risk their lives by saying so. It didn't matter. Most them died, any-way. In July of that year the attack went ahead, and the German forces encountered an intricately constructed series of defensive lines stretching back hundreds of kilometres, each one of which had to be assaulted and overcome at the cost of so much German manpower and machinery that, in the end, the Battle of Kursk turned into one of the most expensive defeats of the entire war. More than half a million men were killed and twelve thousand heavy tanks were lost. After the loss of the 6th Army at Stalingrad earlier in the year, Germany had reached a point where our losses could not be replaced.'

Although Ritter was staring intently through the wind-shield, he did not appear to see the road ahead. It was as if his eyes had rolled back into his skull and he was witnessing again not just the loss of a battle, but the crumbling of his entire world.

'I found out later that this was all due to the work of a single Russian spy. His name was Nikolai Ivanovich Kuznetsov, but he called himself Paul Siebert. There actually was a Paul Siebert. That was the brilliance of his disguise. Siebert, a German Army lieutenant, had been captured earlier in the war and he had been interrogated in much the same way as I interrogated those Russian officers – without violence, using only the relentlessness of courtesy, patience and seemingly harmless enquiry. After learning everything there was to learn about Lieutenant Siebert, down to the tiniest eccentricities and details of his life, he was taken out and shot. And then Kuznetsov, armed with every detail of Siebert's life, was smuggled back behind German lines.'

Carter had heard of this man from Wilby, who spoke the name Kuznetsov with fear as well as admiration. That the Russians could engineer a human weapon so perfectly adapted for its purpose had sent a pulse of dread through their British and American counterparts from which they had yet to recover.

'He not only gathered information,' continued Ritter, 'but also carried out assassinations and sabotage. On one of these missions, he had gone to murder the military governor of East Prussia, a man named Erich Koch. He gained access to Koch's office and began a conversation with him. During this conversation, Koch told Siebert that the war would soon be over, thanks to a massive attack soon to take place in the Kursk region. That fragment of information saved Koch's life, temporarily at least, and Siebert alerted his Russian masters about the planned assault. And unlike my own masters, the Russians actually listened. One man did all that. One perfectly placed spy destroyed an army. So if I seem overly cautious to you, it is only because of the fact that, if someone had actually taken my advice, you might be driving me about, instead of the other way around.'

Arriving at the rendezvous point, Carter directed Ritter to a spot just down the road, where they had a view of all the streets feeding into the intersection.

Galton's van was already there.

Carter could see the shadow of somebody sitting in the passenger seat. He unbuckled the leather straps on the canvas bag and looked inside. It was filled with bank notes, bundled into stacks as thick as his fist.

'It's all there,' said Ritter. 'I counted it myself.'

'Given how little you trust me,' said Carter, 'you won't mind if I return the favour. If this is even a little bit short, this guy will never work with us again.'

'It is correct!' snapped Ritter. 'Now go! The man is waiting.'

Carter was staring at the van. A sense of uneasiness was crackling like static in his mind, but he did not know why.

'What are you waiting for?' demanded Ritter.

'Cut the engine,' said Carter.

'Why?' demanded Ritter.

'Because the only people who would leave a parked car running in this town are either the police or the army.

They're the only ones with enough fuel not to run out of gas while they're waiting.'

Ritter sighed. 'I can't guarantee this thing will even start again.'

'Do it now,' said Carter.

Ritter turned the key and the car shuddered into silence. 'Now what?' he demanded.

'We wait,' Carter told him.

'Wait for what?'

'Just wait.' Carter stared at the blue van, trying to understand why something didn't feel right. He looked for the old woman knitting on her balcony, but the place was empty except for a chair with a cushion. The blind accordion player had also disappeared. The street was entirely empty except for Galton's van.

'Would you mind telling me what this is about?' asked Ritter. 'I don't see anyone.'

'That's the problem,' said Carter.

'It's time. If you don't move soon, he's going to leave.'

'Then let him leave.'

'Dasch won't like that.'

'There are things he would like a hell of a lot less. Now shut up and let me do my job.'

Ritter sighed and folded his arms. But he kept quiet from then on.

Carter searched the street, hunting for some definite sign that his instincts were telling the truth. He could feel sweat beading on his face. The time for the meeting came and went. Minutes passed. Just when Carter had begun to wonder if his fears had got the better of him, he caught sight of a faint grey haze as a puff of exhaled cigarette smoke drifted through a half-open doorway in the shell of a building next to the hospital. A moment later, the door swung wide open and a man wearing an unbuttoned trench coat walked out into the middle of the road. He put his hands on his hips, revealing a gun in a shoulder holster. The man looked up and down the street, then threw up his arms and swore. Now the man who had been sitting in the passenger seat climbed out of the van. It was not Galton. He joined the man already standing in the street.

'Police,' whispered Carter. 'They're plainclothes, but that's who they are.'

'My God, I think you're right,' said Ritter.

Now two more men appeared through the doorway, one of them shoving the other, who fell to his knees in the road.

Carter recognised the person on the ground.

It was Galton. He struggled to get up, but one of the policemen kicked him over again. This time Galton stayed down, cowering with his arms around his head.

A car pulled out of an alley.

Galton was hoisted to his feet and thrown into the back seat along with the man who had kicked him. The car sped away, passing by Ritter and Carter. Two remaining men piled into the van and that, too, drove away.

Then the street was empty once again.

Ever since the first policeman had walked into the street, Ritter had not moved. It seemed he had not even breathed. Slowly he put one hand on the steering wheel and took hold of the gearstick with the other.

'You'll want to start it first,' Carter told him quietly.

Flustered, Ritter got the engine going. Then he slammed the Wanderer into gear and they drove back the way they had come, moving carefully through the narrow streets, as if Ritter had only just learned how to drive. Neither of them spoke. They headed straight for Dasch's compound on the outskirts of the city and Ritter would have driven straight through the gate if the guard had not opened it in time.

Ritter pulled up outside Dasch's office, got out, slammed the door and walked inside.

Carter remained where he was. His heart was beating too fast and he was having trouble thinking straight. He had no idea whether he would be blamed for what had happened and, if he were, exactly what Dasch would do about it. Finally, he took hold of the satchel that contained the money, opened the car door and climbed out.

At that same moment, Dasch emerged from his office, followed closely by Ritter, whose face was still the same chalky shade of white as it had turned in the moment he'd seen Galton kicked into the street.

Dasch walked right up to Carter and took hold of his shoulders. 'Are you all right?' he asked.

'I'm fine,' Carter stammered.

'Ritter said it was a trap.'

'It was,' replied Carter, 'but we got lucky.'

'That was not luck!' said Ritter. 'If it hadn't been for you, we would both be under arrest by now. We would be finished. All of us!'

'You misjudged him, Ritter!' said Dasch, his voice raised to a shout. 'You've been doing that since the first day you met him. Why don't you finally admit it.'

For a few seconds Ritter's mouth twitched, as if he were trying to suck out something caught between his teeth. But then he blurted out, 'It's true!' He turned to Carter and solemnly he said, 'I will not make the same mistake again.'

For a moment, even Dasch looked surprised at Ritter's admission. Then he got down to business. 'This man you were dealing with,' he asked Carter, 'does he know you are working for me?'

Carter shook his head. 'Of course not.'

'Are you absolutely sure?'

'Positive.'

Dasch stepped forward and embraced him. 'Thank God for that,' he sighed. Then he stood back. 'My friend, you are still trembling with fear!'

Dasch was right, but not for the reasons he believed. To Carter, it was starting to look as if Eckberg had been right, and that he could no longer rely on Wilby's promises to keep him safe.

'The police have nothing on you,' continued Dasch. 'Even if they tracked you down, it would mean nothing. No money changed hands. You never set eyes on the goods he intended to sell. As far as they're concerned, you didn't even show up to the meeting. All you are guilty of is a conversation with this man, and they could hardly convict you with that.'

Now Ritter chimed in. 'Mr Dasch is no stranger to the police, but they always leave here empty handed.'

'I keep meaning to ask how you do that,' said Carter.

Smiling, Dasch patted him on the cheek. 'Patience, my friend,' he said. 'That day is coming soon.'

*

While a freezing wind blew through the streets of Rocherath, snatching away thin streams of smoke escaping from the chimney pots, Lieutenant Carter lay on the floor of the attic, wrapped in his dirty army blanket. As long as he stayed on his back, the hard wooden boards were bearable. It was only when he rolled onto his side that his hip bones began to complain.

People came and went throughout the night. Half conscious, Carter listened to the slam of doors and the sounds of men's voices, oblivious the others who were trying to sleep. He had grown so used to the noises in that Belgian farmhouse, at any time of day or night, that even the loudest of them did not stir him from his rest. But shortly before 5 a.m., a strange shudder jarred him out of sleep. The whole house seemed to tremble, as if a train had rumbled past outside. But there were no trains anywhere near. Carter's eyes snapped open and, for a moment, he just lay there staring at the ceiling while he waited for the sound to reappear.

Another shudder came, and then another, rolling together until he lost track of where one sound ended and another one began. *It must be thunder*, thought Carter, but he had never heard thunder in the middle of the winter before. The

179

idea passed through his head that maybe they were having an earthquake.

Then he heard a metallic shriek that caused all his muscles to tense, followed by an explosion somewhere on the edge of town. He saw the glass in the window of his room appear to ripple, as if it had transformed into liquid.

Another explosion roared out of the darkness, and then more. In between the din of the explosions, he could hear trucks racing past outside.

'Out! Out! Out!' somebody was shouting downstairs.

It was only now that Carter realised they were under attack. He thought of the Belgian prisoner, Grandhenri, raging in his cell in Bütgenbach that death was on its way, and the warning of ther German soldier, which Wharton had refused to believe.

Carter rolled out of his blanket and was halfway to his feet when a dusty red flash lit up the room from outside and he toppled backwards. Struggling to his feet again, Carter glanced through the window and saw the whole horizon towards the German border illuminated with a flickering glare.

The next thing he knew, he was lying on the floor again. The window of his room was gone and flakes of ash were flitting like moths around the room. He sat up and put his hands to his face, certain that he must be hurt even if there was no pain, but the skin was still intact. Hurriedly, he moved his trembling hands along his arms and legs, searching for a wound that was not there. He did not know how long he had been unconscious. It seemed like it might only have been a few seconds, but there was no more shouting in the hallway and the house felt empty now.

Once more Carter got up, weaving and uncertain on his feet, and clattered down the stairs, hand skimming along the greasy banister, not even sure where he was going. Arriving at the ground floor, he remembered that he had left behind the olive green satchel in which he kept his cigarettes, a notebook for his case work and a can of tinned peaches, which Riveira had tossed to him the night before when they parted company out by the field kitchen. Instinctively he spun around, ready to run back up the stairs. In that instant another blast, which seemed to come from right outside the house, knocked open the front door, nearly carrying it off its hinges, and the shockwave dropped Carter to his knees. A wave of smoke rolled in, filling his lungs with the metallic burn of high explosives.

Carter staggered upright and, as he turned to leave, he noticed that he wasn't alone. Someone was sitting at the table in the room where he and Wharton had interrogated the German soldier the night before.

Carter stuck his head into the room. It was dark, but he realised immediately from the silhouette that the person was Wharton himself. 'Major?' he asked.

The silhouette turned slowly, seeming more mechanical than human. 'I'm sorry,' he said.

Carter thought he sounded drunk. 'Sir,' he said, 'we need to leave. This town is getting blown to bits.'

Wharton did not move. 'I'm sorry,' he said again.

Carter stepped into the room, his hand held out to help

the major up. The floor trembled beneath his feet as another shockwave washed over the house. More roof tiles clattered into the street, smashing with a sound like broken crockery. 'Sir,' he said. 'We've got to go.'

'I didn't know they were taking the fuel across the border,' muttered Wharton. 'They told me it was for their farm equipment.'

It took a moment for Carter to understand exactly what Wharton was saying. 'You knew about the theft before it happened?'

'Of course I knew,' said Wharton. 'I'm the one who sold it to them.'

Carter felt his body go numb, stunned by what the major was admitting. Even though Wharton had not been exactly helpful to him, the major's perpetually exasperated explanations had made sense to Carter. He had proved entirely convincing. And Carter, who had made a life's work from the tools of deception, had believed that he could always spot when those same tools were being used against him. Until now. In spite of the fact that German shells were arcing down upon the village, Carter just stood there feeling stupid and amazed.

'I told them where the truck would be and when,' said Wharton. 'All they had to do was wait until the drivers went inside the cafe to buy their lunch, which I knew they would do because the soldiers always stop there if they can. And when the truck showed up in some field a few days later, minus the fuel of course, I would have launched a small investigation. It would have led nowhere and the matter would have been forgotten. Instead of that, an American soldier was killed and the thieves left behind one of their own. If it hadn't been for that, they would never have sent you here. They would simply have filed it away with all the other unsolved crimes, too many to investigate. Too many even to count.'

A set of headlights, narrowed into cat's eyes by the special blinkers used by vehicles in the front line, streamed into the room as a jeep pulled up outside.

Only now did Carter get a good look at Wharton. In the glaring light, which carved out monstrous shadows in the room, it took him a moment to understand what he was seeing.

The major's arms were resting on the table, his shirt-sleeves rolled up to his biceps, and he appeared to be staring at his own reflection in the highly polished wood. But the wood was not polished. Carter could see that now. It was slick and heavy and so dark it seemed like motor oil. And then Carter realised it was blood. He saw the deep-carved gashes running from the wrist towards the elbow of each arm. The blood had seeped across the table and poured down the other side and it had pooled by his feet and sunk into the brown wool of his trousers. Carter had never seen so much blood in his life, not even in the men whose bullet-constellationed corpses he had pulled from the trunks of abandoned cars or the low-tide Hudson mud, criminals dispatched by other criminals before the law could ever track them down.

Somebody stepped into the front hall and then a voice called out for Carter.

It was Riveira. 'Lieutenant!' he shouted above the deafening sound of detonations, which seemed to be coming from all around the house. 'We're leaving! Now!'

'I'm in here!' answered Carter.

Riveira stepped into the room and gasped at the sight of Major Wharton. 'Holy crap,' he said. With fumbling hands, Riveira took the metal first aid packet from its canvas pouch on his belt, opened it and tore the bandage in half.

He and Carter laid Major Wharton on the floor, sprinkled the wounds with the packet of white sulfanilamide powder that came in the medical packets, then bandaged them as tightly as they could. By now, Wharton had lost consciousness.

'Where is the nearest hospital?' asked Carter. 'If we don't get him to one soon, he isn't going to make it.'

'There's a medical aid post in a farmhouse just outside of town,' said Riveira, 'although God knows what it's like there now.'

The two men carried him outside and laid him in the back of the jeep.

Riveira got behind the wheel. 'Why the hell did he do it?' he asked.

'Just drive,' Carter told him.

They had cleared the last cluster of houses in the centre of town and were travelling between two open fields with shallow ditches and barbed wire fences on either side, when a flickering Morse code of light raced out of the woods at the edge of one of the fields. At the same moment, Carter heard a rapid clattering sound, as if someone had thrown a handful of small stones against the side of the jeep. Riveira shouted something and the next thing Carter knew, the jeep had skidded off the road and slammed into the ditch. The impact threw Carter sideways out of the jeep and he ended up on the other side of the road from the vehicle, lying up against the fence, tangled in the claws of barbed wire. In the same moment as Carter realised that they had just been shot at, a deafening roar erupted from only a few paces away. In the shuddering light of muzzle flashes, he caught sight of several American helmets hunched down behind a Browning machine gun. In the woods across the field, he saw more flashes, pulsing manically, and then blue sparks showered down on him as bullets tore through the wire just above his head. As Carter rolled down into the ditch, tearing his sleeve which had become tangled in the barbs, he spotted the rear of the jeep silhouetted against the night sky, one wheel off the ground and its front out of sight in the ditch across the road. There was no sign of Riveira.

Carter lay face down in the gruel of water and half-frozen mud. Bullets snapped past above him and he felt the thudding impacts as they slammed into the dirt all along the edge of the ditch. The next sound he heard was a metallic thump and then a hollow whistle, like someone blowing sharply into the mouth of a bottle. A dusty red flash burst in the forest and someone in the distance shrieked in pain. Carter raised his head, his face cast in mud, in time to see an American soldier dropping a mortar shell down a tube, then twist away, hands covering his ears. The same hard thump filled his ears and a wall of concussion swept past. Once more, the woods beyond exploded into fire.

How long the mortaring continued, Carter had no idea. Time seemed to be expanding and contracting all around him, moving sideways through his brain so that he noticed tiny details, like the way the light of the machine gun fire reflected off his fingernails, and then nothing at all for what seemed like minutes on end.

The firing from the woods died away. Trails of smoke rose from among the trees.

A voice nearby shouted, 'Cease fire!'

Then Carter heard the slap of running footsteps in the mud. He looked up to see a soldier crouching over him. 'Are you all right?' asked the man.

It was only as Carter lifted himself up that he felt the cold in his soaked clothes. He looked around blearily. 'My driver,' he mumbled.

'Are you all right?' the soldier asked again. He reached out and shook him by the arm. 'Are you hit?'

'No,' Carter managed to say.

Two more soldiers darted across the road towards the jeep. A moment later they lifted a man to his feet, one on each side, his arms around their shoulders. They carried him, limping, out of the ditch.

One of the soldiers got behind the wheel of the jeep, restarted the engine and slowly backed it up onto the road.

'There's another guy here!' shouted one of the soldiers. 'He's hurt. It looks like he's hurt pretty bad. Jesus, it's Major Wharton!'

'We were taking him to the field hospital just outside of town,' said Carter.

'Too late for that,' said the soldier who crouched beside him. He pointed to a glow in the distance, capped by shreds of flame. 'The hospital got taken out almost as soon as the Germans started shelling us.'

'Record players my ass!' said another soldier.

Now Carter became aware again of the gunfire over by the Wahlerscheid road, an almost constant roar and crackle, and the skyline shuddering light into darkness and back into light, as if a lightning storm were passing through the woods. Mixed in with the coughing rumble of artillery was the rapid snap of Garand rifle fire and the zipper-like noise of German machine guns, firing so fast that the sound of the bullets merged, one indistinguishable from another. Ever since he had caught sight of the German tracer fire streaming out of the woods, the scope of his senses had shrunk to the tiny space he occupied in the ditch. Now, slowly – too slowly – they were reaching out again.

'They're gone for now,' said the soldier, 'but they'll counter attack as soon as they can get some reinforcements. That's one damned thing you can always count on. They'll be coming back, even if it costs them every man they've got.'

Carter could not see the man's face or any details of the man's clothing. It was as if the darkness itself were speaking to him.

The major was lying in the road.

Another soldier was kneeling over him. 'He's still alive,' said the man, 'but he doesn't look too good.'

Riveira hobbled over to Carter. 'I twisted my ankle,' he said. 'I think you're going to have to drive.'

'Is there another hospital?' he asked.

'There's a big one over in Stavelot,' said the man who had become the darkness, 'but you had better get out of here now, or you won't be getting out of here at all.'

'How's the jeep?' asked Carter.

'I think you're fine,' said the man. 'They didn't hit the engine.'

With the help of two other soldiers, Carter lifted Major Wharton into the back of the vehicle. Then Carter got behind the wheel. Riveira climbed into the passenger seat.

Carter put the jeep in gear and drove and, as they ploughed on through the darkness, the vivid arcs of red and green flares rising from the forest behind them reflected on the mud-splashed windshield.

By dawn, they were west of St Christophe and on the main highway to Liège. The roads were heavy with traffic going in both directions.

Riveira removed his left boot and his ankle had swollen so grotesquely that it was now the same thickness as his calf. Grimly, he chain-smoked his way through a pack of cigarettes, his boot clutched against his chest.

Outside the town of Stavelot, they followed nailed-up signs to a field hospital, where a doctor pronounced Major Wharton dead.

The news did not catch Carter or Riveira by surprise. Several times, Carter had pulled off the road, climbed from the jeep and peered down at the major. Beyond confirming that the man was still breathing, and even this he was not sure about, there was little to be done for him.

The body was taken away on a stretcher, covered with a blanket and laid beside several other bodies outside an operating tent. A light snow was falling now and it collected in the folds of the blanket, forming ghostly outlines of the corpse.

While Riveira went to get his foot bandaged, Carter stood with the doctor, who was wearing a white apron over a heavy civilian sweater. He was in his fifties, slightly overweight, with a round and honest-looking face and a pair of spectacles propped up on his forehead. 'I am curious,' he said.

But he didn't go on to ask the question Carter had been expecting – why the major had committed suicide. Instead, the doctor wondered aloud at the method Wharton had chosen. 'Usually, they just shoot themselves,' he said.

'How often does that happen?' asked Carter.

The doctor shrugged. 'It depends on what's taking place at the front,' he replied. 'When everything is getting blown to hell like it is now, I see very few self-inflicted wounds. It's when things settle down, and people have time to think, that they persuade themselves it's not worth going on.' He pointed at the still form of the major, lying under his blanket outside the tent. 'This is the first time I've seen it done like that. It's slow. It's unreliable. It's also very cruel, even as an act of suicide.'

Carter stared at him and said nothing.

'You think I am callous,' asked the doctor, 'to speak of your friend in this way?'

'I wouldn't have called him my friend.'

'Well, whoever he was,' said the doctor, 'I have no time to pity the dead, or to wonder at the reasons for their passing.'

Within the hour, Carter and Riveira were back on the road, heading for the Military Police headquarters in Liège where Carter would write up his report on the theft of the fuel truck, submit it for review and, with luck, be on the next plane home.

The doctor in Stavelot had said that Riveira's tibia was probably broken and had given him a quarter syrette of morphine for the pain. He then wrote a large red letter M on Riveira's forehead in wax pencil, to guard against the possibility the doctors in Liège might also administer morphine and accidentally overdose the patient. Knowing that the Military Police in Liège had their own medical facility, the doctor had recommended that Riveira wait until he got there for treatment rather than stay behind in Stavelot, which was likely to become inundated with wounded soldiers from the front within the next few hours.

Riveira blinked slowly at the dirt-splashed windshield. His left leg was bandaged with olive drab wrapping almost up to the knee, and he was still carrying his boot.

Just as Carter began to worry that Riveira would doze off and fall out of the jeep, the sergeant turned to him and asked, 'Why did Major Wharton do that to himself?'

There seemed no point in keeping quiet about it anymore and Carter told him what the major had done.

Riveira showed no reaction as he listened. He just lit himself another cigarette.

'You don't seem surprised,' said Carter when he had finished with his explanation.

Riveira was quiet for a while. Then, finally, he spoke.

'And you're going to write all that in your report?'

'Of course. It's what happened.'

'Maybe this is just the morphine talking,' said Riveira, 'but did you think about maybe blaming it on someone else?'

'Like who?'

Riveira shrugged. 'That crazy Belgian in the jail at Bütgenbach. He was part of it, after all.'

'Why would I do a thing like that?' asked Carter. 'They sent me here to find the truth. That's my job, the same as it is back in New Jersey.'

'But this isn't New Jersey, sir, and those guys you track down on the docks back in Elizabeth are just regular thieves. They aren't soldiers, out here in the middle of a war.'

'And you think that makes it all right, the fact that Major Wharton is a soldier? As far as I'm concerned, that makes it worse. The Germans are using that fuel to drive their tanks across the border now. Right now! And a man got killed because of it.'

'I don't know what to believe,' he replied. 'I've seen so much thieving since I came ashore in France that I don't even think about it anymore as something no good man would do. A guy like me, maybe he walks into a house and steals himself some candles to take back to his bunker in the forest, so he can see well enough to write a letter home to his wife. Or he steals a jar of cherries from a shelf down in somebody's basement when he's taking cover from an artillery bombardment.'

'Those things are not the same as what the major did.'

'I understand, sir,' said Riveira, 'but I think you are missing the point.'

'Which is what?'

'That I am a sergeant and Wharton was a major. The bigger the fish, the bigger the food they go after. I once drove a colonel halfway across France, stopping at one hotel and then another, and carrying the heaviest duffel bags I've ever had to lift. Right when we were almost at our destination, one of those bags just tore open from the strain and out poured silver plates and cups and candlesticks and cutlery, and that man didn't even flinch. He just ordered me to go and find another duffel bag to pack it all back in again. You see, all I took was a candle, but that officer stole the candlestick and everything else he could find. And like it or not, Lieutenant, rank had everything to do with that.'

'The major is dead,' said Carter. 'We're never going to know for sure what was going through his mind when he did this. Maybe he thought he'd been sticking his neck out so long it was time he did something for himself. Maybe he was in debt and couldn't find another way to pay it off. But the fact that he took matters into his own hands tells us he knew exactly how much of a mistake he had made.'

'I'm not talking about what he thought of himself,' said Riveira. 'I'm talking about what other people are going to think. People back home, for example. They want to go to sleep each night believing what they read in the papers, which is that American soldiers do not shoot women and children, or soldiers with their hands in the air, or that we don't bomb towns by accident, and they sure as hell don't want to know that our officers are selling gasoline to the Nazis.'

'You think they really believe that?'

'Maybe not. Maybe they have doubts. But I'm guessing they would rather live in the dream that has been made for them where all of those things are true. That's what you are going up against, Lieutenant, and I don't know if you realise how strong those dreams can be. But maybe the Germans will break through and none of it will matter. It's like I said' – he leaned out of the jeep and spat – 'maybe this is just the morphine talking.'

*

The night of Galton's arrest by the German police, Carter left a message for Wilby at the drop point, requesting a meeting for the following day.

This time, he chose Vorgebirgs Park for their rendezvous. It was an oddly shaped clearing, hemmed in on all sides by the houses of the Raderberg district and cut through with numerous bicycle paths. Chestnut trees cast leafy shadows on the grass, in which the dew glistened like glass beads from a broken necklace.

The two men sat side by side on opposite ends of the bench, not looking at each other as Carter explained what had happened. This was Carter's first meeting with Wilby since Eckberg had tracked him down at the cafe, and he was worried about how Wilby would take the news of this setback. To Carter's surprise, Wilby did not seem at all fazed by the latest turn of events.

'And when you got back to Dasch's place,' asked Wilby, 'what was his reaction?'

'I think he was mostly just relieved that the whole thing hadn't blown up in his face the way it could have done.'

'And is it fair to say that whatever doubts Dasch might have had about you have now been set aside?'

'Yes. On that he was perfectly clear, and so was Ritter for that matter.'

'Good,' said Wilby. 'Then it was worth it.'

'Worth it?' echoed Carter. 'Those aren't the words I'd use exactly.'

'You would if you saw the whole picture,' Wilby told him.

'Then what am I missing?' asked Carter.

'Well,' said Wilby, 'let me put it this way. Have you wondered how the police found out?'

'Of course I have,' replied Carter, 'and I'm pretty sure I know the answer.'

'And what would that be?'

'Galton wasn't careful enough. He was also over-confident. He didn't seem to care who knew what he was up to. And I guess he must have bragged about it in front of the wrong person.'

'All that makes perfect sense,' said Wilby, 'but there is a simpler explanation.'

'There is?'

'Yes. I'm the one who tipped off the police.'

It was as if Wilby had grabbed Carter by the throat. For the next few seconds, Carter had to force himself to breathe. 'Why would you do that,' he finally managed to ask, 'when the whole thing was your idea to begin with?'

'Because I wanted Galton to get caught. I was gambling

on the fact that you had better instincts than he did for spotting a police stakeout. And it turns out I was right. There was no way he would be able to siphon off army supplies in the quantity he had in mind without making the authorities suspicious. He would have been caught eventually, even without our help.'

'Why didn't you tell me that?'

'The only guaranteed way of selling the plan to Dasch was if you believed it yourself. And when it went wrong, I had to be certain that your surprise was genuine. A thing like that, at a moment like that, is too hard to fake, even for someone like you. You know who I learned that from?'

'I have no idea.'

'Adolf Hitler!' said Wilby. 'Back in 1933, when it looked like the Nazis might lose the election against the rival Communist Party, Hitler decided that the only way he could derail his opponents was for them to do something so terrible that no one would even consider voting for them. Of course, the Communists weren't just going to oblige him by doing this terrible thing, so Hitler ordered his men to carry out this atrocity themselves, and do it in such a way that they could blame the Communists for it. The thing is, Hitler knew that when the news broke, everybody would be looking at him. Cameras. Newsmen. Even people in his own party who weren't in on the plot. In that moment, he knew he would have to look shocked. Genuinely shocked. The only way to guarantee that was for him not to know in advance what had happened. That's why, when the German parliament building went up in flames, and when the Nazis trucked out some Dutchman named Marinus van der Lubbe – whom they had picked up before the fire even started and who just happened to be a card-carrying member of the Communist Party – and blamed the whole thing on him, what mattered most was the look on Hitler's face when he found out what had happened. That's what clinched it. And the Communists were finished in Germany. The most effective lie a man can tell is one he believes is the truth. And that's what you just did. Sure, it was a risk, but it was one we had to take, and it paid off.'

'That risk you took,' said Carter, launching himself to his feet, 'was with my *life*!'

Wilby leaned forward suddenly, clenching his hands into fists. 'But that's exactly what it needed, don't you see? Men like Dasch are conditioned to be suspicious of everything. That's the only thing keeping them alive. He may have wanted to trust you right from the start, but his instincts wouldn't let him, no matter how convinced he might have seemed. From now on, the man you have deceived will become a part of your deception. He will turn upon anyone who doubts you. He will stare your lies right in the face and he will ignore them and do you know why? Because he has given himself no choice. To do otherwise would go against the instincts that have kept him alive. It would mean he can no longer trust them, and if he does not have those, he has nothing.'

Carter still didn't know if what Wilby had done was the work of an increasingly desperate man, as Eckberg had made him out to be, or that of someone operating at a level which he had never encountered before.

'Are you going to stand there and tell me I am wrong?' asked Wilby.

'No,' admitted Carter. Whether it was recklessness or genius that had set these events in motion, Carter could not deny that the gamble had paid off. 'In fact, he said he would soon be telling me how it is that the police can't get anything on him, which is just as well. Except for what he loaded on that plane, I haven't seen any trace of black market goods or how he transports them.'

'Good!' Wilby said sharply. 'Now why don't you sit down? We're not done talking yet.'

Carter returned to his side of the bench. 'What else is there to say?' he asked.

'The truth is,' Wilby told him, 'not everything went according to plan.'

'What do you mean?' asked Carter.

'Galton was due be handed over to the military authorities. He would have been court martialled and sent to jail, probably for a very long time, but he would have been getting off lucky. In wartime, he would have been hanged. As it turns out, and I don't know quite how this happened, Galton has managed to escape. He was in a local jail cell in the Sülz district, waiting to be transferred to US authorities, but when the Military Police showed up to take custody of Galton, his cell was empty. At first, they thought there might have been some bureaucratic foul-up and that he had been transferred to the inner city jail, which would have been a more secure location, but it turned out he wasn't there either. By the time they figured out that he had actually escaped, he'd already been missing for over ten hours. He could be anywhere by now.'

'How the hell did he get out?'

Wilby shrugged and shook his head. 'The cell had been unlocked from the outside, so somebody set him loose. He may have friends in the police, or his wife might know somebody. The point is, it doesn't matter now. He served his purpose. He may turn up some day, but I doubt it. My guess is we'll never hear from him again.' He stood up to leave. 'Any word on Garlinsky?'

'Nothing yet,' said Carter, 'but the plane is due back any day now and he might show up then.'

'Start asking questions,' said Wilby. 'Dasch trusts you now. He'll tell you anything.' Slowly he stood and faced Carter. 'And, for your own sake, do what I say from now on, whether it makes sense to you or not. I told you this before, but it's time that you heard it again. I'm the only one keeping you alive.'

Why should I believe you, Carter thought to himself, *when even your own people don't?*

*

The headquarters of the US Military Police for the district of Liège was located in a manor house belonging to a horse breeder by the name of DeVont, who had made the unfortunate choice to supply a German cavalry regiment with mounts after the invasion of 1914. When that war ended, he spent the next twenty years trying to rebuild his reputation and his business, but when the Germans invaded again in the summer of 1940, he jumped at the offer of another lucrative contract: to board and train horses for the private stable of General Matthias Grob, German military governor of eastern Belgium. DeVont's wife, who had stood by him through the nearly vertical ups and downs of his business dealings, finally snapped in September 1944, when the last Wehrmacht truck drove out of town, heading back towards Germany. That night, she took a bottle of 1896 Lafite Rothschild from their secret and well-supplied wine cellar and broke it over his head, killing him outright. Since DeVont was already on a list of collaborators to be rounded up by the Allies, American Military Police were the first to arrive on the scene. They handed Mrs DeVont over to the Belgian police, then took over the manor, quickly discovered the secret cellar and, over the next few months, quietly drank up the half-million dollars' worth of wine that it contained.

When Carter and Riveira pulled up in front of the DeVont manor, they found the place in chaos. Cardboard boxes of files were being carried out of the building and pitched into a fire, which had been kindled in the waterless basin of a fountain just outside the main entrance. A concrete statue of a naked woman holding a large sea shell against one ear stood in the middle of the basin, flames roaring all around her.

Carter and Riveira were immediately relieved of their jeep. Then each man was handed a rifle and told to prepare for an imminent assault by German forces approaching along the same road Carter and Riveira had just taken to get there. When Carter tried to explain that they had not encountered any German troops on that road, and also that Riveira had a broken leg, they were ignored.

The two men spent the next twelve hours behind a hastily prepared barricade, waiting for an attack that never came. Although by morning they were allowed to stand down and Riveira was finally admitted to the field hospital, Carter spent another week helping to man the barricade in shifts. The rest of the time he was on standby, sleeping in the corrugated iron Quonset hut that the Military Police had built on what had once been the DeVonts' tennis court.

Finally, on New Year's Day 1945, news filtered back from the front that the great German offensive, which became known as the Battle of the Bulge, had ground to a halt.

Only then was Carter able to begin writing his report on the fuel theft. He spent the next several days hunched over a collapsible table in the hut, typing up his account. Given the short time he had been given to carry out his investigation and the limited access to information and interview subjects, his report was largely incomplete. If he had been following the rules of his police training, he would have diverted the whole matter to internal affairs, who investigated crimes within their own branch of service. But he had not been given instructions to do this by the Military Police. In fact, his orders clearly specified that his account would go directly to them.

On 6th January 1945, Carter finally finished the report. He left his perch beside a rusty potbellied stove, which was the only source of heat in the Quonset hut, and set out across a muddy parking lot towards the command post headquarters.

Carter presented his report to the commanding officer of the detachment and returned to his Quonset hut to await instructions. In the days that followed, Carter ate his meals in a draughty mess tent and supplemented the bricks of peat that were his fuel allotment by foraging for sticks in the nearby woods. It gave Carter something to do, and took his mind off the fact that he had no idea whether he was being sent home or back to the front, wherever the front was now, to continue his investigation. He prayed that they might send him home, and he fastened on this idea until it became, in his mind, a virtually foregone conclusion. Already, the days he had spent here in Belgium seemed to be folding back into his memory, as if he were already home.

One week after handing in his report, two military policemen arrived at his hut and escorted him back to the manor house. There, he was brought into what had once been the dining room and was told he was under arrest.

The effect those words had on him were almost the same as if someone had set off a firecracker right next to his ear. While one of the policemen handcuffed Carter, the commander of the detachment read out the charges, but all Carter could hear was a high-pitched ringing sound and the soft pummelling thump of his heartbeat throbbing in his neck. When the commander asked if Carter had understood the charges, the look on Carter's face was so obviously one of total confusion that the commander read them again.

He was being charged with wilfully concealing information about enemy activity, specifically relating to the recent attack by German forces in the Ardennes.

Then he was marched off to a cell that was, in fact, a former servant's bedroom, whose window had been fitted with metal bars and the door reinforced with metal plating.

The next day, an army lawyer came to visit him. His name was Captain Ottway and he brought cigarettes, a thermos of coffee and a reassuring smile.

It turned out that he had been named in a complaint originally filed by the woman whom Carter had seen pushed down in the street in Rocherath, after she had got into an argument with the soldiers who brought in the German deserter. The army authorities in St Christophe who received the complaint from the woman had been anxious to make amends, in whatever small way they could, for the accidental bombing of St Christophe the month before. Taking the woman's complaint seriously, or at least pretending to, appeared to show some measure of compassion. The fact that she had been pushed into the mud while trying to defend a member of the SS would not have got her anywhere, but the fact that he had offered up a warning of an impending attack, which had turned out to be correct, was something entirely different.

Only three days after his arrest, a military court was convened in the same dining room where Carter had been taken into custody. By then, he was no longer confined to handcuffs. He sat at a table with his lawyer, still too stunned to fully comprehend what was happening to him. He had never actually attended a trial before, since undercover officers

202

usually did not testify in public. Carter thought of the trials he had read about, and the number of times reporters mentioned that the accused had remained impassive as the sentence was read, as much as if to say that the convicts were admitting their guilt. Never having seen it for himself, Carter had no cause to doubt what he had read, but now he wondered if those people had simply felt the way that he felt now, like strangers in their own bodies. It was fear. A terrible chasm of helplessness had opened up inside him and the only thing his mind could do was to plunge him into numbness, so that he became like a spectator at his own surgical dismemberment.

Captain Ottway argued that Major Wharton had been the officer in charge of interrogating the German soldier and that, given the specifics of his task, Carter was merely a bystander.

The prosecutor argued that Carter's job description did not relieve him of his obligation to report that kind of information.

When Carter tried to explain that Major Wharton had ordered the boy to be transported to division headquarters for further interrogation, the prosecution countered with the assertion that no German prisoner had been delivered, and that no American soldiers had come forward to back up Carter's claim.

At that point, Captain Ottway had jumped to his feet. 'So where is he?' demanded Ottway. 'Where is the boy? Where is the proof that he said anything at all?'

The judge turned to Carter. 'Do you deny that he predicted the attack?'

Ottway turned and stared at Carter, a meaningful look on his face.

Carter understood that if he lied and said that the boy had not mentioned an attack, or even if he could not remember what the boy had said, the case would most likely collapse, since it would rest entirely upon the testimony of a Belgian woman who had intervened on behalf of an enemy soldier belonging to a branch of service that was guilty of innumerable war crimes, including upon American soldiers in the recent offensive.

'You will recall that you are under oath,' said the judge.

For one strange, hovering moment, Carter seesawed back and forth in his mind about whether or not he should lie. He found himself thinking about everything Riveira had told him on their drive from Rocherath. The world in which they found themselves now was so filled with contradictions that the contradictions themselves became the only things that made any sense. But it became suddenly clear to him that if he lied now, a part of him would always be marooned here in this twilight world.

'He told us there would be an attack,' said Carter and, as he spoke, the fog of disbelief that had surrounded him since he'd first been put under arrest suddenly dispersed. He felt no less helpless than before, but he was no longer afraid.

Ottway showed no emotion. He just looked down at his notes, scribbled something in the margin and then dropped his pencil on the page, the soft, tapping sound carrying with it a strange but unmistakable finality.

'What kind of an attack?' asked the judge.

'Big,' replied Carter.

'And when?'

'Soon.'

'That's it?'

'Yes, sir.'

'And what did Major Wharton think of that?'

'He said the boy was lying,' Carter told the judge. 'He compared it to the noises of those tanks we were hearing in the distance and how they were just recordings played to intimidate us.'

The judge and the prosecutor glanced at each other.

Ottway looked up suddenly. 'Things,' he said, 'which had also been reported to headquarters, and which headquarters chose to ignore. This is in addition to accounts from other German deserters who crossed the lines last month, bringing stories of an impending assault.' He reached into his briefcase and pulled out a thick file of documents. 'Not to mention reports from civilians who had seen and heard things that made them suspect something was coming.' He lifted the file. 'Shall we take a look at these as well?' he asked. 'All of them ignored by men who should have known better. And now you want to court martial a man who had no training as a soldier, whose only crime, if you can call it one at all, was to sit in the same room as a veteran officer who reached the same conclusion as the generals to whom he reported?'

The judge flapped one hand, lazily commanding Ottway to sit. 'That will do,' he said.

The trial lasted two hours.

When Ottway and the prosecuting lawyer had finished their closing arguments, the judge ordered Carter to stand. 'Do you have any questions?' he asked.

'Yes, sir.'

The judge looked a little surprised, as if no one had ever taken him up on that offer before. 'Go ahead,' he told Carter.

'What would you have done if you were me?' he asked.

The judge thought about this for a moment. 'Probably the same as you,' he said at last, 'but that doesn't change anything.'

Carter went back to his cell, a white-helmeted military policeman walking close behind him. This time, he left the door open and Carter just sat on his bunk in the corner, with no idea how things were going to pan out.

He didn't have long to wait.

Ottway came to fetch him. He was smiling.

'What happened?' asked Carter.

'We're about to find out,' replied Ottway.

They walked back to the room where the trial had been held, in order to be present for the verdict.

Standing once more before the judge, Carter was informed that he had been found guilty of failing to report information, but not guilty of deliberately withholding that information.

Apparently, this was all the difference in the world.

The judge then informed Carter that he had been dishonourably discharged from his temporary commission and would no longer be allowed to continue his investigation into the theft of military fuel. 'Do you understand?' asked the judge.

'Does this mean I'm going home?'

'I would, if I were you,' said the judge.

'What about my report?'

'You mean the one in which you accused a decorated front line commander of selling fuel to the enemy?'

'I'm glad somebody read it.'

'Oh, you can be sure of that,' said the judge.

Ottway rested a hand on Carter's shoulder. 'It's time to go,' he whispered.

'Take your lawyer's advice,' said the judge, 'and travel safely.'

*

After his meeting with Wilby, Carter pedalled his bicycle to the compound. He wondered if Dasch had learned about Galton's escape from prison. *Even if the news has reached him,* thought Carter, *there is nothing he can do about it now and, grateful as he might be to have avoided arrest, he still doesn't have the black market goods I promised to deliver.* Carter doubted whether Wilby would set up another purchase, which meant that he had to find some other way to make himself useful. With these thoughts rattling like dice inside his skull, Carter arrived at the compound.

Dasch was there to meet him at the gate. 'You're just in time,' he said.

'In time for what?' he asked.

'You'll see.' Dasch beckoned for Carter to follow. Instead of leading him inside, Dasch brought Carter around the edge of the fence and they set out through the tall grass, across the open stretch of wasteland that bordered one side of the compound.

As they walked, grass seed clung to their legs and startled crickets launched themselves out of their path with a snapping of bristly legs.

Carter began to see objects lying half buried in the undergrowth – a large curl of metal from what had once been the cowling of a car, a half-melted eagle from a bronze lamp stand, a bed frame still laced with rusty springs, and a strip of corrugated iron, its scalloped edges grinning from the weeds.

'What is this place?' asked Carter.

'Better to ask what it was,' replied Dasch, and he went on to describe what had once been a bustling village of workshops where the car mechanics, wheelwrights, tool and die makers and welders of Cologne had run their small and nameless businesses. On weekends back before the war, the dusty alleyways that ran between the booths would be filled with the crackle of welding sparks and the growl of engines as they were coaxed back to life. It had been known as the Eisengasse, and it was said that anything that had broken in the city of Cologne, no matter how obscure or badly damaged, could be brought here and someone would be on hand to fix it. A single 5,000lb bomb, dropped from a Royal Air Force Lancaster the night of 1st June 1942, had landed in a storage area containing hundreds of propane cylinders. This had ignited a fire that burned out of control for a week, since the fire crews were too busy with damage caused to the inner city during the same raid. By the time a heavy rainfall finally extinguished what was left of the Eisengasse blaze, not a single structure remained intact. Many had been so obliterated that their owners, returning to the spot, could find no trace that anything had been there at all. 'It was two years before anything grew here again,' said Dasch. 'But now there are dandelions, thistles, chickweed and poppies. Nature will reclaim everything in time. It always does.'

'Do you think they will ever rebuild it?' asked Carter.

'One day, perhaps,' replied Dasch, 'but there will never be another Eisengasse. No one sets out to build a place like that. It simply evolved over time until it took on a life of its own. It was not just a village of workshops that died when this place ceased to exist. It was a place where the world could not see in, where people came and went and no one ever asked their names. A lot of secrets were buried in this place when it all got blown to bits, but there's still room for more, as you're about to see.'

In the distance, out beyond this shadeless wasteland, lay the rail yard from which Carter had heard the clank and rattle of carriages when he first arrived. Even now, he could see the haze of smoke from a coal-fired locomotive, shunting a set of brick red goods wagons into the siding. Shielding his eyes against the glare of the sun, he thought he glimpsed a figure standing out there in the tall grass. The heat haze quivered around this solitary figure, who appeared and disappeared again as if he were only the mirage of someone halfway round the world.

As they approached, Carter realised it was Ritter, stripped to the waist and leaning on a shovel, dust and sweat caked on his face.

When Carter finally reached the place where Ritter was standing, he found himself at the lip of a large basin, a hundred feet across and easily twenty feet deep which, he realised, must be the crater left by the 5,000lb bomb that had destroyed the Eisengasse.

A shallow puddle had formed at the bottom. There, in the muddy soil, a hole had been dug. Beside the hole was a man on his knees, arms behind his back bound at the elbows, and a bag pulled over his head.

'Who is that?' asked Carter.

'Why, it's your old friend, Sergeant Galton,' said Dasch.

'Mother of God,' whispered Carter. 'How the hell did he get here?'

'Ritter has some friends in the police, as well as in the military, who have managed to keep their pasts hidden. These men owe Ritter their lives. They would do anything for him. How do you think we knew when you were getting out of jail?' Dasch gestured at the kneeling figure in the pit. 'All Ritter had to do was ask, and Galton was delivered to our door.'

'Let's get this over with,' said Ritter. 'This ground was hard to dig and I'm not even sure the hole is deep enough.'

'What does it matter?' asked Dasch. 'This whole country is a carpet of bones. You people saw to that!'

Ritter glared at him, but said nothing in reply.

Dasch turned to Carter. 'Shall we?' he asked. Then he set off down the slope towards the place where Galton knelt beside his grave.

Helplessly, Carter followed, until he stood beside Galton.

The sergeant made no sound. The cloth bag over his head billowed faintly with his breathing.

Dasch nodded to Ritter.

Ritter reached into his pocket and withdrew a Mauser HSc pistol. He drew back the slide, chambering a round.

Galton heard the sound. He knew exactly what it was. 'Wait!' he called out, his voice muffled and faint under the hood.

'What is it?' asked Dasch.

'I haven't told them anything,' said Galton. 'They didn't even have a chance to interrogate me.'

'Do you know who I am?' asked Dasch.

'No, and I don't care,' replied the sergeant, 'and I'm not asking now.'

'How did the police find out about your meeting with my friend?'

'I don't know,' answered Galton. 'Maybe you should ask your friend about that.'

'And what possible reason would he have to stop the sale from going through?'

Galton paused. 'I don't know that, either,' he said. 'All I know is that I got picked up by the local police as soon as I arrived at the rendezvous point with everything you asked for right in the back of my truck. The next thing I know, I'm getting pushed up against a wall in some bombed-out building and told that if I make a sound, they'll smash my teeth back down my throat. I never even saw you guys and, obviously, neither did they. And that's good, don't you see? They don't know who you are and I sure as hell didn't tell them. Look, maybe this whole thing was just bad luck.'

'It was bad luck,' said Dasch, 'but I don't think that is all it was.'

'I can still make good on the deal, if you'll give me half a chance,' pleaded Galton. 'I know people. As long as they get paid, they'll get you anything you want.'

Dasch snapped his fingers at Ritter and held out his hand, asking for the gun.

Ritter turned the weapon in his palm and handed it to Dasch.

Then, to Carter's astonishment, Dasch gave the gun to him. At first Carter tried to refuse, holding up his hands and shaking his head.

But Dasch insisted, slapping the gun flat against Carter's chest so that he had no choice except to take it.

Dasch pointed to Galton. 'Do it,' he commanded.

Carter's breathing came shallow and fast. 'I can't,' he whispered.

'Guys?' Sweat had soaked through the bag on Galton's head, making a silhouette of his face in the cloth. 'Guys, what do you say? Are we ready to make some real money?'

'Do it now,' said Dasch.

Carter pointed the gun towards Galton. The sun was beating down on his head and sweat trickled into his eyes so that he could barely see. He thought of what Wilby had said, about winning Dasch's trust and how nothing could break it from now on. And he wondered if Wilby had been wrong. Perhaps the final test of loyalty for Dasch had not been their escape from the trap set by the police. Maybe it was this. Now. And, if it was true, Carter knew that he had failed.

There was a stunning crash, which seemed to come from all around them.

A tear appeared in Galton's hood, and through the fog of his sweat-blurred vision, Carter saw a white gash of mangled flesh where the sergeant's right cheekbone had been. His face became instantly misshapen, appearing grotesquely elongated, like a reflection in a broken mirror. The torn white flesh bloomed suddenly red and Galton's whole body swayed to the side, as if he knelt on the deck of a ship which had pitched unexpectedly in a wave, but instead of righting himself, he tilted forward past his centre of gravity and slumped face down in the dust.

The sound of the shot was deafening in the confined space of the crater. It seemed to ricochet from one side to another, growing smaller and smaller until the only noise left was a flutter of wings as birds scattered from their hiding places in the tall grass.

Carter's first thought was that he must have accidentally pulled the trigger, but then he saw Dasch, one arm held out and a US government-issue .45 gripped in his hand. Smoke was sifting from the barrel and the receiver.

Ritter set one dusty-booted foot against Galton's back

and rolled him into the grave. A smear of blood and some-thing pinkish-grey lay on the dirt where he had fallen.

Dasch turned to Carter, the pistol still clutched in his fist.

Ritter stepped over to Carter and gently took the Mauser from his hand.

Carter did nothing to stop him.

'I should never have asked that of you,' said Dasch.

Carter only stared at him, too stunned to speak.

'Come now,' said Dasch, putting his arm around Carter's shoulder. 'Let us leave Ritter to his work.'

Carter caught one last glimpse of Galton, curled up in the bottom of the waist-deep hole. The bag that had covered his head was completely torn away now, revealing a crater of blood and bone, all of it filmed with a yellow-green dust of pollen, which drifted thickly in the air.

Carter climbed from the old bomb crater and started off towards the compound in the distance. He kept his eyes on the curls of barbed wire that ran like pencil scribbles along the top of the fence. In between the rustle of his breaths, he could hear the sound of Ritter's shovel scooping dirt into the grave.

'In the old days,' muttered Dasch, 'that would never have been necessary.'

'Why the hell was it necessary now?' demanded Carter. As soon as the words had left his mouth, he knew he should have stayed silent.

Dasch stopped and turned to him. 'It used to be that everyone was simply trying to stay alive. Sometimes, with the help of a glass of wine or a decent cigar or a little piece of chocolate, they could be reminded of why they even bothered. Some people say I am nothing more than a thief selling stolen goods to other thieves, but the people who say that do not know how it feels to have lived through a war that we lost. What I sell, Mr Carter, is hope that life will someday be worth living again. It was only a matter of time before hope itself became just another black market item. As it turns out, that has a higher price than most people are willing to pay. The man I shot back there was dead before I ever met him, not because of who he was but because his way of life was over and he had simply failed to adapt. It may have been Galton himself who chose to break the law, but who decided to make it a crime for people to enjoy the simple pleasures he and I are selling? If I had not sold the chocolate and champagne that have passed through my hands over the years, do you think they would not have been consumed? Of course they would, and by the same people who criminalised their consumption. They will not give a second thought to Galton or his exit from the world. He will simply be chalked up as a necessary sacrifice, something I am trying very hard to avoid having done to me. Or to you, for that matter.'

Carter didn't answer. The sun was prising apart his skull. All he could think about was what Eckberg had said – that sooner or later he would find himself in a place where he would either be part of the problem or else a part of the solution. And he knew the time had come to choose between one and the other.

Later that day, he put in a call to Eckberg from one of the pay phones at the Cologne central station. The phones were located in cramped little booths painted pale green with yellow trim, lined up along a wall near the men's and women's waiting rooms. The doors that closed off the booths were battered, the paint chipped off where people had shoved them open with their boots rather than take hold of the dirty brass knobs. Inside, there was a tiny wooden seat, too small to be comfortable, in order to discourage people from falling asleep. The phone's heavy black receiver smelled of smoke. From the pack of Camels Eckberg had given him, Carter removed the cigarette with the phone number written inside and pulled it apart, spilling shreds of tobacco onto the floor. The numbers had been written in pencil, almost too faint to read. He kept the paper pressed between two fingers against the wall of the booth while he dialled the numbers with his other hand. Outside, he could hear the announcements of trains arriving and departing, the sound echoing around the cavernous building with its glass-roofed ceiling made dingy by the smoke of locomotives.

Eckberg picked up almost at once. 'Who is this?' he asked.

'Carter.'

There was a pause. 'I wasn't sure you'd call.'

'Something has happened. I think it's time we talked.'

'I can meet you tonight, but it will have to be late. Say around ten.'

'Where?'

'Go to the cafe where I met you before.'

'Won't it be closed?'

'Yes, but go around back. I have a key. I'll let you in.'

He was about to hang up when Eckberg spoke to him again.

'How bad is it?' he asked.

'You remember when you told me that people were going to get hurt?'

'Yes.'

'Well, you were right about that.'

*

Following his discharge from the army, Carter spent several days waiting for his transit papers to come through. His lawyer, Captain Ottway, was trying to secure him a seat on a plane heading back to the States. If that fell through, a berth would be found for him on board a ship. In the meantime, he had nothing to do but sit in his Quonset hut waiting for mealtimes so that he could shamble over to the mess hall.

At first, Carter had been nervous about the reception he might receive from the military policemen who were constantly coming and going from the base. He assumed that everybody must know why he was there and what judgement had been handed to him. As soon as he entered the mess hall, which still smelled mustily of horses, he had the urge to get up onto one of the long collapsible tables where soldiers took their meals, and explain his side of things.

To his surprise, nobody looked his way when he walked in and took his place in the food line, a sectioned tin plate in his hand. He spotted the same military policemen who had put him in handcuffs and escorted him to and from his cell during the trial. They seemed completely oblivious to his presence, as if he were a phantom they could not even see.

The relief he felt to find himself anonymous again was so profound that he lingered in the mess hall, alone but suddenly not lonely, until the cooks finally tossed him out.

Captain Ottway had been gone four days when he finally reappeared, rapping softly with his knuckles on the flimsy door of the Quonset hut.

When he heard the knocking, Carter swung off his bed and let the captain in.

Ottway smiled weakly. It was not the same smile as before. 'Listen,' he said. 'We have run into an obstacle.'

When Carter heard those words, the worst thing he could imagine was that he would be travelling home by ship, which might last the best part of two weeks instead of the couple of days it would otherwise take to go by plane.

But it turned out to be worse than that. Much worse.

Ottway explained that the trial, such as it was, had made its way into the newspapers back in America. Celebration of the Ardennes victory had been tempered by the thousands of Allied casualties suffered during the German attack. Reports of the SS massacre of almost a hundred American prisoners in a field outside St Christophe had provoked outrage in an already outraged population. The story of Carter's dishonourable discharge, although it mentioned that he had been cleared of the most serious accusations, implied that he might singlehandedly have been able to forestall or prevent the attack. It made no mention of the dozens of other deserters who had previously warned of the assault, or of the generals' refusal to act upon reports from American troops of enemy activity along the Belgian–German border.

'So you see how it looks,' said Ottway. 'And consider the alternative, which is to acknowledge that the US Army was caught with its pants down. Nobody wants to hear that. Some weeks before you got here, American forces were attacked in the Hürtgen Forest, not far from the Ardennes, and they suffered such massive casualties that the battle was scarcely reported at all because it was considered to be too demoralising.'

'But it's OK if they hang it all on me. Is that what you're saying?' asked Carter.

'I'm not saying it's OK, but I am telling you it's what they did.'

As Carter listened to this, he had the sensation of being swept away down a river somewhere deep inside himself, with no way to fight against the current.

'I'm afraid there's more,' said Ottway. 'The police back home have relieved you of duty.'

'Permanently?'

'I'm afraid so. Apparently, the mayor of Elizabeth, who was taking all kinds of flak from his constituents, insisted on it personally.'

'My father . . .' Carter heard himself muttering the words, but he had already been carried so far downstream that it felt as if he were speaking about a person he had never met.

'Your father is doing all right,' said Ottway. Reaching into his pocket, the lawyer pulled out a telegram message typed on a thin, yellowy-brown piece of paper. 'I cabled him two days ago, after the story broke. I explained that there were extenuating circumstances that would be made clear in time. His reply came in this morning.'

Carter took the telegram and stared at it, struggling to focus, as if the letters were rearranging themselves as he tried to read them.

YOU HAVE MY TRUST AND CONFIDENCE STOP REMEMBER THIRD RULE STOP

'What is the third rule?' asked Ottway.

Carter lowered the page. 'To survive,' he said quietly. 'You got any suggestions for that?'

'I do have a plan,' said Ottway, 'which I think, under the circumstances, might be your only course of action.'

Carter struggled to hear the man over the thundering Niagara in his brain, in which his body turned and twisted, almost lifeless now, down and down onto the anvil of the rocks below.

'The war will be over in a few months,' continued Ottway, 'and most of these soldiers are going home. But the American Army is still going to maintain bases here in Germany – in fact all over Europe – and civilian contractors will be needed to help keep those bases running. The wages are decent and, since you're getting paid in dollars, that money will go a lot further over here than it would back home. You'll get housing, food if you can stand to eat off mess hall trays indefinitely, and some day, when this whole thing has settled down, you can go home and start over if you want to. People might be angry now, but they won't stay that way. Other stories will come along to distract them. The day will come when they won't even remember what happened here.'

'How long is that going to take?' asked Carter.

'I'm not sure,' answered Ottway, 'but for now, I think this is the only chance you've got.'

That night, he went to visit Riveira in the hospital ward, which was located in what had once been the servants' dining room. The ceiling was low and the room was poorly lit, but the red tile floors were clean and smelled of carbolic and, of the six beds in the room, only two were occupied now.

The break in Riveira's leg had been worse than the doctors originally thought, and the delay in his treatment had caused infection to set in. In the end, his left foot had to be amputated at the ankle. He lay in a corner of the ward, his leg in a sling that kept it raised above the level of his head.

'Lieutenant!' he shouted, when Carter walked into the room. He slapped his hands on the clean white sheets, like a child who wanted to play. He had lost a lot of weight and his face looked drawn and shadowy. Nevertheless, he seemed happy, not only to see Carter but at the news he had just been told. 'They're sending me home!'

The other man in the room, his head bandaged so that only his face was showing, sighed and put down the book he was reading. 'Are you ever going to shut up about that?' he asked. 'You already told me a hundred times.'

'And now I'm telling him,' said Riveira, pointing at Carter as if to single him out from a dozen other strangers in the room.

'You can still drive a jeep with one foot,' said Riveira.

'Did you know that? They fix your leg into some kind of a stirrup and you can work the clutch like that. And you know what I'm going to do when I get home? I'm going to buy myself a taxi. I'm set. I'm all set. I wish they'd damned well send me home today!'

'Sounds like you got it all worked out,' said Carter.

'I do,' he replied. 'That's a fact.'

The other wounded man sighed again. With his face haloed in bandages, he looked like a nun. 'I got all my hair burned off,' he said, 'and my ears just melted like wax so that there was nothing left. And I don't think they're sending me back. Can you believe it?'

'You should have burned your foot,' said Riveira.

'I know it,' muttered the nun.

'I came to say that you were right,' Carter told Riveira.

Riveira blinked at him. 'About what, Lieutenant?'

'About everything you said when we were driving out of the Ardennes. It all came true, more or less.'

Riveira shook his head. 'I don't recollect any of it, sir. That morphine does a number on your brain.'

Carter wondered if Riveira was telling the truth. It didn't matter now. 'Anyway,' he said, 'you're smarter than you look.'

Riveira grinned. 'Who'd have thought it?' he said.

'That's for damned sure,' laughed the nun.

Carter raised one hand to say goodbye.

As Riveira did the same, the smile disappeared from his face. It was only for a moment, but there was something in Riveira's expression that told Carter the man remembered every word he'd said.

*

As Carter cycled through the Höningerplatz, he noticed that the makeshift store where the legless man sold razor blades was gone now, and the place seemed strangely desolate. The sun had just set and the murky lavender of twilight filled the air. Pedalling towards the fenced-in sprawl of Dasch's compound, Carter could smell the white blossoms on a crooked old apple tree which had somehow escaped the war. In a patch of tall and reedy grass the tree clung stubbornly to life, its coarse bark scabbed with moss and its branches arthritically twisted.

He arrived at the front gate just as the guard was opening it for Ritter to drive through in his Tatra. Ritter made no move to greet Carter as he sped past, raising the dust.

The guard let Carter through. 'You might not want to go in there,' he said, gesturing towards the office.

In the half-light, Carter could see broken glass strewn in front of the building. Its window was shattered and the chair that had flown through it only a short time ago lay splintered on the ground outside. 'What happened?' he asked the guard. 'Was there a police raid or something?'

The guard shook his head, eyes hidden under the brim of his cap. 'Mr Dasch did that all by himself, and I think it's even worse inside.'

'But why?' demanded Carter.

'I'm damned if I know,' said the guard, 'but whatever it is, I have a feeling we're all going to take the blame, one way or another.'

Carter made his way across the dusty expanse of the compound. The garage was closed up now, and a warm night breeze muttered through the overlapping slats of corrugated iron that made up the roof of the building. For an instant, it reminded him of the warehouses back on the docks of Elizabeth, and he half expected to smell the brackish, muddy water of the Hudson.

Cautiously, he stepped through the open doorway of the office. His boots crunched on broken glass. It was dark in there, and it took him a moment to realise there was someone else in the room.

A figure sat at a desk in the corner, head in his hands, hunched over like a bear. 'I said get out!' roared the man.

In that moment, Carter realised it was Dasch. Without a word, he turned to leave.

'Carter, is that you?' Dasch's voice sounded strained and unfamiliar.

'Yes,' he replied, 'but I'll leave you alone.'

'Nonsense!' With a sweep of one hand, Dasch beckoned to Carter. With the other, he clicked on the desk light, which had somehow remained unbroken. 'Come in,' he said, 'and marvel at my handiwork.'

In amazement, Carter looked around. The large map of Europe had been torn down and kicked into a corner of the room. A filing cabinet had been tipped over and lay like a coffin on the floor. A smell of old cigarettes from an overloaded ashtray, whose contents had been hurled against the wall, mixed with the blossom-scented air sifting in through the broken window.

'This must look like the result of a brawl in one of your Wild West saloons,' said Dasch. 'I just sent Ritter out to get some wood to make repairs. God knows where he'll find what he needs at this time of day, but he always manages somehow.'

'Was there a fight?' asked Carter.

'Only me against the world.' As Dasch spoke, he began arranging things that had been scattered around the desk – pencils, a ledger, a stapler – as if somehow to atone for the damage he had done to the room. 'One day, it will sink into my skull that this is a struggle that I cannot win.'

'And how did it beat you this time?'

'By crashing my plane.'

It took a moment for Dasch's words to sink in. 'I'm sorry to hear that,' Carter said at last.

'Garlinsky called with the news,' explained Dasch. 'He's on his way over here now. God help me.'

'Why are you so afraid of Garlinsky?' asked Carter. 'What power does this man have over you that a million others don't?'

Dasch was silent for a while before he replied, and then he answered with a question of his own. 'What are we, Mr Carter? What kind of men would you say that we are?'

'That all depends on who you ask.'

'I'm asking you.'

The wind whistled in through the fangs of broken glass still clinging to the window frame.

'We are men who work outside of the law,' said Carter. 'That is the thing which defines us, to the world and to ourselves.'

'Very good.' Dasch raised a finger and wagged it at the ceiling. 'No matter which side of the law we choose to stand on, one thing remains a constant – what we do is who we are. Although the world imagines that there are many of us on our side of the line, wallowing in our riches, the actual number of those who truly prosper is very small indeed. In this little universe, we come to know each other, by reputation if not by association. Do you follow me, Mr Carter?'

'So far, I guess,' he said.

'So when a man appears out of nowhere, the way Garlinsky did about a month ago, not only with a plan to expand my business beyond what even I had thought was possible, but with enough money in his briefcase to actually make the plan work, it is natural enough that I would make enquiries as to who this man might be.'

'Sure,' said Carter, 'that makes sense. And did you?'

'Of course.'

'What did you learn?'

Dasch leaned across his desk. 'Nothing,' he hissed. 'He is a ghost, Mr Carter, and even here among the ruins of the Reich, where almost everybody must keep secrets from the past, no one has the skill to make them disappear completely the way this Garlinsky has done. No one but the devil, anyway.'

At that moment, the guard appeared in the doorway, his rifle slung across his back. The silhouette of the gun barrel jutted from his shoulder, as if an arrow had been plunged into his neck. 'Somebody's coming,' he said. 'I think it is Mr Garlinsky.'

Dasch rose to his feet. 'I didn't hear a car.'

'There is no car,' replied the guard.

'What?' asked Dasch. 'Is he on a bicycle?'

'No, sir. He is on foot.'

'But it's an hour's walk back to the city, and nobody lives out here!'

'Nevertheless, sir,' said the guard, 'somebody is coming.'

'Well,' Dasch said exasperatedly, 'when he gets to the end of the road, open the gate and see what the hell he wants.'

'Sir,' said the guard, 'he is not walking on the road.'

There was something about the way the guard spoke that sent a shudder down the length of Carter's spine. Leaving the carnage of Dasch's office, the two men followed the guard across the compound until they came to the fence. Beyond it, shuddering blue in the moonlight, lay a wide, open tract of land, stretching featurelessly out towards the Rhine. A shallow mist had settled on the ground, weaving in amongst the nodding stalks of milkweed.

Across this space came a figure in a long trench coat, carrying a briefcase whose polished leather sides caught a glint of moonlight now and then. His face was hidden in shadow. He did not move quickly, but his pace never slackened and the trench coat billowed about his legs, stirring the mist as he walked.

'It's him,' whispered Dasch.

Only now, as Carter mutely watched the man's approach across the wasteland, did he understand the fear that Dasch had spoken of, and he thought back to the last time a stranger had walked into his life.

The year was 1948.

By then, he had been working as a civilian contractor with the US Army for over three years, moving from base to base wherever he was needed. He had begun in England. From there, he had shifted to France and, once the war ended, into Germany, where bases were quickly established in the American zone of occupation.

Carter's job as a contractor guaranteed him a decent wage, as well as healthcare, two weeks' vacation a year and time off for all major holidays. In spite of the good working conditions, Carter had lost count of the number of men who had taken civilian jobs at the base and then left soon afterwards, returning to the States. After the war, there had been an initial slump in the job market as returning veterans competed for employment, and many of those who returned to Europe immediately after being demobilised had done so because they'd had no choice. By 1947, as the big American manufacturers in the car, aircraft and construction industries had completed their transition from wartime to peacetime operations, most of those men who had come over decided to return stateside. For most of them, whether they had fought there or not, Europe was still haunted by the carnage that had swept across it. It would take years, if not decades, to restore the cities that had been bombed and, beyond those cities, in the forests and the fields, the dead could still be found huddled in the foxholes where they had perished. Liberation had come at such a terrible price that the word itself was seldom used, except sarcastically, by those who had been liberated. For those who had been left to clean away the wreckage, it was not the outcome of the war that tormented them. It was simply the cost.

For the soldiers of the occupation, the lack of choice about whether or not to remain there was its own solution to the problem. But for men like Carter, the choice was real and present. It gnawed at them constantly as they weighed steady work and steady pay against the dream of going home. For most, the dream won out. Only a few, like Carter, became regulars in the seemingly endless shift from base to base, never staying long enough to feel like they belonged and never knowing when they would be asked to leave again. The majority were veterans, but few of them talked about their war experiences and, since it was considered rude to enquire about such matters, it was always left at that. These men, and women too, learned to live among the gaps in what they knew about each other. Their pasts became blurred and redundant. Carter found, to his surprise, that this existence suited him, at least for now. Most days he could convince himself that he had made his peace with it, but there were moments, when certain sounds and smells would jolt him back into the life he'd once taken for granted, that he realised how fragile this peace really was and that he could not endure this forever. But as to how and when he might move on, that stayed a mystery to him until the day Marcus Wilby appeared.

Carter was sitting outside a cavernous warehouse at the US Army base in Dornheim, not far from Wiesbaden. He had just finished unloading several pallets of ration boxes, which had been flown in that morning. These packages, each stamped 'CARE – USA', contained canned food and sundries which were to be handed out to German civilians who might otherwise starve while the rebuilding and reorganisation of the country was underway.

Now he was on his lunch break, eating army-issue baked beans out of a can, with a canteen of water to drink and a Hershey bar for afterwards. It was a sunny morning in late summer, with a stiff wind blowing up from the south that had caused several planes to be diverted from the Dornheim base where Carter worked.

From the corner of his eye, Carter glimpsed two men approaching. He could tell, just from the way they walked, that they were military personnel, even though they were wearing civilian clothes. Carter guessed that they must be intelligence officers – SI, SO, X-2, or whatever they were calling themselves these days. The only thing he didn't know was if they were here to see him, or whether they were simply lost.

At first, Carter did not look up. He scooped another spoonful of beans from the can and was about to shovel them into his mouth when the strangers came to an abrupt halt a few paces away.

'You really going to eat those cold?' asked one of them.

Now Carter raised his head.

The man who had spoken wore a trench coat made from the particular pinkish-beige gabardine popular with men who had been officers. The cuffs of his trousers were so high that his ankles were nearly exposed – another

230

bizarre fashion statement known as 'flood pants', common amongst Ivy League men. Carter could also tell, from the sag on the man's left side, just below the armpit, that the stranger was carrying a gun.

The other man wore a tweed sports jacket, which barely fitted over his muscle-hunched shoulders. He had a head like a battering ram, with a broad forehead, one cauliflowered ear and a nose that had obviously been broken. He looked as if he had once been thrown into a cage with a gorilla and had to fight his way out.

'I asked if you were going to eat those cold,' the man in the trench coat repeated.

'I have no choice,' said Carter. 'It's too far to go to the mess hall. That's way over on the other side of the base. By the time I got there, my lunch break would be half over.'

'Cold beans.' The man winced. 'That takes me back.'

Carter dropped his spoon into the can and held it out. 'Help yourself,' he said.

'Oh, hell no,' replied the man.

There was an awkward silence.

'Well, since you aren't here for my lunch,' asked Carter, 'is there something I can help you with?'

'I hope so, Mr Carter,' said the man.

He knows my name, thought Carter, and he felt the muscles tighten in his neck.

'My name is Captain Wilby,' said the man, 'and I work for the US government.'

Carter nodded at the man in the tweed jacket. 'And who's your friend?'

'Oh,' said Wilby, 'he's just a figment of your imagination. There's no one here but you and me.'

The man in the tweed jacket scowled at Carter and said nothing.

'All right,' answered Carter, 'then what do you want, you and your imaginary pal?'

'To reassure you that there are some of us who know you were not treated fairly by the military court.'

It threw Carter off balance to hear this. No one had ever said that to him before.

'Those men who convicted you,' continued Wilby, 'were trying to save themselves from having to admit that one of their own people had committed the crime they sent you in to investigate. In effect, you were punished for doing your job. But none of this is news to you, I'm sure.'

'Then why are you telling me now?' asked Carter.

'Because the same cruel god who trampled you into the dirt can lift you up again and dust you off and send you on your way if he so chooses.'

'And that god would be you, I guess.'

'Not at all, Mr Carter. I'm just the guy who works for him.'

'And what does your god want for this favour?'

'A little help, perhaps.'

'You're going to have to forgive me,' said Carter, 'but the last time someone like you showed up and asked for help, I climbed on board a plane to Belgium and that's the last I saw of home.'

'I know about that,' said Wilby.

232

'I figured you would. What kind of help are you talking about?'

'The kind you could perform as an Agent of Opportunity.'

'A what?' asked Carter.

'An Agent of Opportunity,' repeated Wilby. 'Sometimes we make use of people who are not officially a part of our organisation, but whose credentials and motivation match the tasks that must get done.'

'What credentials?' He gestured at the mountain of packages. 'Loading and unloading boxes?'

'No,' answered Wilby. 'Your real skill, as an undercover detective. I assume you haven't forgotten who you used to be.'

'It's not something a person forgets.'

'Exactly.'

'And you're telling me you can't find someone else to do this, whatever the hell it is?'

'Not someone as well placed by time and circumstance. In fact, you are perfect for the job.'

'And how exactly would you lift me up again,' asked Carter, 'you and your trampling god?'

'On completion of your task,' explained Wilby, 'we will announce that you have been working for the US government, and that your dishonourable discharge was simply a part of your cover. You would receive a public apology for your unlawful dismissal from the police department, as well as back pay, reinstatement, a pension and a medal of commendation, and I'll even throw in a parade down the main street of Dunellen if you want it, so that no one, ever again, would be able to question your honour or your service to society. I know it isn't fair that you should have to bargain to get back something that has always been properly yours. But I'm not here to make things fair. I'm here to make them right.'

'In other words,' said Carter, 'you're blackmailing me.'

'Don't think of it as blackmail,' said Wilby. 'Think of it as an incentive, without which nobody does anything in this world. I realise that what I'm asking of you is more than anyone in their right mind would accept, especially a civilian. You don't owe me anything. This isn't a question of rank. I can't just give you orders and expect you to obey them. So I have to offer you some kind of reward. Something that will make this worthwhile. I could have appealed to you as a patriot, but that ship has already sailed. I could have offered you money, but everything I know about you tells me that this would have backfired. I could have tried to entrap you in some compromising situation, but you'd have seen that coming. So what was left, except to give you back your life? That is, if you still want it. You're smart enough to know that the only power on this earth that can restore what has been taken from you is the same one that took it away. You're also smart enough to know that I'm only going to make this offer once, so if you send me away empty handed, I'm never coming back. And what you have now' – he raised his hands and let them fall again, taking in the windswept runway and the warehouse and the empty can of beans – 'will be all you ever have, and there'll be no one to blame but yourself.'

Carter knew there was no point having a conversation about any of this. There wasn't going to be a conversation. Neither did he doubt that this man could do, or not do, everything he said. 'How's it going to work?' he asked.

Over the next few minutes, Wilby described how the press would receive notification of a crime at the Dornheim base, involving the theft of thousands of American cigarettes which had just arrived in the country and were due to be distributed to military bases all across Europe. A few days later, American occupation authorities would announce that they had arrested someone in connection with the robbery. That person, Wilby's Agent of Opportunity, would be Nathan Carter. After a short trial, from which the press would be excluded, Carter would be sentenced to three years in the Allied military prison at Langsdorf. He would serve nine months of that sentence before being released, after which he would approach Hanno Dasch, a known criminal specialising in the distribution of black market goods. Once enough information had been gathered on Dasch and his accomplices they would be arrested, and Carter would return to the United States and the promises Wilby had made to him would be fulfilled.

As Carter listened to this his mind kept slipping, like a needle dragging across a damaged record. He had worked so hard to leave behind the person he had been and the things he had done that the idea of returning to that life, so suddenly and so completely, was hard for him to grasp.

'Are you getting any of this?' asked Wilby.

Carter realised he had been staring at the ground this

whole time. The taste of the beans was sour in his mouth. He reached for his canteen, fumbling with the cap until at last it slipped to the side, rattling on its little chain. Then he drank, cold water splashing down inside him. 'How long do you need?' he asked.

'Give me one year,' replied Wilby, 'starting from the day you get out of jail. After that we'll cut you loose, no matter where we are.'

'And nine months on top of that, locked up in a military prison?' he asked.

'It's the only way this could ever work.'

'Would you really be putting me on trial?'

'No,' said Wilby. 'We'd just announce it, and in the three weeks that it's supposed to be going on, we'll give you a holiday. You name it. The south of France. Morocco. London. Whatever you want.'

'I would like to visit my father,' said Carter.

'You mean go back to New Jersey, when I'm offering you Paris?'

'That's what I said.'

Wilby sighed. 'Well, I'm afraid it is out of the question. You show up in New Jersey at a time when the rest of the world thinks you're supposed to be on trial in Germany, and people are going to ask questions. The operation would be ruined before it had even got started.'

'Think of all the things I could have asked for, which you would hand me on a platter if you really needed me the way you say you do. But all I'm asking for is this.'

Wilby glanced across at the man in the tweed jacket.

Throughout this conversation he had not spoken, nor had he taken his eyes off Carter. He seemed to be studying Carter, appraising him according to some scale of checks and balances known only to himself. But now the man turned and, almost imperceptibly, he nodded at Wilby.

For a moment, Wilby looked surprised. Then he shrugged and turned back to Carter. 'Consider it done,' he said.

Those words reached Carter like the slamming of a door as he realised that, in the space of only a few minutes, the course of his life had changed forever. 'What happens now?' he asked.

Wilby looked at his watch. 'In fifteen minutes,' he said, 'you are going to be arrested.'

*

The stranger was only a hundred paces from the fence when Dasch snapped out of his trance. He turned to the guard and whispered, 'Let him in!'

The guard set off at a run towards the gate. There was a creak of metal and then more hurried footsteps as the guard set out towards the stranger.

Garlinsky stopped. He stood there waiting as the guard approached, his face still hidden in shadow. He appeared to be completely bald, almost as if there was no flesh at all but only a skull, softly reflecting the moonlight.

Carter felt an instinctive hostility towards the man, primitive and dark, rising from some nameless vortex of emotions deep inside him.

The guard came to a stop in front of Garlinsky and the

two of them spoke in voices too faint for Carter to hear. Then they made their way towards the gate.

As Garlinsky passed in front of them, Carter caught a glimpse of the man's narrow cheekbones, thin lips and sharply angled jaw. There was a drawn, pinched quality to his expression, which Carter likened to the faces of men he had known around the docks, who slept in the hulks of old ships and lived off greasy po' boy sandwiches handed out of the back doors of diners and made up from the food left behind by paying customers. The harshness of the lives they lived was tattooed on the faces of these men, and they had no way to hide it.

Dasch rested his hand on Carter's shoulder. 'I'll see to this,' he said. 'You go and find Teresa.'

'Where is she?'

'The last I saw of her, she was heading for the dining room.'

'Are you sure?' asked Carter, remembering what Wilby had said about doing whatever it took to find out who Garlinsky really was. 'You might need some help.'

'That time may come,' said Dasch, 'but it will not be tonight. Just make sure Teresa is doing all right.'

Before Carter could ask what he meant by that, Dasch began walking towards the office, where the guard had brought Garlinsky. Already the lights had been turned on, and there was the crunching sound of footsteps treading cautiously on broken glass.

Carter found his way to the dining room, a flimsily built structure connected to the office by a narrow corridor. The room was lit by bulbs in dusty metal shades, whose conical shapes threw spreading pools of light upon two long wooden tables at which the workers could sit and eat their lunches. A sink for washing dishes stood in the corner, with drawers on either side of it and, on a shelf above it, a stack of enamelled cups and plates, the rims all chipped and rusty.

On the walls hung tattered posters advertising tourism in the Rhineland. They all seemed to date from before the war. In one, taken from high ground far above the river, the Remagen bridge spanned the murky water, flanked at either end by grey stone towers. Nothing remained of it now but those two towers, the bridge itself having been wrecked by the Germans themselves in 1945 as they attempted, unsuccessfully, to stop American forces from crossing the river. In other posters, their colours faded like the ribbons on cemetery wreaths, girls in the feathered hats and white-aproned dresses of traditional Rhineland costume clutched bouquets of flowers and smiled into the sun.

At the end of one of the tables sat Teresa. With one hand, she held a bundled dish towel to the side of her head. With the other, she covered her eyes, shielding them from the light bulb glowing just above her head.

'Too much champagne?' asked Carter.

As soon as she heard his voice, Teresa straightened up and scowled at him. 'What do you want?' she demanded.

'Your father sent me here to see if you were doing all right.'

'You can tell him I'm fine,' she replied.

Carter pointed at the dish towel. 'Do you need some more ice for that thing?'

She lifted the bundle of cloth, revealing that the side that had been pressed against her head was soaked with blood.

Carter gasped. 'What the hell happened?' he asked. 'Did your father do this to you?'

'It was an accident,' she told him.

Instinctively, he stepped towards her. 'Let me take a look.'

'Leave me alone!' she snapped. 'It's just a little cut.'

Carter halted in his tracks. 'Please,' he said. 'I think you might need stitches.'

Her face turned suddenly ashen. 'Is it really that bad?' she asked.

'Just let me take a look,' he pleaded with her.

This time, she did not protest.

Gently, Carter moved aside some strands of hair that had become tangled in the clotted blood.

She breathed in sharply with the pain.

'I'm sorry,' he whispered.

The cut was about an inch long, not deep but cleanly done, as if it had been made with a knife.

Carter went over to the sink, pulled open one of the drawers and removed a clean dish towel. Then he turned on the tap, soaked the cloth, squeezed out some of the water and gave it to Teresa. 'Give me that,' he said, holding out his hand for the cloth that had been soaked in blood.

'Will it need stitches?' she asked.

'I think you might be OK,' he replied.

'Good.' She pressed the clean cloth to her head. 'I don't want to see any doctors.'

'Why not?'

'I don't want to have to explain to them what happened.'

'Then explain it to me, at least.'

'I was walking past the window of the office when my father threw the chair through the window.'

'And it hit you?'

'No! Only a little piece of glass. He didn't mean to do it. People don't understand.'

'You make it sound like this has happened before.'

'It is an occupational hazard of working with my father.'

'What is?' asked Carter.

'Sooner or later, everyone gets hurt.'

'And what about him?'

'He has already been hurt enough,' she muttered.

There it is again, thought Carter, *this past no one will speak about.* Now would have been the time to press her about where she had come from and what she had lived through to make her the person she was, the time to push past all of her sarcastic answers until he arrived at the truth. But Carter couldn't bring himself to do it. Neither could he hide from himself that the reason for his hesitation lay in the fact that he would probably have succeeded, but only by exploiting the pain that she was in. None of that should have mattered. He had been taught never to feel sympathy, never to forget what he was there to do.

But one single fact had overwhelmed the brutal logic of his trade. Carter could no longer deny feeling drawn to her in ways that were both irresistible and frightening to him, because he could not control where his emotions were leading him. From the moment Carter had first laid eyes on Teresa, he had sensed the presence of the barricades this woman had built to keep the world at bay, even if he still didn't know why. He had grasped at once this fragile illusion of strength, because it was no different from his own. To hunt her down inside that labyrinth of secrets, destroying what held her world together, would have been the greatest act of cruelty in a career which had been filled with cruelties.

So Carter let the moment pass, trusting that the opportunity might come again. But the true meaning of what had just happened did not escape him. From now on, Carter realised, he would not only be lying to everyone around him. He would also be lying to himself.

'Why is it so quiet out there?' asked Teresa.

'Garlinsky is here,' replied Carter.

'Since when?'

'He just arrived.'

'What does he look like?'

'You mean you haven't seen him?'

'Nobody has seen him,' said Teresa. 'Not even my father. All he has heard is a voice on the phone. That's why my father is so frightened of Garlinsky. He wasn't even sure the man was real.'

'He is flesh and blood all right,' said Carter, 'and that is one more reason to be scared.'

'You'd better see what's going on,' said Teresa, 'before my father smashes anything he might have missed the first time.'

'Are you going to be all right?' he asked.

'Go!' She waved him away.

Carter turned to leave.

'And I'm sorry,' she muttered, so quietly that Carter almost missed what she had said.

Carter looked back over his shoulder. 'Sorry for what?' he asked.

'For thinking you were like the others.'

Carter stared at her, afraid that she could tell what he was thinking. It would have been better, he wanted to say, if you had just kept hating me.

*

The day after his staged arrest at the Dornheim military base, Carter boarded a plane bound for America. Two days later, after an overnight stay in Lisbon, where he had slept on the metal floor of the aeroplane with a life jacket for a pillow, Carter stepped out onto the tarmac at Fort Dix in central New Jersey. It was a hot summer day and he could feel the humid air like butter between his fingertips. Huge cauliflower clouds, which the pilot of his transport plane had jockeyed past on his way down, now passed by majestically above them.

There to meet him was Captain Tate, the officer who had walked into Pavel's cafe all those years ago.

Tate was not in uniform this time. He wore an unpressed pair of chinos, boondocker boots and a white T-shirt. 'It's Jersey camouflage,' he said. 'We don't want to stand out, after all.'

'You mean you're coming with me?' asked Carter.

243

'I guess you're too valuable for us to let you out of our sight.'

'You don't trust me on my own?'

'I trust you just fine. It's the people we work for who don't. Say, are you really flying out of here tonight?'

That was the deal he had struck with Wilby. Two hours with his father. That was all. Wilby dared not risk any more. 'They drive a hard bargain,' Carter said.

The tarmac shimmered with heat haze as they made their way to the parking lot, where Tate climbed behind the wheel of a Packard Super Eight sedan with purplish-black paint like the skin of a ripe eggplant, white wall tyres and a fat chrome bumper that looked as if it could push down trees.

It startled Carter to see such a beautiful, clean and new machine. Most of the vehicles he encountered back in Germany either belonged to the military and were painted olive drab or else were civilian cars which somehow survived the war and had been resurrected by their owners. In many ways, the technology had gone backwards in Europe, not forwards, as people turned to the only working machinery they could find, which had remained intact simply because it had been obsolete by the time the war began.

'And this won't draw attention?' asked Carter.

'This isn't so fancy.' Tate looked at him and grinned. 'You've really been away a while, haven't you?'

Just outside the base, Carter asked Tate to pull over at the same gas station where he had telephoned his father to say goodbye. 'I need to make a call,' he said.

Tate pulled off the road and the bell clanged as he rolled

over the air tube laid out in front of the pumps. He tanked up his car while Carter went over to the phone booth.

'All set?' asked Tate, when Carter returned.

'All set.'

'Any chance you'd care to tell me who you called?' asked Tate.

Carter said nothing but, for the first time in a long while, he smiled.

They drove up through the Pine Barrens, the long, straight roadways lined with orange-khaki sand and withered-looking trees. Carter rolled the window down and breathed in the smell of the scrub pines and the scorched tar of the road surface. He had dreamed so much of coming home that he could not be sure he was actually here. He thought he must do something – scream or cut himself – and by the sound or sight of blood convince himself that he was home, even if only for a day.

A block short of the cottage where Carter's father lived in Belmar, Tate pulled up to the kerb and cut the engine. 'I'll wait here,' he said. 'Make sure you keep an eye on the time.' When Carter moved to open the door, Tate reached across and rested his hand on Carter's shoulder. 'I hope you're not thinking of running.'

Carter settled back into his seat. 'I have a choice,' he said. 'I could bolt, knowing you would find me in a day or two, and let you turn my world into something even worse than you did last time. Or I can let some guy, whose name you maybe know and maybe don't, blackmail me into working for him, in which case I'll be home in two years and you and all your kind can slink back into the shadows where you came from and let me get on with my life.'

'Fair enough,' said Tate, releasing his grip. 'Just make sure you're back here in two hours.'

Carter walked around the corner and, as soon as he was out of sight, he turned in the opposite direction from his father's house and made his way along the narrow streets towards the boardwalk, beyond which lay a stretch of beach the locals called the Irish Riviera, and then nothing but ocean until you reached the shores of Spain or Africa.

It was a weekday, so the beach was not crowded. A few families had set up towels and umbrellas and were eating sandwiches out of metal-sided coolers. Children played in the lazy surf and on the stone breakwaters. Along the wooden boardwalk, people rode by on bicycles or pushed strollers. Some, too old to walk, were pushed along in wheelchairs, wool blankets covering their legs, vacant looks upon their faces. The smell of lemonade and fried dough stands flooded Carter's senses.

There was a little coffee shop on the corner of 16th and Ocean Avenue where, for as long as Carter could remember, they had made cider doughnuts and sold them for a nickel a piece. They were still selling them, but the price had gone up to a dime. He bought one anyway and stood there, letting the sugar dissolve on his tongue with each bite, just as he had done when he was a kid.

'I was surprised to get your call,' said a voice.

Carter turned.

It was Palladino, his father's old partner in the police,

who had looked after Carter during his time with the Office of Price Administration. Palladino wore a short-brimmed panama hat and an untucked shirt with a Hawaiian print on it, which helped to hide the half-moon of his belly.

'Thank you for coming,' said Carter.

'I heard you'd left the country.'

'I did,' replied Carter.

'Heard you were in some trouble, too.'

'I was, but I'm setting that straight.'

Palladino nodded. 'Glad to hear it.'

'It wasn't like they said.'

'I never thought it was.'

'I have to go back,' said Carter. 'I might be gone a while.'

'And you want me to keep an eye on the old man?'

'I'd be grateful if you did.'

Palladino smiled. 'I do that anyway,' he said. 'He knows it, too, a fact he's too proud to admit. We just keep having these coincidental meetings. He never asks me why. You know how it is with your father. As a matter of fact, he's over there now' – Palladino pointed towards the boardwalk – 'keeping an eye out for U-boats. That's what he always says, even though the war's been over for years.'

Carter turned and looked.

The old man was sitting on his usual bench, looking out to sea and oblivious to the people passing by. His hands were folded on the top of an Irish blackthorn walking stick and his chin was resting on his hands.

'You want to say hello?' asked Palladino.

Carter paused, as if willing his father to turn around. But

the old man just kept staring out to sea, his eyes peeled for the German submarines that now lay rusting on the sea floor, the bones of their crews lying in heaps of sticks down in the green-grey silt of the Atlantic. 'I think I'll leave him be,' said Carter.

'I expect that's for the best,' answered Palladino. 'You go and do the things you have to do. And don't you worry. I'll be watching over him.'

There was nothing more to say. Carter shook Palladino's hand and watched him plod across the road towards the boardwalk, his flat-footed gait like a baby just learning how to walk. Palladino stopped beside the old man and slapped him on the shoulder. Carter's father turned and jerked his chin in greeting.

The last Carter saw of the two men, they were sitting side by side, both of them looking out to sea as if the U-boats might still be there, after all, like iron sharks prowling the deep.

On his way back to Tate, Carter stopped at his father's house. The front door was locked but he knew the screen door around back would be open. As he stepped inside, Carter filled his lungs with the familiar smell of his father's laundry soap and tobacco and the lemony-scented polish he used on the furniture in the dining room where he never sat, since he never had guests and preferred to eat his meals at a small, bare wooden table in the kitchen.

He made his way into the family room.

Nothing had changed. The same overstuffed chairs. The same unread pile of newspapers. The ashtray full of cigarette butts.

Carter stood there for a while, suddenly aware that if he stayed any longer he would never have the strength to leave. He spun on his heel and walked out of the house, closing the screen door carefully behind him. He returned to the car, where Tate sat with the windows rolled down, one arm sticking out of the window and a cigarette pinched between his fingers.

'You've only been gone half an hour!' said Tate.

'I did what I came to do,' replied Carter.

'That is the damnedest thing,' said Tate. He sipped at the smoke from his cigarette and exhaled against the inside of the windshield, sending the grey cloud arcing back into his face. Then he flicked the half-smoked stub out of the window.

That single, careless gesture made Carter realise how far he was from the place in which he had just spent the past few years. If Tate had thrown that cigarette into the gutter of a German road, people would have rushed to pick up what he had thrown away. But now it just lay there, smouldering and ignored. This part of the world had always been Carter's home but, even though he could have found his way blindfolded through these streets, he felt so out of phase with everything around him that he wondered if he could really belong here anymore.

Tate's voice snapped Carter out of his momentary trance. 'I guess we had better be going,' he said.

Before the sun had even set upon that day, Carter found himself in a cargo plane bound for Europe as it climbed steeply over the gunmetal blue sea, and the shoreline of New Jersey faded back into the clouds.

Leaving Teresa to nurse her injured head, Carter made his way down the narrow corridor to the office.

Some attempt had been made to kick the broken glass into the corner and the furniture had been dragged outside, leaving the room half empty.

Dasch was sitting at his desk. His skin looked deathly pale under the glaring bulbs, whose green glass hoods had all been smashed away.

Garlinsky stood in the middle of the room, his back towards Carter and the briefcase on the ground at his side. He turned as Carter stepped into the room. 'Ah,' he said. 'The American.' The gabardine wool of his overcoat shimmered softly as he moved, like the wings of an insect in the sun.

Now that Carter could see him up close, Garlinsky did not appear as dangerous as he had seemed before. But he looked very much like the kind of man who worked for people that were.

Slowly, Garlinsky turned away again.

'You were saying,' muttered Dasch.

'The plane overshot the runway,' explained Garlinsky, 'and crashed in a thickly wooded area, possibly as far as a kilometre beyond the airstrip. Our contacts were waiting to receive it. The weather conditions were bad. There was rain and there were crosswinds. Your pilots made two aborted attempts to land and then, on the third one, they crashed.'

Slowly, Dasch subsided back into his chair. 'So my plane has been destroyed,' he whispered.

'We assume so,' said Garlinsky.

Carter walked around until he stood beside Dasch's desk. 'Did it burn?' he asked.

Garlinsky shook his head. 'It must have been almost out of fuel by the time it crashed. My contacts saw no smoke.'

'And what about the pilots?' asked Carter.

'We assume that they are dead.'

'Why do you assume?' demanded Carter. 'Didn't anybody check?'

Garlinsky paused before replying. Even in those few seconds, the silence seemed to settle upon them like a layer of dust. 'The plan,' he said, 'was for our contacts to unload that plane in twenty minutes and be gone within thirty. The longer they remained in the area, the greater the likelihood that they might be found by the authorities, and I do not need to tell you what would happen to them if they were arrested. As soon as the plane crashed, they left the area as quickly as they could, and they have not been back.'

'Where is this airfield?' asked Carter.

'As I have already explained to Mr Dasch,' said Garlinsky, 'it is located in Czechoslovakia, in what you once called the Sudetenland. It is near the old spa town of Carlsbad, known to the Czechs as Karlovy Vary. It was a popular resort before the war. The Czechs built the runway not far from the town as an emergency landing strip for a nearby military airbase. If there was a crash on the runway at the base, other inbound planes could divert to the emergency strip. The base was taken over by the Germans when they marched into the Sudetenland in 1938, but they never used it because the runways weren't long enough for their heavy bombers. So, instead, they built a different airbase one hundred kilometres to the north. The emergency runway was forgotten. That is why we thought it would be safe, as long as everyone moved quickly. As of last year, Czechoslovakia is under Communist control, but people from the west still come and go and planes from western countries, military and civilian, still overfly the area on their way down to Turkey and Greece. The sight of a Canadian transport plane in the skies above Karlovy would not have aroused suspicion, and as far as we know the wreckage has not been discovered, but that situation could change at any moment.'

'Tell your people,' said Dasch, 'that I will pay for the whisky they lost.'

'It's not the whisky I'm concerned about.'

'Then what?' demanded Dasch.

'Our concern,' explained Garlinsky, 'is that the discovery of that plane, along with its cargo, will somehow lead the authorities back to us.'

'We all share in that risk,' said Dasch.

'Perhaps,' replied Garlinsky, 'but the responsibility lies entirely with you. If the aircraft had exploded and everything on board had been incinerated, the equation might be different. But since this did not happen, it is safe to say that the discovery of that cargo by Communist authorities is inevitable. When that occurs, the Russians will learn of this and they will waste no time finding out where it came from, whom it belonged to and where it was going. I know the Russians, and I can assure you that this is a matter that they will pursue beyond what you and I would consider sane. They will get to the bottom of it, and that is where they will find us. In the meantime, you will have created an international incident, the type of which both the Soviet and Allied governments are painstakingly trying to avoid. Do you have any idea what will happen to you then, Mr Dasch?'

'I can't say that I do,' he replied.

'At the very least, you would spend the rest of your life in prison,' replied Garlinsky. 'That is if the Allies get to you first. More likely, it will be the Soviets, in which case you and everyone around you will simply be found dead. Am I making myself clear, Mr Dasch?'

'Yes,' answered Dasch, 'in everything except what you would like me to do about all this!'

'Make sure that any trace of the cargo that might lead back to us has been destroyed.'

He still hasn't mentioned the money, thought Carter. *How does he expect to keep that secret?*

'Very well,' Dasch said. 'I'll send Ritter first thing in the morning.'

'I'm afraid that will not do at all,' said Garlinsky.

'Why on earth not?' demanded Dasch. 'Ritter can get the job done.'

'Mr Ritter is wanted by the Soviet authorities, a fact of which I'm sure you are aware. If he should fall into their hands—'

'Enough!' boomed Dasch, bringing his hands crashing down upon the desk.

In the seconds that followed, Garlinsky did not move. It was as if the man had turned to stone.

Finally, Dasch spoke again. 'Are you suggesting that I go myself? The German police are watching me. I am convinced of that.'

'Not you,' answered Garlinsky.

'Then who—' Dasch began.

Garlinsky cut him off. 'Why don't you send Mr Carter?' he asked.

Carter felt the breath catch in his throat.

'Well,' said Dasch, 'I suppose I could do that, provided Mr Carter agrees.'

Garlinsky smiled at Carter. 'Surely you would not want to disappoint your employer, after all he's done for you.'

Carter said nothing. *Does he know who I am?* he wondered. *Does he know that I have seen the money?* None of that seemed possible, and yet the idea would not leave his head, rushing in circles around the inside of his skull like a fish trapped in a net.

'Then it is settled!' Garlinsky glanced at his watch. 'Our time is up,' he said.

Carter and Dasch walked him out to the gate and watched in silence as Garlinsky set off across the field, the moonlight like a cape upon his back, until at last he vanished in the mist.

'How did he know I was an American,' asked Carter, 'before I even opened my mouth? Did you tell him?'

'No,' replied Dasch. 'I just assumed he heard your voice before you walked into the room.'

'Was he right?' asked Carter. 'Is Ritter really wanted by the Russians?'

Dasch sighed heavily. 'Did he tell you what he did in the war?'

'He said he was an interrogator.'

'That is correct,' answered Dasch. 'And did he tell you what happened to those Russian officers after he had finished questioning them?'

'No. He never mentioned that.'

'They were shot.'

'All of them?' asked Carter.

'They did not make exceptions.'

'Then how do the Russians know about it, assuming the bodies were buried?'

'Because wherever Ritter had been, they dug up those bodies by the hundreds. Or thousands. Ritter told me he lost track of their numbers. But the Russians didn't. They remember everything. And who can blame them? The war you fought may be over, Mr Carter, but what happened between Ritter and the Russians will not come to an end until the last of them is dead, and probably not even then.'

'And you really think he would have gone if you had told him to?'

Dasch turned and looked at Carter. 'Ritter would do anything I ask, and that is my burden, not his.'

'What Garlinsky's asking for,' said Carter, 'it won't be easy.'

'Ah, but you haven't heard my plan.'

'Whatever it is, it better be a good one.'

'It might just be the best I've ever had.'

At the end of the road leading to Dasch's compound, a set of headlight beams cut through the darkness. It was Ritter, returning from his errand to fetch supplies to repair the broken window.

Carter helped him carry sheets of plywood from the car to the office, along with a bag of nails, a saw and some hammers. Along the way, he explained what had happened.

'I knew he never should have bought that plane,' said Ritter. 'If we had just kept things small and manageable, none of this would have happened.'

'Too late now.'

'It was too late from the beginning,' said Ritter, 'but we did it anyway.'

Inside the office, they found Dasch pacing back and forth like a cat locked in a cage. 'You can put all that aside!' he said, when the two men entered the room. 'We have important business to discuss.'

Ritter and Carter dumped the wood and nails and hammers on the floor.

'You told me you had a plan,' said Carter.

'Not just a plan,' replied Dasch. 'It is a work of genius.'

'What are you going to do?'

'It's not what I am going to do,' replied Dasch. 'It's what you're doing. You are going on a vacation to the spa town of Karlovy Vary, where people go to sit in vats of mud and lounge around with cucumber slices on their eyes.'

'That does not sound like something I would do,' muttered Carter.

'You might' – Dasch paused dramatically – 'if you were on your honeymoon.'

'But since I'm not—'

'Oh, but you are!' exclaimed Dasch. 'You will be married to my daughter. Temporarily, of course, but you will travel together as newlyweds. If anyone asks you why you are going, that is all you'd have to tell them, and they would understand.'

'And when we get there,' asked Carter, 'assuming that Teresa doesn't murder me before we arrive?'

'You will travel out into the countryside, perhaps to take a picnic. You will go walking in the forest where you will stumble, quite by accident it seems, upon the wreckage of that plane. And then you will see to it that nothing remains by which its cargo can be traced back to us, or to our client.'

'It won't work,' Carter said flatly.

The expression froze on Dasch's face. 'Why not?' he asked.

'Because of Teresa. It will put her at risk! You have kept her away from your affairs until now – you know the ones I mean – but all of that will be for nothing if you drag her into this.'

'Don't you think I have considered that?' asked Dasch, his voice rising with indignation. 'We simply won't tell her why she's going. All she will know is that she is accompanying you on a trip, on which you have some business to conduct. If anyone asks her, that's all she'd be able to tell them.'

Carter shook his head, still unconvinced. 'That will not be enough to keep her out of danger. Let me go alone, instead. This way, she does not need to be involved.'

'That is a fine gesture,' said Dasch, 'but any man travelling by himself to such a location is bound to raise suspicions, and even if you can conjure up some rationale for being there, questions would remain. But a former American soldier setting out on a honeymoon with his young German bride – now that makes perfect sense. Thousands of GIs have married German women since the end of the war. The purpose of your visit is so obvious that no one would think twice about it.'

'What about a marriage certificate?' asked Carter. 'They might ask for that.'

With a wave of his hand, Dasch brushed the question aside. 'The way bureaucracy works now, it can take months to process those. Even if you were getting married, you wouldn't receive the document for months, so there's no need to worry about that.'

'Have you talked to your daughter about this?'

Dasch's back stiffened. 'I was just about to,' he announced and, with a confident smile bolted to his face, he strode down the narrow hallway towards the dining room, where Teresa was still sitting with a wet towel pressed against her head.

A few moments later, the sound of raised voices reached Carter's ears. He could not hear what they were saying. Their words were muffled by the walls that stood between them. Carter glanced across at Ritter.

Ritter shrugged and shook his head.

The argument continued for a few more minutes. Then Dasch appeared in the hallway. 'Be reasonable!' he shouted back into the dining room.

Carter heard no reply, but it seemed clear that Teresa had found some other way to answer her father, because Dasch threw up his hands and growled with frustration. Then a plate crashed into the wall beside him. Dasch flinched, then quickly turned and made his way back to where Carter and Ritter were waiting. By the time he reached them, the confident smile had returned. 'She'll be fine,' he whispered to the men. 'She just needs a moment or two to think it over.'

'When is all this supposed to happen?' asked Carter.

'There is an overnight train to Vienna which leaves from here once a day. From there, you can catch another one heading into Czechoslovakia.'

Ritter looked at his watch. 'That train has already left,' he said.

'Then you will leave tomorrow,' announced Dasch. 'Ritter will make the arrangements. Now, if it is possible.'

Ritter nodded sharply, spun on his heel and walked out. The engine of the Tatra fired up. The glare of headlights swept across the wall and then Ritter was gone, leaving Dasch and Carter alone in the room.

'Are you sure Teresa will agree to go?' asked Carter. Some part of him hoped that she might still refuse.

'She will,' Dasch assured him, 'if not for my sake then for yours.'

'What do you mean by that?' asked Carter.

'In spite of everything she says, and all those scowling looks, Teresa has grown fond of you.' Dasch tapped a finger against his temple. 'I know how her mind works, you see.' Now he held out his hand towards the corridor, at the end of which stood the dining room. 'Will you join us for dinner?' he asked. 'A little company might help defuse the situation.'

Carter suddenly realised how hungry he was.

The two men walked down the hallway, stepping over shards of crockery from the thrown plate. In the dining room, they found Teresa laying out plates for their meal. She did not speak to them, or even acknowledge that they were in the room.

Dasch seemed to be expecting this. He made no attempt to coax her into conversation, which even Carter knew would only have made things worse. Instead, Dasch began to prepare the meal, as if no angry words had ever passed between them.

Carter imagined that he might at last catch sight of some of the luxury goods for which Dasch had become famous. But there was none of that. Instead, from one of the cupboards, he produced a head of garlic, rustling in its papery white skin, a bowl of eggs and a few potatoes, which even the most humble of households could have purchased in the markets of Cologne.

Next, Dasch took a knife out of the drawer and honed it with long, precise strokes against a sharpening rod.

Carter watched in quiet admiration as Dasch began chopping the garlic upon a little wooden board, the tips of his fingers only a hair's breadth from the blade.

Dasch lit the stove and melted butter in a pan. He whisked the eggs and poured them in.

In a few minutes, he had made a large omelette, which he sectioned into three pieces and slid onto the plates.

Teresa had brought out a bottle of white Mosel wine from the Black Cat vineyard down in Zell. She poured it into the tin cups, which were the only things they had from which to drink.

They sat down at the bare wooden table.

'You are full of surprises,' said Carter.

Dasch grinned and picked up a fork. 'Eat,' he commanded, 'before it gets cold.'

With his first mouthful, Carter thought back to what the chef at Logan's had told him during one of his summers working as a dish washer: *You want to know if a chef can really cook? Just get them to fry you an egg. You can eat eggs all your life and never know for sure how they can taste until a good chef cooks them up for you.*

And here, in this dingy little hut on a rusted enamel plate, was proof of what the chef had told him. Now Carter stared in amazement at his plate.

Teresa still wasn't speaking, so they sat there saying nothing, the only sound the scrape of the forks on the plates and the splash in their mugs of the sharp, sweet wine. But it was not an uncomfortable silence. It seemed clear to Carter that Dasch and Teresa were used to it, perhaps that they even preferred it, and this was such a contrast to the rapid chatter Carter had come to expect from Dasch that he realised it was the first moment in which he had actually seen them as they really were.

At last, Dasch pushed his plate away and settled back into his chair. From around his neck he pulled a leather cord, from which dangled something small and glittery. He set it down upon the table before Teresa. Looped onto the cord was a gold ring fitted with a single lozenge-shaped diamond. 'I suppose you had better wear this,' he said.

Teresa stared at it for a while. Then finally she spoke. 'Is that Mother's?' she asked.

'It is,' Dasch confirmed, 'but it will not be enough to convince anyone that the two of you are married.'

'Why not?' asked Teresa.

'Because first you must master the art of looking at him' – he waved his fork at Carter – 'as if the only thought in your head is not to shoot him and leave him for dead.'

She glanced at Carter and then back to her father. 'You ask a lot,' she said.

Ritter returned just as their meal was ending, bringing a file decorated with the logo of the Josef Schmieder travel bureau. 'I know a man who works for them,' he said. 'I had to wake him up. But it's all here. They are booked in for one night in the presidential suite at the Orlovsky hotel. Full meal plan. Unlimited access to the spas.'

Dasch took the file from Ritter's hand and opened it. He made approving grunts as he inspected the tickets. Then he lifted out the itinerary and squinted at the print. A frown appeared on his face, the creases to his forehead deepening as he read to the bottom of the page. Then he looked up suddenly and glared at Ritter. 'This is what it costs for a single night!' he shouted. 'Are you trying to bankrupt me, Ritter?'

'You told me to make the arrangements,' answered Ritter, 'and that is precisely what I did. They are on their honeymoon. It is the most magical time of their lives! Why would you settle for anything less?'

'Because it's not true!' wailed Dasch.

'And you would want people to know that?'

'Of course not,' spluttered Dasch.

Ritter leaned over the table and set one finger on the travel agent's file, as if to stop it from blowing away in an imaginary breeze. 'Then this is exactly as it should be.' He straightened up, indignant, but as he turned to leave he caught Carter's gaze. For a fraction of a second, Ritter arched one eyebrow and then, before anyone else could notice, his face returned to its usual stony self.

After the meal, Carter cycled back towards his apartment, the dynamo headlight casting a weak, wavering glow upon the dirt road. Arriving, he parked his bicycle next to the old staircase, but did not climb the stairs. Instead, he stepped back to where the alleyway connected with the street. For a while, he just stood there in the shadows, looking up and down the road. It was deserted. Clouds slipped past the gibbous moon, filling the street with a steely blue light and then snatching it away again. The cafe across the road, where he was due to meet with Eckberg, was dark and empty. He wondered if Eckberg was even going to make the rendezvous. Carter felt sick to his stomach at the thought of going behind Wilby's back, but the man had given him no choice.

Carter dashed across the street and into the alley that ran behind the cafe. He came around the corner, next to a row of garbage cans set out behind the building, and almost collided with Eckberg. It took Carter a moment to realise that Eckberg was holding a gun.

'Right on time,' said Eckberg, tucking the pistol back into his jacket.

'Are you sure about this place?' asked Carter.

Eckberg dangled a key on the end of his finger. 'I guess we'll find out.' He opened the back door, which was plated with iron, and the two men stepped inside.

The air was still and greasy-smelling. The chairs had been stacked on the tables. Carter could see out into the street, where the cobblestones were outlined with moonlight.

Eckberg showed him to a small table at which the employees could take their breaks. The only light came from the pilot on the grill used for cooking the sausages. It was enough to cast a pale, orangey glow across the faces of the men.

'So somebody got hurt,' said Eckberg.

'Before I tell you anything,' replied Carter, 'I need to know that the station chief has approved my talking to you.'

'I told you he did.'

'And he knows you're talking to me now?'

'You want to call him?' asked Eckberg. 'There's a payphone down the street. How much time have you got?'

'Not enough,' admitted Carter. 'I was just making sure. I don't know what this is going to do to Wilby.'

Eckberg breathed out sharply. 'Look, Carter, you need to stop thinking about him and start worrying about yourself.

Whatever happens to Wilby he has brought upon himself by withholding information from people he's supposed to be working with. Not just me. I'm the low man on the totem pole. He can cut me out of the loop if he wants. But the station chief – that's another matter altogether. Nobody's faulting you for anything.'

'When Wilby finds out, he will.'

'But he isn't going to,' insisted Eckberg. 'In fact, it's very important that you don't mention any of this to him. That's for your own security. He's still running this operation. If he finds out that we suspect him, either of not sharing information or, even worse, of leaking it, that could jeopardise the whole station. So until you hear otherwise, the station chief's orders are for you to carry on as if everything is fine between the two of you.'

'It's never been fine. You know that.'

'Well, as normal as it's ever been – you understand?'

'All right. So how much do you need to know?'

'I'll take whatever you've got,' replied Eckberg, 'starting with the reason you called me.'

Carter sat back in his chair and drummed his fingers lightly on the table. 'How much do you know about Galton?' he asked.

'Who?' Eckberg narrowed his eyes.

'Sergeant Galton, the guy Wilby set me up with for the purchase of black market goods.'

Eckberg shook his head. 'I guess you'd better start from the beginning.'

So Carter told him everything – about Galton, about the

plane with its cargo of whisky and counterfeit currency, and then about the meeting with Garlinsky.

While he listened, Eckberg cupped his hands over his mouth and nose, struggling to take in all that he was hearing.

As Carter spoke, he heard the muffled rustling of Eckberg's breath, like a deep-sea diver sucking in air through a tube.

'The thing is,' said Carter, 'I think Garlinsky knows I am aware of the counterfeit currency.'

Eckberg lowered his hands to the table. 'What makes you say that?' he asked.

'He specifically asked for me to be the one who travelled to Karlovy Vary.'

'Did he give a reason for that?'

'Yes,' admitted Carter. 'Something about Ritter being wanted for war crimes by the Russians, and Dasch himself is convinced that the German police are monitoring his movements. Or at least that they are trying to.'

'He's probably right,' said Eckberg. 'So that makes you the obvious choice.'

'I guess. I don't know. It didn't seem that way to me.'

'You're starting to sound as paranoid as Wilby, for Christ's sake.'

'What if Wilby leaked the information?'

'Well, that's why you're talking to me now, isn't it?' said Eckberg. 'When do you leave for Karlovy?'

'We leave tomorrow,' said Carter.

'Who is "we"?' he asked.

266

'I'm travelling with his daughter, Teresa. Dasch has made it up to look like we are newlyweds.'

'And when you get there?'

'I find the wreckage and make sure no trace remains of the money. Teresa doesn't even know why she's going, only that it is important, and she is smart enough to know what questions not to ask.'

'You know where the plane is?' asked Eckberg. 'Where exactly, I mean? Otherwise you could be out there for weeks trying to locate it.'

'There's an old runway from before the war, somewhere east of the town. I have a map which shows where it's supposed to be. Garlinsky said the plane overshot and crashed into the woods just beyond it.'

'Does Wilby know about this?'

'Not yet. I was going to set up a meeting for tomorrow.'

Eckberg looked at his watch. Then he sighed. 'You'd better get going,' he said. 'The last dead drop check is at midnight. That gives you a little over an hour. Do you think you can get there in time?'

'If the wheels don't fall off my bike, I should be fine.'

They made their way back into the alley and Eckberg locked the door behind them.

'You did the right thing, coming to me,' said Eckberg.

'I wish it felt that way.'

Eckberg took hold of Carter's arm and shook him gently. 'Listen to me,' he said. 'You know as well as I do that nothing ever goes according to plan. It's how you react to things going wrong that determines whether you succeed or fail. And I'm telling you, whether it feels right to you or not, you're part of the solution now.'

'Did they teach you how to give that kind of pep talk,' asked Carter, 'or is that something you picked up on your own?'

'That's not something you can teach.' Eckberg smiled reassuringly. 'We all have to learn it the hard way.'

Carter wondered what he meant by that, but there was no time to ask.

Eckberg slipped away into the dark.

Carter climbed onto his bicycle and started riding.

It was almost midnight by the time he reached the alleyway behind Maximinenstrasse, just outside the Cologne central station. The local trains had ceased operating for the night, but there were still passengers on the platforms waiting for the overnight express trains that would take them to Paris, Brussels or Rome. The place for the dead drop had been well chosen, since there were always people coming and going in the area around the station and the alleyway was lit by a single streetlamp jutting from the wall of a brick building that formed one side of it.

Carter climbed off his bicycle and pushed it through the alley, since there was a couple approaching from the other side and not enough room for him to cycle past them.

The couple were laughing and speaking in hushed voices. From the sway in the man's walk, Carter judged him to be drunk. There were many bars around the station, some of them little more than collections of tables and chairs under half-collapsed roofs, but even these had their charm and also loyal customers. During his time in this country, one thing Carter had always marvelled at was the fact that, even when almost nothing else was available, you could always get a decent glass of beer.

He knew he would have to pass the couple and then double back to the dead drop. He had already written the note, and it would only take him a couple of seconds to stash it behind the brick. What occupied his thoughts was the possibility that no one would get to the drop before it was time for him to leave. If that happened, Wilby would not be there for the meeting, which Carter had scheduled for 11 a.m. the following morning. They had never discussed what to do under such circumstances. Without Wilby's permission, Carter didn't know if he was supposed to follow through with Dasch's plan or to abandon it completely and disappear. Carter knew that if he did not guess correctly, he would find himself in a world of trouble – with Dasch, with Wilby or with both of them.

The couple were passing by, heads lowered, muttering to each other in voices too low for Carter to hear.

Carter was already looking past them, trying to spot the loose brick in the wall somewhere up ahead.

At that moment, the man weaved towards him, and Carter had to turn the front wheel of his bike to avoid crashing into the couple. The man moved suddenly, as if to right himself, and then Carter felt a deep, wrenching pain in the side of his head. Blackness flooded through his eyes and he stumbled back, still trying to keep hold of the bicycle. He hit the wall and tried to stay on his feet, but only slid down onto his haunches, finally letting go of the bike, which crashed to the ground.

Suddenly, the man and the woman were standing over him. They hauled him upright and, with one on either side of him, began to drag him down the alleyway in the direction from which they had come.

Dimly, Carter grasped what was happening, but he was so dazed that he could not find the strength to fight back. His nose was bleeding.

A car pulled up at the end of the alleyway, its engine revving loudly.

Carter tried to wrench himself free but the man hit him again, this time on the top of the head, and from the sound it made, Carter could tell that the man was wearing a set of iron knuckles. The streetlamp's orange-yellow blurred and spread across his vision, as if his eyes were filled with oil. He knew that he was passing out. The light began to tunnel, closing to a single point of clarity and, just as that was about to disappear, the couple dropped him on his face.

At first, Carter wondered if he had been dumped in the trunk of the car, but then he realised he was still in the alley. Someone fell to the ground just beside him. Blearily, he saw the face of the woman. Her front teeth had been smashed out and her upper lip was split all the way to her nostril. She rolled onto her back and groaned, pale hands reaching to her face. Someone stepped on Carter, a heel digging into his back, and then he heard a soft and heavy thump and the harsh, barking sound of a man getting the wind knocked from his lungs.

Once more, Carter was lifted to his feet by a man he now recognised as Wilby, and who seemed to have appeared out of nowhere.

The driver climbed out of the car and started coming down the alley towards them, moving cautiously since his view was obscured by the streetlamp that stood between him and the others.

Wilby pulled a gun from his shoulder holster. He aimed it at the man.

The driver stopped.

Wilby set his thumb on the hammer and cocked it.

The man's arms moved slowly outwards from his sides. He backed up, then got into the car and drove away.

Carter looked down and saw the couple. The man had been rammed head first into the wall. He lay face down and unconscious. The woman was spluttering with a mouthful of blood and broken teeth. She had rolled onto her stomach and was trying to get up. She had got as far as her hands and knees before Wilby kicked her underneath the jaw, swinging his leg like a football player making a field goal. The blow lifted the woman up and she came to rest in a sitting position with her back against the wall, her head lolling so grotesquely sideways that Carter thought her neck must be broken.

Leaving the bicycle where it lay, Wilby wrapped Carter's arm around his shoulder and ran with him down to the far end of the alley. Carter tried to run along, but mostly his toes just dragged along the ground. They kept moving for some time, past the cathedral to Bechergasse and from there down side streets to Frankenwerft, which ran along the west bank of the Rhine. There, Wilby helped Carter into the ruins of a building and they both collapsed in the dirt, exhausted.

'Can you hear me?' gasped Wilby.

'Yes.'

'How badly are you hurt? Can you tell?'

'Nothing's broken. I think I'll be all right. Who were those people?'

'I don't know,' answered Wilby, 'but whoever they are, they weren't just mugging you for your wallet. They were planning on taking you with them. They might have guessed you were an American and figured they could hold you for ransom. That's happened before in this town. The only other possibility is that your cover has been blown. Do you have any reason to suspect that?'

'No,' said Carter. 'There's nothing I've seen to make me think so.'

A car drove past out on the road, and both men held their breaths in case it stopped. But the car kept going.

'I spotted you when you went into the alley,' said Wilby, 'and I was going to wait until you'd left before I checked the drop. But then I saw what happened and came running. Lucky for you.'

Carter told him about the meeting with Garlinsky, as well as Dasch's plan to send him and Teresa into Czechoslovakia.

'I hate to say it,' said Wilby, 'but I think Garlinsky is right. If the Russians find that money before you have a chance to destroy it, and if they figure out that he's the one who made it, they'll come after him and whoever he works for with everything they've got.'

'Then shouldn't you just let the Russians find it?' asked Carter.

'The problem,' said Wilby, 'is that they aren't just going to blame Garlinsky. That money went down in a military plane. They're going to convince themselves we are involved. And when that happens, they're not going to sit back and do nothing. This kind of thing will be answered, and the Russians can be very heavy handed when it comes to that. We're already in a war. It's just a question of what kind of war we're fighting. So far, we have managed to avoid firing artillery at each other, but this kind of thing could change that. You never quite know what straw is going to break the camel's back.'

'So what do you want me to do?' asked Carter.

'I want you to do exactly what Garlinsky said. Find the plane. Destroy it. Make sure there's nothing left behind that could lead the Russians back to Dasch or Garlinsky, but not before you've gathered enough evidence to make sure we can track down Garlinsky ourselves.'

'Shouldn't you send in a team of experts for this?'

'Of course, and if I had a month to set it up, or even a week, I might be able to do that, but we have less than twenty-four hours. Besides, if I pull you out now, it won't take more than a few minutes for Dasch and Garlinsky to figure out you're either on your way to the authorities or already working for them, and they'll shut everything down and vanish in the wind and we'll never find them again. It will be as if they had never existed, and everything you have suffered through to get this far will have been

273

for nothing – less than nothing because of how close you got us to the truth. But if you follow through with what they're asking, if you accomplish the task and make them think they're in the clear again, you will have done for them what they could not do for themselves. And they will reward you for that.'

'How?'

'By opening doors you never knew existed and behind which you will see the true face of our enemy. An opportunity like this will never come again, and we cannot walk away from it.'

'All right,' said Carter, and he started to rise to his feet.

'Not so fast,' Wilby told him. 'We're not done here yet.'

'What's wrong?' asked Carter, as he settled back into the dirt.

'I can't let you go without the approval of the station chief.'

It surprised Carter to hear Wilby say this. 'I thought you were keeping this whole thing under wraps.'

'I was,' Wilby admitted. 'Parts of it, anyway. And I told you why, as well. I don't believe the station is secure.'

'So what's changed?' asked Carter.

'This isn't the same mission we began. It's too big to keep in the dark. So even if there's a risk involved, it's one I've got to take. That *we* have to take.'

I wonder if Eckberg was wrong about you, thought Carter. *I wonder if I was, as well.* And suddenly he wished he'd never doubted the man who crouched beside him in the dark. 'So get the approval,' he said.

'It's not that simple,' replied Wilby. 'The station chief is going to have questions, not all of which I can answer, and we don't have time for me to act as go-between, relaying messages back and forth. That could take days, or even weeks.'

'That train pulls out tomorrow evening.'

'I'll set up an emergency meeting for tomorrow morning at the safe house on Nassaustrasse. Do you remember the house number?'

'One hundred and six.'

'That's it,' said Wilby. 'I'll call the meeting for nine. In the meantime, don't go back to your apartment. It's not safe. Do you think you can bed down here for the night?'

Carter looked around. He could see stars through gaps in the roof. 'It's not exactly the Hotel Europa,' he said.

'I told you to enjoy that while you could.' Wilby slapped him on the shoulder, then stood and headed for the gap in the wall.

'Thank you,' said Carter.

Those words stopped Wilby cold. He turned around. 'That's not something I expected to hear out of you.'

Carter shrugged. 'It kind of surprised me as well.'

'Don't get all sentimental on me now,' said Wilby. Then he slipped out into the street.

Carter glanced at his watch, but the crystal had been broken in the fight and it was no longer working. He took it off and put it in his pocket. It couldn't be long until dawn. He felt the cold now, seeping in through the neck of his shirt and slithering down his back. A dusty, metallic odour filled

Carter's lungs, the same as in the house where Ritter had almost blown his brains out on the first day they met. What had Dasch called it? The smell of the war? Something like that. And he had been right. Once you smelled it, you never forgot what it was. And from then on it would always be there, lurking in your blood.

Carter woke to the sound of somebody slamming a door.

He opened his eyes.

It took him a moment to remember where he was.

The morning sun was shining on his face, streaming down in bolts through the lopsided mosaic of slate tiles which were all that remained of the roof in the ruined building where he'd spent the night.

Out in the street, people passed by on their way to work. Beyond them, he saw a barge making its way down the Rhine. Some of the people had stopped and were looking across the river at something.

Carter lifted himself up on one elbow. His joints felt stiff and the side of his body that had rested on the ground was numb with cold. He staggered to his feet and wandered about in the ruins until he came to a puddle of water. There, Carter tidied himself up as best he could, crouching down on his haunches and washing the dried blood from his face where the man in the alley had hit him. Then he wetted his hair and smoothed it back, combing it through with his fingers. He slapped the dirt off his clothes and made sure his buttons were fastened. There wasn't much else he could do.

A moment later, he stepped out of the ruined building and joined the flow of people. A number were still looking out across the river and, when he followed their gaze, Carter could see a plume of black smoke rising from among the buildings on the other side of the Deutzer bridge.

'What happened?' Carter asked a man who was shielding his eyes from the sun with a newspaper so that he could get a better view.

The man turned to Carter. '*Keine Ahnung*,' he replied. No idea.

'It was a crash,' said a woman. 'Somebody told me there was an accident between a streetcar and a bus.'

'That was bound to happen,' said the man, 'the way those streetcars race around.'

'Could you tell me the time?' asked Carter.

The man reached into his vest pocket and hauled out a pocket watch on a chain. 'Twenty minutes past nine,' he said.

Carter swore quietly, realising that he was already late for the meeting. He thanked the man and crossed the road, making his way as quickly as he could towards the bridge, where tramcars rushed by in both directions, punching the air as they swept past. The pedestrian walkway was jammed with people pushing bicycles and others who, still seeming half asleep, plodded unhurriedly towards their jobs.

Carter weaved among them, trying to make up for lost time. As soon as he was across the bridge, he veered off onto Constantinstrasse and from there onto Grembergerstrasse.

The smoke from the crash was still in the sky and Carter heard the clang of fire truck bells coming from the same direction. Carter imagined how it must have looked after the air raids during the war, with smoke rising not just from one fire but from hundreds scattered across the city.

Turning off Grembergerstrasse, Carter realised that the crash had taken place on Nassaustrasse, the same street where the meeting was taking place. Several fire trucks were blocking the road and hoses were being unravelled by men in black helmets with large, silver comb-shaped fittings on the top, which reminded Carter of the helmets worn by French soldiers in the First World War. Blue lights jutted from the roofs of the green fire trucks, flashing a quick, pulsing rhythm, as if sending out messages in code.

As Carter walked towards the fire trucks, peering into doorways for the house numbers as he searched for 106, he realised that the crash had caused one of the buildings up the street to catch fire and it was this that the firemen were battling now. But the closer he came, the less sense the picture made to him. He could not see the streetcar anywhere, or the bus with which it was supposed to have collided. He was only a hundred paces from the first of the fire trucks before he finally realised that there was no streetcar and no bus, either. The woman had been mistaken. Only the house had been damaged. The whole front of it had collapsed.

The air was thick with oily smelling smoke and feathers of ash rained down upon the heads and shoulders of the spectators. The police had cordoned off the area and a small crowd had gathered to watch. With bronze-tipped hoses, firemen sprayed jets of water at the smouldering wreckage.

'It was a bomb, they think,' said a woman next to Carter.

She wore a housedress and an apron and her hair was bundled in a cotton headscarf.

'A bomb?' asked Carter.

'From the war,' she explained. 'A bomb that didn't go off. There are hundreds of them all over the city. They went right into the ground – deep, deep, some of them – and there they lie until something comes along to wake them up. It might have been a streetcar going overhead. It might have been anything. But there' – she held out a hand towards the burning house – 'is what has come of it.'

'I don't think that's what it was,' said another woman. She was holding a child in one arm. His fat little legs dangled down around her waist. The child made no sound, content simply to stare at the spectacle of the trucks and the firemen and the gushing arcs of water. 'I saw the explosion from my house across the street,' the woman continued, 'and it came out of the second floor. If it was a bomb from the war, it would have come up from below the road.'

'I don't know,' said the woman in the headscarf. 'Anyway, the whole place is gone now, so I guess it doesn't matter how it happened.'

'What number house is it?' asked Carter.

'That's 106,' replied the woman, 'and thank God the owners are never around. I don't think I've ever even seen them.'

Before the shock could settle in his bones, Carter watched as a body was carried out of the wreckage on a stretcher. It had been partially concealed with a blanket. The fact that the head was covered left Carter in no doubt that the person was dead. The two firemen who carried the stretcher were pasted with whitish-grey dust. As they moved towards a waiting ambulance, the blanket slipped away.

As they glimpsed the corpse, a kind of groaning sigh went up from the onlookers.

Carter could see at once that it was Wilby. The front of his head, from the eyebrows upwards, had been completely crushed. Blood from his ears and his mouth had mingled with the dust, forming a frothy crust upon his face.

One of the firemen paused and made as if to put down his end of the stretcher in order to replace the blanket, but his companion put a stop to that with one short, sharp command, and they carried on to the ambulance, which was only another few paces. They slid the stretcher inside and the double doors at the back of the ambulance were immediately slammed shut. The ambulance departed, its bell clanging, towards the Hohenzollern bridge, which would take it, eventually, to the Lindenburg hospital on the other side of the river.

'Was there no one else?' Carter asked a policeman, who stood with shoulders squared, holding back the crowd by force of will alone.

'Who knows?' replied the policeman. 'It will take them a week to dig through that mess.'

With bile rising in his throat, Carter turned and stumbled away down the street, until he came to the Kalk train station on Gottfriedhagenstrasse. There, he found a phone booth cubicle and shut himself inside. He put in a call to Bonn station.

A woman answered. 'Embassy,' she said.

'I need to speak to Eckberg.'

'Who is calling, please?' she asked.

'You can tell him it's Carter. Please hurry. It's important.'

There was a pause. 'I'm afraid the person you are asking to speak with isn't here right now. If you would like to come to the embassy, I'm sure we can find someone who will help.'

Carter hung up the phone. He breathed in the smell of stale cigarette smoke that had sunk into the cramped walls of the booth, and stared without seeing at the calling cards of prostitutes, jammed between the wall and the metal coin receiver of the phone. Carter wondered if Eckberg was dead. Maybe the station chief, too. Both of them could have gone to that meeting at the safe house. Until he found out otherwise, it only made sense to assume that they were gone.

Only one thing seemed perfectly clear – that the explosion was no accident. Whoever set the charge must have known about the meeting, and also who would be there. That information must have come from somewhere inside Bonn station, after Wilby broke with his own protocol to keep everyone else in the dark. So Wilby had been right all along. The station had been compromised, which also explained what had happened in the alleyway the night before. Only someone with access to the inner working of the station could have known the location of the dead drop.

Without any idea of where he was going, only that he needed to put some distance between himself and the ruins of the safe house, Carter wandered down Am Grauen Stein road until he came to the Deutzer cemetery, its wide expanse bristling with tombstones and the occasional stone angel, arms held out as if waiting for raindrops to fall into their palms. Carter turned into the cemetery and walked among the graves until he found a bench, shaded by the serrated green leaves of a horse chestnut tree. He sat down and tried to think straight.

Carter realised that there was nowhere for him to go where he knew he could be safe. There had been no plan for this eventuality. None of the escape routes, which had been put in place in case anything went wrong, could be trusted anymore. As far as the rest of the world was concerned, the cover under which he had been living, as an ex-soldier working on the black market, was not a mask at all but his actual identity. He had no documents or contacts he could trust which might prove otherwise. For that, he had relied entirely on Wilby. The station chief might have been able to vouch for him, and maybe Eckberg, too, but both of those men were probably dead now, which left Carter out in the cold.

The tornado of these fears whirled in Carter's mind, so vast and deafening that he pressed his hands to the side of his head, as if to stop the debris of his panic crashing like shrapnel through the walls of his skull.

Eventually, Carter managed to force aside his confusion long enough to remember what Wilby had said to him the night before – that everything he had suffered through would be for nothing if he bailed out now. If he ran, he knew he'd be running for the rest of his life, which probably wouldn't last long, since the way things stood right now he didn't even know who he was running from. The only people he could trust now were the ones he'd been sent to betray.

That night, Carter and Teresa boarded the overnight train to Vienna.

Cologne central station was busy, with porters wheeling trunks of luggage towards the baggage car and people milling around with tickets in their hands, looking for which wagon to board. The lights were yellowy and glaring and the sweaty smell of steam from the locomotives mixed with a haze of cigarette smoke. Conductors prowled the platforms, whistles clamped between their teeth and flag batons gripped in their fists. Policemen, armed with submachine guns held against their chests, strolled about in pairs.

Carter carried a suitcase full of new clothes. It was all that he owned in the world.

Teresa wore a dress and high-heeled shoes, and a long coat tied with a belt. Her dark hair was shining in the station platform lights.

Carter looked at her. It was the first time he had seen her in a dress. 'Shut up,' she told him.

'I didn't say anything!'

'That was for what you were thinking,' she replied.

Dasch had come to see them off. Unapologetically, he stared.

Finally Teresa turned to him. 'What is it?' she demanded.

'Well, I . . .' Dasch began. 'I was just going to say . . .'

'Yes?'

'That you are a beautiful couple.'

She stared at him incredulously.

Dasch ignored the glance. He put one hand on each of their shoulders. 'When you arrive in Carlsbad,' he said, 'if it is possible, and without forgetting what you're going there to do, or how much I am paying for all this, try to find a moment when the weight of the world isn't resting on your shoulders.' Without another word, he turned and walked away.

Both Carter and Teresa became suddenly aware that they were alone now.

Whistles blew along the platform.

A conductor leaned out of a carriage doorway and shouted, '*Alle einsteigen!*'

'I guess maybe we should get on board,' said Carter. His words came out faint and hollow, like a voice almost lost in the static of a poorly tuned radio.

'Where is that cocky American confidence now?' she asked.

'Same place you left your trousers,' Carter replied. Then before she could say anything else he held out his hand, and to his surprise she took it without sarcasm or reluctance and they climbed on board the train.

A barrel-chested porter, wearing a dark blue uniform with silver buttons, picked up their bags and escorted them to their private compartment in one of the first class carriages. There, he accepted the bills Carter awkwardly stuffed into his hand, and delivered the bags to the first class steward, a slightly built man with a small potbelly and a narrow face, who moved effortlessly in the cramped space of the train.

Carter, meanwhile, seemed to be banging his elbows into

284

everything he passed and felt the narrow space of the corridor close in as if it were shrinking around him with every step he took.

The steward swung open the door to their compartment, revealing a small room with a window at one end, a table, whose surface was taken up mostly by a lamp with a red shade, and a couch that spanned the length of one wall. The other wall was panelled with mahogany veneer and had a gold-framed mirror in the centre.

Realising that this couch would fold down into their bed, Carter immediately broke out in a sweat. He had imagined that there might be some kind of bunk arrangement, since that was the only type of bedding he had ever seen on trains before, but he had never travelled first class.

Their bags were placed upon a railing that ran along the length of the opposite wall and was fitted with a net in which the suitcases could rest without sliding around.

'Dinner will be served in half an hour,' said the steward.

Carter reached for his wallet, ready to tip the man just as he had tipped the one before.

With one sharp, commanding movement, the steward held up one hand, keeping it close to his body. 'It is not necessary,' he said quietly.

Carter felt the sweat run down his face.

The steward left, closing the door behind him.

For the first time since they had entered the compartment, Carter looked at Teresa.

She was smiling at him.

'What?' he asked.

'You seem uncomfortable.'

'I am!' he almost shouted. He wanted to tell her that he had spent the previous night in a bombed-out building and that he had slept well, so well that it had saved his life, because a part of him knew he belonged there, on the ragged edges of humanity. But this rolling cell, with its cushions and delicately crenellated lampshade, was almost more than he could bear.

Whistles blew out on the platform again. They heard the sound of running footsteps. The train jolted as it began to move.

Teresa gave a short cry and tipped backwards onto the couch.

The lights of the station flickered past. A moment later, they slid into a sheath of darkness, fractured by the lights of houses that overlooked the tracks. Carter glanced around the compartment in case there was a chair somewhere that he might have missed. But there was no place to sit except beside her. Slowly, he lowered himself down, careful not to put himself too far away and also not too close.

Minutes passed.

Neither of them spoke.

Carter got up and opened the window to let in some air, but it was loud and cold and rain came in, so he closed it up again and took his seat once more.

'I suppose there is no point in my asking why we're on this honeymoon,' said Teresa.

The word 'honeymoon' rang like a gong in Carter's ears. He had already given up the struggle to conceal how he felt about Teresa. In spite of what Dasch had told him, it seemed an affection so entirely one-sided that any revelation of his feelings would only cause the walls to close on him completely, smothering him to death between the first class cushions, first class lamp and first class mahogany veneer. 'No,' he said. 'There would be no point in that.'

'Is it going to be dangerous?' she asked.

For the past few minutes Carter had been staring at his shoes, but now he looked up and the first thing he saw was her reflection in the mirror. 'It might,' he said to the reflection, 'but the fewer questions you ask now, the safer you will be.'

There was a sudden sharp, clattering sound, which made both of them jump. It was a moment before they realised that the steward was knocking on the door. 'Dinner is served,' he announced, his voice muffled through the polished wood. Then they heard him knocking on the next door down the corridor, and the one after that, telling them dinner was ready.

Carter and Teresa stood. It was really too small a place for them both to be standing at the same time and they had to shuffle past each other to get to the door. For a brief moment, as she stood directly in front of him, as close as partners in a waltz, he had to stop himself from looking her in the eye, convinced that she would know each thought that trampled through his mind.

The dining car had actual chairs, upholstered in red cloth with yellow piping, the same colour scheme as the exterior paint on the carriages. The tables had been set with white cloths and lamps that were the same as the ones in the compartment. Curtains gathered with silk bell ropes had been drawn back from the windows, even though there was almost nothing to see outside except the occasional cube of light from some window out there in the night.

They were shown to their table by a waiter in a short, white tunic who spoke only one word – champagne – in a way that seemed less like a question and more like a guarantee.

The dining car quickly filled up, mostly with couples, most of them older, and all of them, it seemed to Carter, well accustomed to the wealth of their surroundings. But they seemed happy and intent only on themselves and, for the first time since they had boarded the train, Carter felt the muscles in his shoulders begin to relax. He glanced up at Teresa.

There was a softness in her face and in her eyes which he had never seen before. 'You look very pretty,' he said, and he wondered where the hell those words had just come from.

'I'm glad you think so,' she told him. 'We are married, after all.'

'I didn't say it because of that,' he muttered hoarsely, as if his lungs were filled with smoke. 'I actually meant it.'

'Well, I'm still glad,' she replied.

He picked up the heavy silver cutlery and weighed it in his hands. 'I don't know if I could ever get used to this.'

'And you think I could?' she asked.

'Yes, actually, with all the caviar your father must have heaped upon your plate.'

She shrugged and shook her head. 'I never saw it. He

made sure of that. He never much cared for it himself. His tastes were always simpler than those of the people with whom he was dealing.'

'Well, for a man with simple tastes,' said Carter, 'he can cook one hell of an omelette.'

'He would be pleased to hear you say so.'

'Where did he learn to do that?' asked Carter.

'He was a chef,' she replied, 'and the people for whom he cooked had tastes even simpler than his.'

'How does a man go from that place to where he is now?'

'Why don't you ask him yourself?'

'He isn't here.'

'There's no short answer.'

'We have plenty of time.'

'We do not speak of this,' she told him, her voice almost lost amidst the clatter of wheels on the tracks.

'I know.'

'So why are you asking me now?'

'Because if I don't ask now, the time will never come again, and then we will always be strangers.'

'And that matters to you?' she asked.

'I wish it didn't,' he said, 'but I can't help that now.'

She sighed and took up her purse, which was lying on the table beside her. It was black, rectangular and closed with two gold prongs that locked together with a twist. She opened the purse and removed a small, creased photograph, about two inches square, but she kept it hidden in her palm. 'Did it ever occur to you,' she asked, 'that afterwards you might wish you'd never known?'

'All the time.'

'And still you ask me.'

'Yes.'

She handed him the photograph. 'When you figure out that it's too late to undo what's been done, just remember I gave you the chance.'

Carter took the crumpled piece of paper and laid it on the table. It showed two men standing side by side on some kind of stone balcony, with snow-capped mountains in the distance. In front of them stood a girl in a dark skirt and white shirt with a thin scarf hanging down her chest. She was holding a bouquet of flowers. He recognised both men immediately. One of them was Dasch. He wore a white apron and what looked like grey checked trousers. In his hands, he clutched the tall white hat of a chef. He was smiling, but he looked afraid. The other man was Adolf Hitler, in a double-breasted jacket and black trousers. His face looked calm and serious. One hand rested on the shoulder of the girl. It took Carter another moment to grasp that this was Teresa. She looked so young, he barely recognised her. He looked up and caught Teresa's eye. 'When was this taken?' he asked.

'About 1936,' she replied. 'I must have been about twelve years old. My father cooked for Hitler and for those with whom he dined. That was his job. His only job. Hitler had a very specific and unusual diet. For breakfast, only milk and toast or little cakes. For lunch, only vegetables. For dinner, vegetables and rice or pasta. No alcohol. No tobacco. No coffee. Of course, even when these things became scarce, he could have had whatever he wanted. He also ate at odd hours. Breakfast at 1 a.m. Lunch at 4 p.m. Dinner whenever it pleased him. From the day he was hired in 1935, my father travelled with him everywhere. And in January 1945, when Hitler went down into his bunker in Berlin, my father went with him, while my mother and I lived in a house nearby. A few months later, Hitler died in that bunker but, long before then, my father had reached the conclusion that anyone who remained with him would end up dead as well.

'By the beginning of April, the Russians had begun shelling the city with their long-range artillery and air raids struck night and day. One morning, just after the all-clear sirens had sounded, my father showed up at the door of our house. He was wearing clothes I'd never seen before. He told my mother she had fifteen minutes to pack a bag and then we would be leaving. When she asked him where they would be going, he told her, "Anywhere but here." She asked where his clothes had come from and he told her he had pulled them off a dead man who had been caught outside in the air raid of the previous night. He had dressed the man in his own clothes and thrown him into a house that was on fire. Because he was a part of Hitler's private staff, my father had a special pass that allowed him to travel anywhere he wanted and by whatever means were available. By the end of that day, we were already far to the west. We were somewhere near Hanover when our train was attacked from the air. Royal Air Force planes fired rockets into the locomotive and shot bullets along the length of the carriages. The rear of the train exploded. It must have been carrying munitions. The whole train left the tracks and fell on its side. I remember seeing the ground rise up to meet us and the windows shattering. The next thing I knew, I was lying out in a field with my father standing over me. His jacket was smouldering. My hair had been burned. I could smell it. When I sat up, I could see that the whole train was on fire. A few people were walking around in the field, some of them terribly injured. My mother never made it out of the train.'

'I'm sorry,' said Carter.

'People always say that,' replied Teresa, 'and what they really mean is that they're sorry they asked. So are you sorry you asked, Mr Carter?'

'No,' he told her. 'Keep going.'

'When the fire died down,' she continued, 'my father went back into the wreckage of the train, found her body and carried her out, wrapped in a blanket. We buried her in the field. Until yesterday, I'd never known he took the ring from her finger. At the end of that day, trucks from a passing army convoy stopped and told us we could climb aboard. By then, my father had stolen the identity cards of a man who had died of his wounds. His name was Hanno Dasch. My own passbook had already been lost, but nobody cared as long as he had his.'

'So what is his real name? And yours?'

'None of that matters,' she said. 'Those people are dead now, and we should let them stay that way.'

'And who else knows about this?' asked Carter.

'No one,' she said. 'Aside from my father, only you.'

'Not even Ritter? I wouldn't think he'd object to what your father used to do.'

'It's not the job he'd mind. It's the fact that my father deserted. A man like Ritter sees the world in black and white. Each German soldier took an oath of loyalty, and for Ritter such things become a part of you, as real as the bones beneath your skin. It cannot be removed. It cannot be undone.'

'Not even at the end of the war?'

She shook her head. 'This might be hard for you to understand, but it has nothing to do with the war, or even the fact that Hitler is finally gone. An oath is a sacred thing. It is a line you have drawn in the sand. Break it, and the world dissolves into a pack of lies.'

Her words felt like needles jabbed into his flesh. This whole idea of loyalty, which men like Ritter thought of as their greatest strength, could be transformed by men like Carter into their greatest weakness without them even knowing what had changed. Carter thought of all the times that he had pierced through the armour of such people, just as he was doing now, and how he had learned to accept the collateral damage to those whose lives had been caught up in the crime rings he'd helped to break apart.

This time, it was different. Teresa was the only person he had ever met who had lived so long with her secrets that, like the oaths of Ritter's comrades, whose bones lay strewn across the Russian steppe, they had become a part of her. It seemed so unfair to Carter that the thing they had most in common he would never be able to reveal. He did not know the precise moment when he had begun to care about the woman who sat before him. If he had known, perhaps he might have been able to prevent it, and to strangle those emotions before they ever reached the surface of his mind. But it was too late now.

'On the day the war ended,' continued Teresa, 'we had passed through the Allied lines as refugees. We finally reached Cologne, and that was where my father began to reinvent himself as the man he has become.'

'But why did you pick Cologne?' asked Carter. 'The place was in ruins, after all.'

She smiled at him. 'Because that's where the treasure had been buried.'

'What treasure?'

'Everything he has been selling since the war ended. The champagne. The wine. The cigars.'

'He buried it?'

She laughed. 'No. Hitler did. He had ordered the construction of various fortresses scattered around the Reich. Some, like the one at Rastenburg he called the Wolf's Lair, were completed. Others, like one in the Alps he called the Giant, were never used, even though kilometres of tunnel had already been dug into the sides of the mountains. And some, like the underground complex Hitler had ordered to be constructed beneath the city of Cologne, were destroyed before they could ever be completed. My father never even knew of it until one evening late in the war, after Hitler had gone down into the bunker, bringing his entourage with him. My father was expected to cook for them, but he had trouble finding any ingredients. When my father apologised for the quality of the meal, Hitler remarked that if they had been in Cologne instead of Berlin, they could have had anything they wanted. He explained that the construction of a bunker complex beneath Cologne, similar to that in Berlin, had been permanently derailed by a single bomb which had fallen on the Eisengasse, causing all four levels of the complex to collapse.'

Carter thought of the crater where Galton had been shot, and he tried to imagine the tunnels and the rooms below, one crashing down into another as the Eisengasse was cremated above it.

'By the time the fires had burned out,' said Teresa, 'the builders of the Cologne complex decided that the damage was so severe it made no sense to re-start the excavation. Instead, they began work on a different fortress in Belgium and the Cologne project was forgotten. Or almost forgotten. Hitler told my father that night that an underground storage facility, which had been created to supply the Cologne bunker, had actually survived the bombing. He unrolled a great blueprint, which showed where the complex was located and how it would have looked if it had ever been completed. The entrance to the storage area had been blocked by rubble, but Hitler's engineers had confirmed that the contents had almost certainly remained intact. The plan was that at some point in the future it would all be retrieved, but for now it was safe and Hitler had other things on his mind. In the end, Hitler's engineers never reopened the storage facility. But my father did.

'It took him a month to locate the entrance and another month to dig his way down through the rubble, but finally he found his way inside. Until that moment, he wasn't even sure if Hitler had been right about the contents of the facility. He gambled everything on the chance that it might have been true, and it turned out he was right. He woke me in the middle of the night to tell me the good news. Until then, we had been living in an abandoned rail car in a siding not far from the field where the Eisengasse had once stood. We were starving. He led me out across the field and down into a tunnel, lighting the way with a candle in a jar. We came to a set of huge iron doors, one of which had been bent almost in half by the weight of stone that had come down upon it in the cave-in caused by the bomb. We stepped through into a huge room, and there I saw row after row of wine crates, food crates – tobacco, chocolate, canned fruit, canned vegetables. Anything you could have wanted was there. We sat down on the dusty floor, and my father opened up a tin of cherries and we ate them with our fingers. The next day, my father began selling small amounts of what he had found. Not too much, you understand. A bottle of wine. A box of cigars. The sort of thing any scavenger might turn up if he was lucky. Within a few weeks, he had bought a truck for moving things around the city. We rented a house. He bribed city officials to give him contracts transporting construction materials around. He bought more trucks. Within a year, he had become the most successful dealer in black market goods that this part of the country had ever seen.'

'But how did he do it?' asked Carter. 'The police raided

the compound. They searched the trucks dozens of times. Your father told me so himself, and they always went home empty-handed.'

'Because they were looking in the wrong place,' explained Teresa. 'He never used the trucks to move black market merchandise.'

'Then how?'

'The trains,' she said. 'On the far side of the Eisengasse, trains were constantly moving wagons through those sidings. That's how he did it, and they never thought to look.'

'Then why did he need me?' asked Carter. 'If he had it all worked out, why take the risk of bringing someone new on board?'

'He had to,' explained Teresa. 'The storage area was almost empty – at least the part that he could reach.'

'You mean there was more?'

'Yes,' said Teresa. 'Sometime after he first entered the storage area, my father discovered that there was actually a second adjoining area, connected by a steel door, behind which the ceiling had collapsed. The door frame had buckled and he couldn't open it, but he was convinced that more provisions had been stored there or perhaps even something more valuable. He had all sorts of theories – a temperature-controlled room for artworks, a cellar for the finest of the wines, a vault for precious gems. Or maybe nothing, an empty concrete space just filled with tons of dirt. It used to keep him awake at night. He once told me that if even half of what he had imagined lay behind that door was actually there, he could retire off the proceeds.

But it might as well have been on the moon, because he couldn't get to it and the fact was he needed a new source of products. As far as he was concerned, there was only one solution to that – the Americans. He knew they were unlikely to deal with him directly, so he needed a middleman, someone who understood how their minds worked and who could speak their language. And that's why my father picked you. He always said he had an instinct for knowing who to trust.'

Back in the sleeping car the bed had already been pulled down, and a flask of cocoa was set upon the little table, flanked by two cups upturned in their saucers, rattling faintly with the movement of the train.

'I'll sleep on the floor,' said Carter.

'No,' she told him, 'you won't.'

They sat down, side by side.

'I ask so many questions,' said Carter, 'but you ask almost none of me.'

'And you wonder why?' she replied.

'Of course.'

'Perhaps,' she said, 'it is because I am afraid you'd tell the truth, and that I could not bear to hear it.'

Hearing those words, Carter leaned forward, resting his elbows upon his knees and pressing his hands to his face, as if to stop his mask from crumbling to dust. Her hand rested softly on his shoulder. She was so close now. He could feel her presence like static in the air. 'I wish we weren't pretending,' he told her.

'We're not,' she whispered.

He looked up.

She kissed him before he could speak.

And the barricades that he had built to withstand any siege and splintering of bone began to slip and fall, dissolving back into the particles from which they'd been created, like the castles he had built as a child out of the gritty sand at Belmar, when they were swept away by the incoming tide.

*

It took another twenty-four hours to reach Karlovy Vary, passing through Vienna, where they boarded a much smaller train, and then changing again at Prague, travelling in carriages barely half the size of the ones in which they had begun their journey.

The town was nestled in a valley, surrounded on all sides by thickly wooded hills. Instinctively, Carter found himself looking for traces of where the war had left its scars upon the landscape, but he found none here. The sight of burned-out buildings, pyramids of rubble and the skeletons of tanks and trucks lying half buried in weeds beside the tracks had been such a constant until now that Carter felt as if they had travelled not just into a different land, but into a parallel universe where the war had never taken place, and where the lifeless stones still held the memory of those who had gone before.

Arriving at Karlovy, the locomotive groaned to a halt beneath a rusted metal roof that covered only one of the tracks. The station building was a sandy yellow colour, with scabs of plaster showing where the paint had peeled away. Although it looked run down, it seemed that way by choice, surrendering gracefully to time.

The cab that drove them to the Orlovsky hotel was a white Skoda with a narrow, curved front grille. 'Are you here for the cure?' asked the driver, as he motored through the narrow streets. He was a nervous-looking man who wore a knee-length canvas coat of the type drivers used to wear in open-topped cars. He sat very close to the wheel, hands gripping the top, and as he steered the Skoda along the narrow zigzag streets, his whole body swayed with the effort.

It was evening now and the tall houses, with their brick red roofs and the same dusty yellow paint as the station, glowed in the setting sun.

The architecture was so ornate and colourful, like something out of a child's picture book about fairytales, that to Carter it barely seemed real.

'The cure?' asked Teresa.

'The Karlovy Cure,' explained the man, with a stern patience that implied she must surely know about this but had simply forgotten in the moment. He talked quickly, as if the thoughts were piling up inside his head. 'It is a regimen of sulphur baths and water from our thermal springs. It was once named the Carlsbad Cure, which had a better ring to it, in my opinion, but the past is the past, and Karlovy Vary is what it's called today. Whatever the name, most people come here seeking to mend their broken and neglected constitutions. They have done for a thousand years and a thousand years from now, they'll still be coming here. Sometimes we can undo what has been done, but in spite of everything you see, we do not deal in miracles.' He studied them in his rear-view mirror. 'But I see you have not come here seeking those.'

'Not yet, anyway,' said Carter.

The driver pulled up in front of the hotel and carried their bags into the lobby. Giant potted ferns made an archway just inside the door and a red carpet stretched towards a wide stone staircase which twisted to the left, passing out of sight beneath a stained glass window depicting a stag look-ing at its own reflection in a forest pond. Sunlight passing through red and green and yellow chips of glass seemed to fill the air, as if a ghostly flock of birds were flying around the room.

The concierge at the desk was an elderly man with a stiff grey moustache and piercing whitish-blue eyes, like the eyes of a sled dog. He wore a red tunic with a collar buttoned tight against his throat and brass buttons emblazoned with the willow tree logo of the Orlovsky.

He watched the couple approach, his face unreadable.

Carter paid the cab driver, who touched the brim of his cap and walked out beneath the archway of ferns into the almost blinding summer light outside, as if passing into a different dimension.

Then Carter handed his reservations to the concierge.

The man studied the documents. Then suddenly he looked up, and his expression was so stern and fierce that Carter felt sure that something had gone terribly wrong.

But it was nothing like that.

'The Orlovsky welcomes you,' the concierge said solemnly.

He raised one arm above his head and snapped his fingers with a sound like cracking bones.

A porter appeared from a back room, buttoning his uniform as he dashed out to gather their bags.

Instead of going straight to their room, they walked out into the street and strolled along a boulevard beside the river that ran through the centre of the town. Rows of leafy trees sheltered benches on which people, some of them clearly very ill, sat and watched fountains of water rising from the shallow river. Music drifted from the cafes where some patrons, instead of wine, drank yellowy, sulphur-smelling water from glasses nestled in brass holders.

As Carter walked beside Teresa, his thoughts tripped back and forth with the relentlessness of a metronome between the work he had come here to do, along with all the danger that came with it, and the unmistakable sensation that he and Teresa had emerged from the lifeless twilight that they had once believed was the entire world into a hovering, in-between place where they were both dreaming the same dream – which was so real and yet so fragile that if either of them even breathed out of pace with the other, the whole thing would vanish like smoke and they would find themselves once more inside a cage of rust and rock.

There was a moment late that night after they had returned to their hotel when, half conscious in the gauzy veils of moonlight shining through the window, Carter felt himself falling away into the darkness which, for the first time in his life, he did not fear.

Carter woke at 5 a.m.

He sat up in bed and looked down at Teresa, still fast asleep beside him, and in that moment, seeing her hair spilled out across the pillow, he realised that he had fallen in love. Until this moment, there had been a part of him that still believed that, when the time came, he could walk away and simply add her to his tally of regrets. But the possibility of that had slipped away from him. Perhaps it was when she handed him the photograph. Perhaps when they were walking the streets the night before. And perhaps it had always been that way, from the moment he first saw her, and it had taken this long for him to admit it to himself. *You have either killed me or saved me*, he thought as he looked down upon her, *but I'm damned if I know which it is.*

He slipped from the bed and got dressed, careful that his belt buckle did not clink as he fastened it. He took the map that Ritter had given him, picked up his shoes and stepped out of the room, closing the door soundlessly behind him. Still moving carefully, as if across a sheet of ice, he made his way along the carpeted corridor to the stairs. There, he sat down and put on his shoes.

There was no one at the front desk as he passed through the foyer of the hotel. He opened one of the great double doors at the entrance and stepped out into the dove grey light before the dawn. Mist hung in tatters in the mountains. He looked at the map, turning it this way and that until he found his bearings. Then he set off towards the old airfield, six kilometres outside town. The streets were empty and at first he only walked, so as not to draw attention from anyone who might be looking from a window, but as soon as he cleared the last of the houses, he began to move more quickly. Soon he was running, not flat out but at a steady pace. The first rays of sunlight showed through the trees, lying across the road like scattered bolts of brass.

The road narrowed as it climbed into the hills, and the old map showed a turn-off to the south, which led to the airfield. But when he came to the place where the turn-off should have been, he found the path so overgrown that he felt sure it must lie further up ahead. He kept on, sweating through his shirt, his shoes unfit for the punishment they were taking. He went for another kilometre and then realised he had gone too far. Doubling back, he returned to what seemed to be the path, but whole trees with trunks as thick as his leg had grown up in the ruts where vehicles had once passed through. He knew he must be close, but the thought that he could spend hours searching for the last section of the path that would get him to the airfield sent a flutter of panic through his chest.

He set off down the overgrown trail, sweeping aside undergrowth as if he were swimming to his destination. The sun was up now, and mosquitoes whined around his face. He heard birds singing off in the forest and the chuntering of squirrels in the branches above his head.

Just at the moment when he thought he might have to turn back, he saw a clearing in the woods ahead. A minute later, he emerged onto the old runway. It had been tarmacked years ago and, although the surface was cracked and wavy, exposing a bedrock of concrete below, he saw at a glance that it was a well-chosen location. He walked out into the middle of the runway, his feet brushing through the hazy globes of dandelions that had grown up through fissures in the ground. After the closeness of the forest, Carter felt uneasy to be out there in the open. He made his way to the other side of the runway and skirted the edge from then on.

Garlinsky had said that the plane went down south of the runway, and that it had been on its final approach when that happened. Carter knew that the wreckage couldn't be too far, but the forest was so dense here that he might not see the aircraft until he was practically on top of it.

He forced himself to be calm, knowing that the work which lay ahead of him might take hours. He might not even find the plane in a day, in which case he would have to return and keep looking. He hoped it didn't come to that. The longer he spent out here, the more likely it was that he would be noticed, and yet still in the back of his mind was the nagging fear that the wreckage might already have been spotted and was being watched, in which case he would be walking right into a trap.

Carter pushed forward through the first screen of trees, which grew more thickly than those that lay deeper in the forest. The ground was uneven, with stones banked up by some ancient force and fallen trees blocking his path. Soon his clothes were filthy, smeared with dirt and streaks of frog-back green from the moss that grew on the rotted trunks.

It was almost half an hour before he found his first clue

that he might be heading in the right direction. A tall, spindly birch tree had been snapped off at a height of about twenty feet, leaving a pale gash of bark and branches.

A little further on, he came across two more broken trees and one of them bore traces of pale blue paint, which he realised must have come from the underside of the plane.

He moved more quickly now, oblivious to his torn shirt and the way his feet were sliding in the stretched-out leather of his shoes.

He almost ran right into the first piece of wreckage before he realised what it was. A large wheel, still attached to its strut, lay by itself, almost hidden among a tangle of young pine trees. A little further on, he glimpsed the forward section of the plane, the sloping shape of its nose reminding him of a whale he had once seen beached upon the Jersey shore when he was a child. The tail had broken off and lay to one side, exposing bare metal where it had torn away.

Carter stopped, panting. He had been so focused on finding the wreck that only now did it occur to him how difficult it might be to dispose of the cargo without drawing unwanted attention. His original idea had been to burn the money using fuel from the plane, if there was any, or the whisky itself to start the fire. But now he wondered if it might be better to bury the money instead, and avoid the risk of any smoke being spotted by somebody else in these hills.

Garlinsky's contacts had been right. The aircraft had not burned. Its fuel supply must have been exhausted by the time it crashed. It may even have been the reason for the crash.

The plane had nosed into the woods and come to an almost immediate halt against the tall maples and oaks that made up the surrounding forest. The front section had crumpled into the ground and several trees, snapped off nearly at ground level, had fallen over the cockpit. Carter could tell at a glance that if the pilot and co-pilot had been in their seats at the time of the crash, neither of them would have survived. Both wings had broken off. One port-side engine lay half buried in the ground and the starboard engine had torn loose, tumbling past the crash site until it had come to rest in the undergrowth. Now it was nothing more than a tangle of pipes, valves and an engine block already filmed with rust. Only the tail section had remained more or less intact. Most of the cargo had been thrown forward and lay crushed in a large pile where the broken-off section had slammed into the ground. Only a few of the crates had been disgorged from the severed mid-section. These had disintegrated into shards of wood and broken glass, some of which were now embedded in the nearby tree trunks. And now, almost buried amongst the carpet of dead leaves, ferns and moss-scabbed stones, he saw the mangled confetti of rouble notes. Here and there, stray bills, some of them torn to shreds, twitched in a breeze blowing through the tops of the trees.

Carter realised that very little of this crash could have been seen from the air. The camouflaged topside of the aircraft had been further concealed by a matting of leaves and branches torn loose from the surrounding trees. The plane had come in at such an angle, and must have been travelling so slowly when it crashed, that there was no scar of cleared vegetation that might otherwise have been visible if anyone had thought to look. Given how dense the forest was and the fact that he was far from any path, Carter thought it might be years before anyone stumbled across the plane, and even then they might ignore it as just another of the thousands of wrecked aircraft that lay scattered across Europe after the war. As Carter stepped around to the other side of the tail section, he came across a body spread-eagled and face down on the ground. He swore and stumbled backwards. He had tried to prepare himself for the sight of the dead crewmen, but it still caught him by surprise to find one of them lying here. A moment later, once the initial shock had passed, he realised that it wasn't one of the crewmen, after all. This man was not wearing flight gear. In fact, he was dressed in a pair of thick corduroy breeches, long woollen socks and a pair of hobnailed boots. He also wore a turtleneck sweater. It was the same kind of walking gear he had seen worn by people back in town.

As Carter struggled to piece together what a hiker could be doing this far from the path, he heard a twig crack behind him. Spinning around, he found himself face to face with a man who was holding a gun.

Carter recognised him, but he seemed so out of place that it took him a moment to grasp that this was the same man he had met at the American airbase in Dornheim, when Wilby first made him the offer, who had neither smiled nor said a word and whom Wilby had refused to identify, calling him a figment of Carter's imagination. He was even wearing the same tweed jacket, which barely contained the bulk of his muscular shoulders.

Carter knew that if the man had intended to kill him, he would already be dead. But that didn't mean he couldn't change his mind.

'I guess I didn't dream you up, after all,' said Carter, slowly raising his hands.

And then, to Carter's surprise, the man laughed. 'It's your lucky day,' he said, and put away the gun.

'Who are you?' asked Carter.

'My name is Babcock.'

'Colonel Babcock? The station chief at Bonn?'

'That's right.'

'I thought you were dead.'

'To paraphrase Mark Twain, that would be a slight exaggeration.'

'What are you doing here?'

'Well, first of all, keeping you alive,' replied Babcock, nodding at the body. He set his boot upon the man and rolled him over, revealing a face half masked with old pine needles that had stuck to his skin as he lay there on the ground.

Carter gasped. 'Jesus Christ,' he said. 'That's Eckberg!'

The dead man's eyes were half open, his teeth outlined in blood. A bullet had gone through his right cheekbone and blown out the back of his head. A piece of his skull, with a shred of skin and blond hair still attached, lay beside his outstretched arm, as if he had tried to catch that fragment of bone in the final moment of his life.

'He tried to dress himself up like a local,' said Babcock, 'but this guy never could figure out how to stop looking like an American. Now, as it turns out, he might not even be one, after all.'

'What are you talking about?'

'You spoke to him, didn't you?'

'Yes,' admitted Carter. 'He tracked me down. He told me you had concerns about Wilby, about how he might be falling apart. He said you had authorised me to tell him about the operation.'

Babcock sighed. 'Unfortunately, I never did that.'

Carter stared at the body. 'You mean he was the leak?'

'Yes,' said Babcock, 'and I wish I could say that we had our suspicions about him, but the truth is we had assumed it was one of the secretaries.'

'You mean the one who turned up dead?'

'That's right,' said Babcock. 'We thought she had committed suicide after realising that we were closing in on her. It now seems more likely that Eckberg killed her to throw us off the trace, and I'm ashamed to say that it worked. At least until today.'

'So he put the bomb in the safe house?'

'It might have been him. It might have been someone he works with. Either way, he's the reason Wilby is dead. It must have been on a timer, or else they would have waited for us to arrive.'

'But why did he do it at all?'

'Because as soon as he learned about that planeload of counterfeit money, he knew he had to stop you from getting to it first. That's why he tried to have you kidnapped in the alley behind the train station. If Wilby hadn't shown up, they'd be finding you in the reeds right about now, with a bullet in your skull. But you got away. Then, when Wilby informed us that he had set up a meeting at the safe house, he decided to get rid of all three of us at once. But that didn't go the way he had planned either and, by then, his cover was blown. As soon as that bomb went off, we knew who must have set it. The only choice he had left was to set out on his own and get here before you. And for once, he actually succeeded. He just didn't count on the fact that I would be here waiting for him when he arrived.'

'You knew he'd come?'

'I knew he had to try,' said Babcock.

'But why was it so important that he stop me from coming here? Surely the Russians would have wanted it destroyed.'

'This was their best chance of tracing the money back to the people who made it. They already knew that someone was producing high-grade counterfeit roubles. This wasn't the first load that had found its way into Russia. It was showing up all over the place, and they had a hunch that it was coming from somewhere in Europe. Of course, they assumed we were behind it. They just didn't have any proof. The fact is, we had nothing to do with it and, until you came across this man Garlinsky, we were no wiser than the Russians as to who it might be.'

'What about now?' Carter gestured at the tail section and the splintered mass of crates and broken bottles, from which the sour smell of whisky drifted through the air. 'Did you find anything that might help?'

'I'm afraid not,' sighed Babcock. 'We'll get them eventually, whoever made this stuff, but not today. Until this plane went down with half a million roubles stashed inside it, I had been inclined to let these counterfeiters carry on as they'd been doing. One day, the Russians would realise we weren't behind it, but between now and then, this whole thing was giving them a heart attack. And that made me very happy. But this crash, and the fact that the Russians know about it, thanks to Eckberg, has changed the whole equation.'

'What happens now?'

'To you?'

'That will do for a start,' said Carter.

'As far as I'm concerned, you are not here. An imaginary friend, if you will.'

'I don't understand.'

'Your contract with us as an Agent of Opportunity has been terminated. We no longer require your services. I'll leave the timing up to you, but all you have to do is put a call in to my office at Bonn station, give me the go-ahead and, as per our original agreement, an announcement will be made that you have been working undercover in western Europe, for which your dishonourable discharge was only a part of your cover. You will receive a public apology from the mayor of Elizabeth, New Jersey, as well as the governor. You will be reinstated into your old job, if you want it, and I seem to remember something about a parade.'

'You can skip that part.'

'As you wish.'

'What about Dasch?'

'I have nothing personal against the man. He was never

anything more than a symptom of human desire, without which crimes like his would not exist. Nor did I care about the goods themselves. Fine wine and liver pâté will not be the start of World War Three. But men who can get their hands on such luxuries, and who can move them so skilfully from one country to the next, will soon develop an appetite for more dangerous cargo. It was only a matter of time before Dasch started running guns, or even worse. That's why we were much more interested in his links to the criminal organisations in other European countries, and the government officials who helped him circumvent the borders.'

'There were no government officials,' said Carter, 'or any criminal organisations that helped him.'

Babcock stared at him. 'But that's impossible,' he said.

Carter told him about the underground depot in the ruins of the Eisengasse bunker complex.

'Son of a bitch,' said Babcock. 'Wilby had Dasch pegged for a genius.'

'I think Dasch knows he isn't one,' replied Carter, 'and that makes him smarter than all the people I've met who thought they were.'

'We have been chasing a mirage,' said Babcock. 'At least we were until Garlinsky showed up. Because this' – he held up a block of the counterfeit money – 'this is every bit as dangerous as guns.'

'So are you going after him?'

'No,' said Babcock. 'We'll make him come to us. We're going to make an announcement about the discovery of the plane and the counterfeit currency it was carrying. And then we're going to let Garlinsky finish what he started.'

'What do you mean?'

'Do you really think Garlinsky and whoever the hell he works for are going to wait around for someone to put together the pieces of where that plane came from, and all the money it was carrying? They're not going to take a risk like that. Since Dasch is the only person who can lead the Russian or the West German authorities back to them, they're going to make sure that can't happen. They're going to find him and they are going to shut him up. Dasch might not know it, but he's just bait for a trap now, like a goat tied up in a clearing. And when the wolf comes we'll be ready.'

'What about Teresa?'

'What about her?' muttered Babcock.

'She has nothing to do with it. She's asleep back at the hotel.'

'That saved her from me. If she had seen my face, Mr Carter, even if only for an instant, this would have ended differently. But that isn't going to save her from Garlinsky. The fact that she came on this journey, even if she didn't know why, is more than enough to get her killed.'

'You really think they'd do that?'

'They might. They might not. Who knows what rules they play by? But one thing is for sure – it's what I would do if I were them. It sounds to me like you might have a personal stake in this.'

'I might.'

'Wilby did warn you about her.'

'He tried. I'll give him that.'

'Well, I can't help you there,' said Babcock. 'You just have to get her back to Cologne, so that her father thinks she's safe and that his problems have been solved, and to get yourself out of there before we make the announcement about the counterfeit money and all hell breaks loose. Which it will, I guarantee you. Listen to me, Carter. You're almost there. Just keep your eyes on the finish line. Keep reminding yourself why you spent the last nine months in prison, not to mention almost getting yourself killed I don't know how many times. In one week, you can have your life back, just as we agreed.'

'I don't even know if she'll be there when I get to the hotel.'

'Then hurry,' Babcock told him. 'And I'll be waiting for your phone call.'

By the time Carter returned to the Orlovsky, he had cleaned himself up as best he could. He made his way through a staff entrance at the back.

He found Teresa sitting on the end of the bed.

She was dressed. Her bag was packed and sitting by her feet. 'You look like you'll need some new clothes,' she said.

He glanced down at the ruins of his suit. 'Yes,' he whispered.

'I didn't know if you were coming back.'

'Of course I was,' he said.

Teresa looked around the room and sighed. 'Do we really have to leave so soon?' she asked. 'I was just getting used to this place.'

Carter sat down on the bed beside her. 'There's one train a day, and it leaves in three hours. You know that we have to be on it.'

The journey took two days. They spoke very little, but the silence did not trouble them now as it had done before.

Babcock's words echoed relentlessly in Carter's head – that in one week he would have his life back, the way it had been before they took it. He thought about those months in Langsdorf prison. He thought about Ritter's gun aimed at his face and the sound of the iron knuckles when they made contact with his skull in the alleyway behind the train station. He looked at Teresa and told himself that none of what he felt for her was real. That it had never been real. It was simply what he had been forced to do. In one week, none of it would matter. He would look back on this chapter of his life as the time he almost fell for his own lies. And nothing more.

That was what he told himself.

They arrived at Cologne station just as the work day was ending. Evening light filtered through the dirty glass panels in the roof, refracting crookedly off the smoke and steam that billowed through the crowds milling about upon the main platforms.

He walked her to the taxi stand.

'Are you coming with me,' she asked, 'or are you going back to your apartment?'

'I'll go to the apartment,' he told her. 'I need to get some rest and some clean clothes. I'll see you again in the morning.' The words felt like stones in his mouth, clattering against his teeth and chipping them down to the nerves.

She stood on her tiptoes and kissed him. 'I'll see you then,' she said.

Carrying his suitcase, Carter walked across the city, heading for his apartment above the electrical appliance repair shop. As he plodded through the darkened streets, all the lies that he had told himself as he sat beside her in the train caught up with him at once. There would be no tidy closing of this wound. The best that he might do was learn to live with it and hide his memories from the world as he had done before, but there would never be peace in his heart. He thought about the people he had seen in that strange little town in the mountains, with their broken bodies and their worn-out souls, pouring sulphur down their throats to burn away the debts they owed the past. And he knew he was one of them now.

He unlocked the door and walked inside, not even bothering to turn on the light. He flopped down on the bed, springs groaning as they took his weight, and it was only then that he realised there was somebody standing in the doorway to his kitchen. 'Oh, shit!' he said, and sat up, heart stamping in his chest. He rolled off the bed and onto his feet, looking around for anything he might be able to use as a weapon. A chair. The bedside lamp.

The figure in the doorway raised his hands to show he wasn't carrying a gun. 'Mr Carter!' hissed a man's voice. 'I mean you no harm.'

'Then what the hell are you doing here?'

'I've been waiting for you,' said the man. And now he stepped forward into the last faint puddle of light still shining through the window.

It was Garlinsky.

Carter felt the dread rise in his throat.

'I have a message from my employer,' said Garlinsky. 'He would like to meet you. He has something for you. Something of great value, which he hopes you will accept in trade.'

'In trade for what?'

'Information that he knows you possess.'

'And if I say no to this meeting?'

Garlinsky breathed out slowly. 'Please, Mr Carter, don't let it come to that.'

There was a car waiting outside. Carter and Garlinsky sat in the back. The driver glanced at Carter in the rear-view mirror and then did not look at him again.

'How did you know I wasn't armed?' asked Carter.

'I didn't,' replied Garlinsky.

'Then you were taking a hell of a risk.'

Garlinsky looked at him and laughed. 'Not for the first time,' he replied.

They drove around the edge of the city, along the Eifelwall, the Zülpicherwall and the Venloerwall, heading north past the Gereon rail yard and into the Nippes district.

By now, the windows had grown a silvery sheen of condensation and when the car pulled up outside a building, Carter wiped away the moisture to see where they were.

It was Thesinger's bookshop.

Carter turned and stared in confusion at Garlinsky.

But Garlinsky said nothing. He just got out, came around to the other side and opened Carter's door.

The lights in the shop were off.

Garlinsky used a key to let them in and Carter followed him to the back room, where he and Wilby had met the owner of the shop.

Thesinger was there, sitting on a stool and wearing the same heavy cardigan. His hair was precisely as dishevelled as it had been the time before. The room was lit by the single bulb of the lamp perched on his work table, where he had examined the counterfeit roubles shown to him by Wilby.

'Garlinsky works for you?' asked Carter.

'I prefer to think it is more of a co-operative arrangement.'

'Why have you brought me here?'

'To express my admiration for your work.'

'Somebody else once told me that,' said Carter, 'and no good came of it.'

'I imagine that person might have been Hanno Dasch.'

Carter did not reply.

Thesinger gave a slight wave of his hand to show that no answer was required. 'The difference,' he said, 'is that Mr Dasch was aware only of the illusion that you created. My admiration, Mr Carter, is for the creation of the illusion itself. A subtle difference perhaps, but a fundamental one nonetheless.'

'If you say so.'

'Believe me, Mr Carter, I know what I'm talking about. You see, like you, I am also a maker of illusions, so complex that they can sometimes be revealed only by those who have created them.' He reached into his pocket and removed something, which he hid in his palm. And then, between his hands, he unfurled the tiny banner of a twenty-five-rouble note. 'This illusion, for example.'

'Wilby didn't let you keep any of that money,' said Carter.

'He didn't have to,' answered Thesinger. 'I have more than enough of my own.'

It took a moment for the truth to sink in. 'You're the counterfeiter?'

'Not just me,' explained Thesinger. 'There are others – Mr Garlinsky for example, and those men you might have seen gathered around the table just inside the front door of this shop the last time you were here.'

Carter remembered the thin man with the suitcase and the clothes that were too big for him.

'We are the survivors of an experiment,' continued Thesinger, 'conjured into life by the Nazis, and by one in particular, a man named Bernhard Krüger. In the autumn of 1942, I was an inmate at the Sachsenhausen concentration camp. One day, when I had just begun my work breaking stones with a sledgehammer, I was summoned to appear before the commandant. I dropped the sledgehammer and ran to the commandant's office. There, I found myself in the presence of an SS officer named Krüger, who asked me many questions about my previous employment at the Reichsbank. I had worked there for more than a decade as an engraver of the copper plates that were used for print-ing German currency. Krüger offered me the chance to take part in a special programme, which would make use of my particular training. In exchange for my full co-operation, I would be given proper clothes, not the grey and blue striped sackcloth worn by regular inmates, as well as three meals a day, a shower once a week and an actual bed, as opposed to the wooden-slatted bunk in which I currently slept. I agreed at once. I did not need to be told what this work might be for. Anything was better than breaking rocks, for which an inmate's life expectancy was less than six months.'

Carter had seen pictures of those death quarries, and of stone staircases that prisoners were forced to climb, carrying heavy loads, day after day, until they inevitably collapsed.

'I was taken to a barracks known as Block 19,' said Thesinger. 'Until that day, I had not even known of its existence. Even though it was within the grounds of Sachsenhausen, it was completely cut off from the rest of the camp by barbed wire and tall wooden fences. No one outside Block 19 could even see into our barracks. In Block 19, I was introduced to a group of men who would become my friends, and my only companions, for the next two and a half years. Each of them had special skills, much like my own. There were engravers, jewellers, graphic artists, photographers and collotypers. It was explained to me by Krüger that I was now part of Operation Bernhard, which was a plan to destroy the British economy by flooding it with counterfeit currency. Although with considerable difficulty – especially with the production of the correct paper and also a seal that could be found in the upper left hand corner of each note, depicting Britannia – we eventually managed to produce millions of notes of such high quality that, as I mentioned to you at our first meeting, even the Bank of England certified them as genuine.'

'The only part of the story you left out,' said Carter, 'was that you were the one who had made them.'

'You weren't ready for the truth, any more than I was ready to tell you.'

'I'm surprised the Nazis let you live after taking part in something like that,' remarked Carter.

'It was never their intention for us to survive,' replied Thesinger. 'Those of us who worked for Krüger had been under no illusion that, once this operation had been completed, we would be murdered and all trace of Block 19 obliterated. So we always knew that we were playing for time, and we would often create delays in production, just to stretch out the process a little longer. In the end, with the Russian and American armies closing in, we and our equipment – which included some very valuable printing presses – were moved from Sachsenhausen to a smaller camp called Ebensee, near the site of a rocket-building facility in the Austrian Alps. By then, the war was almost over. Many of the guards who had accompanied us simply vanished into the mountains. In the end, there were not even enough of them left to execute us, as I am certain they had planned to do. Some, like me, were fortunate enough to be taken prisoner by the Americans. That is how Major Wilby came to know of my existence, since he was the one who debriefed me before I was released back into the world with the status of "displaced person".'

'What about the others?' asked Carter.

'Many were less lucky. They fell into the hands of the Russians as they tried to make their way back to their homes. In spite of the fact that they had been selected from among a population of concentration camp inmates, they were accused by the Soviets of collaborating with the Nazis. In one sense, of course, it was true. Technically, all of us had volunteered to work for Krüger. The fact that we would all have been dead if we did not was, to the Russian mind, irrelevant. Having only just emerged from years of captivity, my friends were now sent to a particularly notorious labour camp in Siberia known as Borodok, some of them with sentences of more than twenty years.

'Could nothing be done to help them?' asked Carter.

'We weren't sure,' answered Thesinger, 'but we knew we had to try. We decided to reincarnate Operation Bernhard, only this time we were working for ourselves and, instead of British currency, we would set our skills towards the forgery of Russian roubles. We traced the equipment we had been using at Block 19, including a top of the line Monopol Type IV flatbed press, to a warehouse outside Vienna, where it had been put into storage and forgotten. Posing as representatives of a German newspaper whose facility had been destroyed in the war, we purchased the equipment from the warehouse manager. Eventually, through several intermediaries, contact was established with the commandant of Borodok and an offer was made to purchase the freedom of our friends.'

'Did this commandant have any idea that the money was fake?'

'None at all, and he had no reason to suspect. Our copies of Russian currency were even more accurate than those

British pounds we made for Krüger.'

'But where did he think the money came from?'

'We passed ourselves off as former Nazis who had looted huge quantities of gold during the war and smuggled it into Swiss banks. From there, with the help of unscrupulous bankers, we were able to exchange the gold for any currency we chose to purchase.'

'But why would former Nazis care about a bunch of concentration camp inmates?'

'We made no secret of the fact that these men had been part of Operation Bernhard, since we assumed the camp commandant would eventually figure it out on his own. We told him that we were planning to begin a counterfeit operation of American dollars, which was actually something Krüger had been working on before the war ended. Whether the commandant of Borodok cared one way or another what we were doing is still a mystery to me. All he cared about, I think, was lining his own pockets in exchange for the lives of a few men who were going to die before long, anyway.'

'How did he get them out of the camp?'

'It could not be done all at once without attracting suspicion, so we agreed that he would smuggle them out one at a time. He was already supplementing his income by selling the bodies of those who had died at the gulag as cadavers to various medical institutions, not only in Russia, but also in Hungary, Poland and Czechoslovakia. The bodies were sealed inside barrels filled with formaldehyde and sent out on flatbed railcars along with wood cut from the forests around

Borodok. Our men, listed as dead but still very much alive, were sent out among these shipments of barrels. For each man, thousands of roubles were smuggled back to Borodok inside the empty barrels, which were being returned so that more bodies could be placed inside them. Our contact worked at a hospital in Prague, so that was the place where our friends were delivered. From Prague, they travelled here to Germany. Seeing these men after they had spent two years labouring in a gulag was enough to break my heart, but at least they are free now. We provide them with housing, clothes and enough money to make a new start.'

Carter thought of the men he had seen that day in the bookshop, and how happy they had looked to see their friend, in spite of his ragged appearance.

'And if they need documents,' continued Thesinger, 'we provide those as well.'

'Are those also forgeries?'

'Of course. It's what we do.'

'So why did you start working with Dasch?' asked Carter.

'We knew that the Russians had become aware of counterfeit roubles in circulation, and that they were searching for a source. It was only a matter of time before one of our shipments of currency was discovered. That was when we realised that we would have to begin working with black marketeers, since their livelihoods, just like ours, depended on being able to outwit the authorities. Our contract with Mr Dasch was to contain the final shipment of currency, which would secure the release of the last two men from Operation Bernhard still in captivity at Borodok. Of course, he thought he was transporting crates of whisky. He had no idea of their true value. When you and Major Wilby showed up with some of the currency, I almost did not recognise our own work! It was only with some difficulty that I spotted a slight variation in the print quality. You see, we took a short-cut in the construction of the intaglio plates, which need to be engraved by hand. This would have taken months to complete, and it was time we simply didn't have.'

'Why have you told me all this?' asked Carter. 'Are you planning on killing me now?'

'No, Mr Carter.' Thesinger gave him a pitying glance. 'That might have been the method of the people who enslaved us, and perhaps even the method of the people for whom you've been working, but as far as we are concerned, there has already been enough killing. I brought you here because, after recent events, it seemed to me only a matter of time before you found your way on your own. And I am not optimistic about the treatment my friends and I would receive, either from your masters or from the Russians, no matter how noble our intentions. But you are the key to their knowledge. Without you, they may have several pieces of the puzzle, but they do not understand the picture they are trying to assemble.'

'So you would like me to keep quiet.'

Thesinger nodded. 'Precisely.'

'Without actually killing me.'

'If at all possible, yes.'

'And how did you plan on doing that? With a slab of your counterfeit money?'

'With something far more valuable,' said Thesinger. He reached into the drawer of his desk and removed a handful of small booklets, which he handed to Carter.

They were passports. Swiss. German. American. Canadian. All of them brand new and unissued.

'What makes you think I might need one of these?' asked Carter.

'Maybe you do and maybe you don't,' replied Thesinger, 'but I imagine one of them might come in handy for Teresa Dasch when Mr Babcock and his friends have grown tired of waiting for us to appear and turn her over to the German police, along with her father and everyone who works for him. This, they will do. I assure you.'

Carter knew that Thesinger was right, and an idea began to form inside his head – no more than a shred of thought, but there was hope in it where no hope had been before. 'You can fill this out correctly, with a photograph and issue stamps?'

'Why not?' asked Thesinger. 'We made the whole passport from scratch. Everything else is child's play by comparison.'

'I'm glad you didn't just stick with faking money.'

'That would have been a waste of so much talent,' said Thesinger. 'So are we agreed, Mr Carter?'

For a while, Carter gave no reply. He was thinking about something his father had once said – that if you wanted to leave on your own terms, you had to wait for the precise moment in time when such a thing was possible. And if that moment ever came, you could not hesitate. 'There is one final thing,' he said at last.

Thesinger opened his arms. 'Name it, Mr Carter,' he said.

Carter turned to Garlinsky, who had been standing in a corner of the room the whole time, waiting and listening, his stare burning into the back of Carter's head. 'Dasch was terrified of you,' he said.

'Indeed he was,' replied Garlinsky.

Carter jabbed a finger against his own chest. 'I was terrified of you.'

'I did have that impression.'

'I have to know,' he said. 'What in God's name are you?' *An assassin*, thought Carter. *Some kind of torturer, at least.*

Garlinsky glanced across at Thesinger.

Thesinger shrugged. 'You might as well tell him.'

'I was a high school history teacher,' said Garlinsky.

'A teacher?' mumbled Carter.

'I spent twenty-five years in the classroom,' explained Garlinsky, 'perfecting a look to make a student's blood run cold, and it has come in handy ever since.'

'So why did Krüger take you on?' asked Carter. 'What do you know about counterfeiting money?'

'Nothing at all,' answered Garlinsky.

Now it was Thesinger who spoke. 'When Krüger asked a group of prisoners at the concentration camp if there was anyone who knew about collotyping, Garlinsky stepped forward.'

'And you knew nothing about collotyping?'

'Not even what it was,' replied Garlinsky.

'But he gave Krüger the look,' said Thesinger, 'and nothing more was needed.'

'Some of the other prisoners taught me the basics,' Garlinsky continued. 'I learned enough not to get myself killed and Krüger never questioned me.'

'He didn't dare!' laughed Thesinger.

'I can't say that I blame him,' said Carter.

*

One hour later, Carter arrived at Dasch's compound. He found the front gate open. The guard was gone, and so were the mechanics in the workshop. The whole place was silent and seemed empty.

He walked into the office, whose broken window had been patched with sections of plywood.

Ritter was there, although at first Carter barely recognised him. He was sitting at Dasch's desk, stripped to the waist and clutching a bottle of brandy, most of which he appeared to have drunk by himself. In his other hand, he held the Mauser pistol that he always carried with him.

He was plastered with grey dust and mud, which had caked in his hair so that it stood up by itself in chalky clumps.

'What happened to you?' asked Carter.

'Mr Dasch is dead,' said Ritter, his voice heavy and slow from the dust and alcohol.

An image of Dasch burst behind Carter's eyes. They were back at the train station, just before he and Teresa departed for Vienna. Dasch had his arms spread wide, his hands resting lightly on their shoulders. He was telling them that they were a beautiful couple. And it seemed impossible to Carter that Ritter was telling the truth. Some people walked around with doom painted on them like a bull's eye. Others had a hold on life so frail and tenuous that no matter how big or strong they were, the part of them that clung to their existence appeared as fragile as a candle flame. And there were some, like Dasch, who seemed to own a kind of armour, protecting them from all the randomness of death. Carter had seen this with his own eyes, and he had learned to trust it, even though he never spoke of it or put it into words. But for Dasch to be gone . . . he simply refused to believe it. 'How?' he whispered.

'He had been trying to open that door,' said Ritter, 'the one down in the storeroom, with crowbars and hammers and ropes. He was convinced that a fortune lay on just the other side. I think he must finally have succeeded, and then the whole ceiling gave way. I heard it. I thought it was thunder, at first. When I realised what had happened, I ran to the entrance and the entire place was blocked. The ground above where the storeroom had been located had sunk into the earth, the way a grave collapses on a coffin when the wood has rotted away. I tried to dig my way in, thinking that perhaps a passageway existed. But it might as well have been solid rock. It was useless. I had to give up.'

'Does Teresa know?'

'She was with me,' answered Ritter. 'She heard it, too, when the roof gave way. We both tried to dig our way in. She knew before I did that there was nothing we could do.'

'Where is she now?'

Ritter jerked his chin in the direction of the narrow corridor that led towards the dining room. 'In there,' he said.

'How is she?'

Ritter blinked, his dust-covered eyelashes like slivers of ivory. 'About the same as me, I think, except without the brandy.'

'How about you put that gun away?'

Ritter ignored the request. 'It's over, you know.' He looked around the room. 'All this.'

'That's why you need to leave.'

'And where would I go?' he asked.

'That's up to you, but I would make it somewhere far away.'

Ritter shook his head. 'It would make no difference where I went. What I am running from is here.' He tapped one grimy fingernail against his forehead.

'There must be something you still believe in, out there in the world.'

'I'm not so sure of that. There are only so many causes one man can fight for in a lifetime.'

'Then don't fight for any of them. Just start again.'

Ritter smiled beneath his mask of dust. 'It's a little bit late for that now.'

Carter nodded at the pistol. 'Are you planning on shooting me?'

'I was thinking about it,' he admitted. 'You, and everyone else.'

'And now?'

Ritter set the gun on the desk. 'Now,' he said, 'I think

you and Teresa should depart while you still can. And take this with you.' As he spoke, he reached below the desk and lifted up the same grey canvas bag in which they had carried the money for the deal with Sergeant Galton. The bag was still full.

Carter found Teresa sitting at one of the tables in the dining room. She was staring at the bare, stained wood with a confused look on her face, as if she couldn't figure out how she had got there. When Carter walked into the room, she looked up but did not smile.

'I didn't think I would see you again,' she said. 'The whole ride back, I had it in my head that you would vanish the first chance you got.'

'It's not the first time you've been wrong about me.'

She sighed. 'Did Ritter tell you about my father?'

'Yes.'

She set one hand upon the table and traced her finger along the grain of the wood. 'From the first day he walked into that room, I think he always knew that it would be the end of him. But he had to try. Not much hope for an unemployed chef in a country without any food.'

'We need to go,' said Carter.

'Where?'

'It doesn't matter. There's no reason to stay, and plenty of reasons to leave.'

'They'll be looking for me. For both of us. How far do you think we would get?'

'You'll just have to trust me on that,' said Carter.

At that moment, they heard a popping noise, which at

first Carter thought was a light bulb exploding. It took another second before he realised what it was. He dashed out into the hallway.

Ritter lay slumped in the chair, his head tilted back so that the tendons in his neck were stretched like wires beneath the skin. The pistol lay on the floor and the wall behind him was splashed with red.

Teresa came up behind Carter. 'What is it?' she asked.

Carter turned and gently pushed her back into the room. 'Ritter,' he said. He led her out of the back door of the dining room, emerging behind the mechanic shop. They came around the building and down towards the gate at the entrance of the compound. There, he stopped. 'When I woke up next to you at the hotel in Karlovy Vary, I thought to myself that you had either killed me or saved me. I just didn't have any idea which one it was.'

She reached up and brushed a hand across his face. 'And now you think you know?' she asked.

'I do,' said Carter, 'and that's why I'm standing here.'

*

Babcock was sitting with his feet up on his desk, a black market Cuban cigar in one hand and a tumbler of bourbon in the other. He could hear the clip-clop of feet down in the street below as people made their way home from work. The office was empty. Everyone else had already gone home. Babcock often lingered in the embassy at the end of the day. His wife did not like him smoking in their apartment and there was no point holing up in some cafe, because the smell of a Cuban cigar was enough to make him the focus of attention from everyone who even caught a whiff of good tobacco. This was the only place where he knew he would be left in peace.

Then the phone rang on his desk.

If his secretary had been there, she would have answered it and told the caller that there was nobody there by his name. She always began things that way.

Babcock stared at the phone, willing it to fall silent.

But the phone kept ringing.

Babcock groaned and swept his feet down to the floor. He looked at the cigar and then at the tumbler, wondering which hand to free up, and decided on the bourbon. Placing the glass on the desk, he took the phone receiver and pressed it against his ear. Through the purr of static, he could hear the sound of train announcements, but it was too garbled to make out the language. 'Who is this?' he asked.

'It's Carter.'

Babcock settled back into his chair. 'Sounds like you're on the move.'

'That's right.'

'Well, you got yourself out of here just in time,' said Babcock.

'Why's that?' asked Carter.

'They're all dead,' Babcock told him.

'All of them, you say?'

'Dasch, his daughter, Ritter. The German police just announced it.'

Carter knew that wasn't true, because Teresa was stand-

334

ing right beside him, but he wondered how Babcock had become convinced of it. 'What happened?' he asked.

'Some guy who worked as a guard at the front gate of Dasch's compound showed up for work two days ago and found Ritter with a bullet in his head. He's the one who called the police. They said it looked like suicide, but who the hell knows? While they were searching the area, they discovered that a whole section of the field beside the compound had caved in. It turned out to be that bunker you told me about. The police went in there with heavy equipment and found Dasch's body buried under the rubble. There was no trace of Dasch's daughter, but they knew she hadn't run away because her passport and all her papers were still there. They think she might have been down in the bunker with Dasch when the cave-in occurred. They tried to look for her, but the roof was too unstable and they couldn't get to her body. As for Garlinsky, and whoever he was working with, there's no way we'll ever find them now. The only person the German police are still looking for is you, so it's a good thing you called when you did. First thing in the morning, I'll send out a notification of how you've been working for us. I've got the draft right here.' He picked up the sheet of paper on which he had scribbled the announcement, then let it slip through his fingers back onto the desk. 'Then you can get your life back, just like we agreed.'

'I don't want it,' said Carter.

'You don't want what?'

'What we talked about.'

Babcock sat forward and put his elbows on the desk, keeping

335

the phone receiver hooked under his chin. 'I don't understand,' he said. 'You don't want me to make the announcement?'

'That's right.'

'But you do realise that I'm the only living person who knows you aren't actually a criminal? If I don't set this straight, there's nothing I can do to protect you.'

It was quiet at the end of the line.

'Carter?' said Babcock. 'Are you still there?'

'Yes.'

'Are you sure about this? After all we put you through?'

'I'm sure.'

'All right,' said Babcock, 'but I wish to God you'd tell me why I'm doing this.'

Again, he received no reply.

'Carter?' Babcock called into the receiver. 'Hey, Carter, are you there?'

There was only the rustle of static, like waves breaking on a beach in the distance. Babcock sighed and hung up the phone. He picked up the piece of paper on which he had drafted the announcement, crumpled it in his fist and tossed it into the wastebasket. Then he slowly put his feet back on the table and puffed at his cigar until the embers glowed again. As the dry, sweet smoke filtered into Babcock's brain, turning lazy pirouettes among the rafters of his skull, his memory of Nathan Carter was already fading from his mind, as if it had never been there.

In the grand foyer of the Orlovsky hotel, early morning sun glinted on the giant ferns that formed the archway on either side of the main entrance. As the doors swung open, the waxy leaves rustled with a sound like gentle rain.

The concierge, with his red tunic and stiff grey moustache, glanced up from the paper that he had spread upon the counter. As the couple appeared in the doorway, passing through the dazzle of light as if emerging from a different dimension, he recognised them at once.

But he did not greet them with a smile. Instead, without averting the gaze of his sled-dog eyes even for a second, he raised one arm above his head and snapped his fingers, summoning the drowsy porter from the back room. Only then did the concierge speak. 'The Orlovsky welcomes you again,' he told the couple, with such gravity and reverence it was as if the stones within the walls had been expecting them.